PENGUIN BOOKS

A CRUEL Twist of FATE

Other titles by H. F. Askwith

A Dark Inheritance

H. F. ASKWITH

A CRUEL *Twist* of FATE

PENGUIN BOOKS

PENGUIN BOOKS

UK | USA | Canada | Ireland | Australia
India | New Zealand | South Africa

Penguin Books is part of the Penguin Random House group of companies
whose addresses can be found at global.penguinrandomhouse.com.

www.penguin.co.uk
www.puffin.co.uk
www.ladybird.co.uk

Penguin
Random House
UK

First published 2024

001

Set in 10.5/15.5pt Sabon LT Std
Typeset by Jouve (UK), Milton Keynes
Printed and bound in Great Britain by Clays Ltd, Elcograf S.p.A.

The authorized representative in the EEA is Penguin Random House Ireland,
Morrison Chambers, 32 Nassau Street, Dublin D02 YH68

A CIP catalogue record for this book is available from the British Library

ISBN: 978-0-241-62964-2

All correspondence to:
Penguin Books
Penguin Random House Children's
One Embassy Gardens, 8 Viaduct Gardens, London SW11 7BW

For Jake

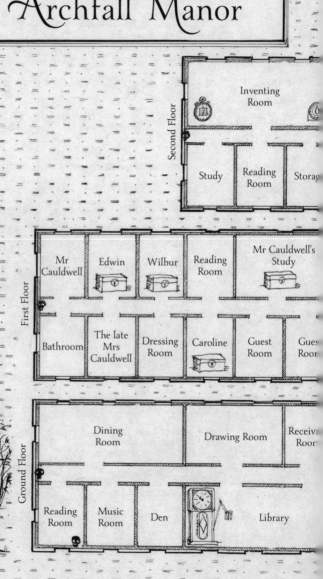

Archfall Manor

Second Floor

Inventing Room

Study | Reading Room | Storag

First Floor

Mr Cauldwell | Edwin | Wilbur | Reading Room | Mr Cauldwell's Study

Bathroom | The late Mrs Cauldwell | Dressing Room | Caroline | Guest Room | Gues Room

Ground Floor

Dining Room | Drawing Room | Receiv Roor

Reading Room | Music Room | Den | Library

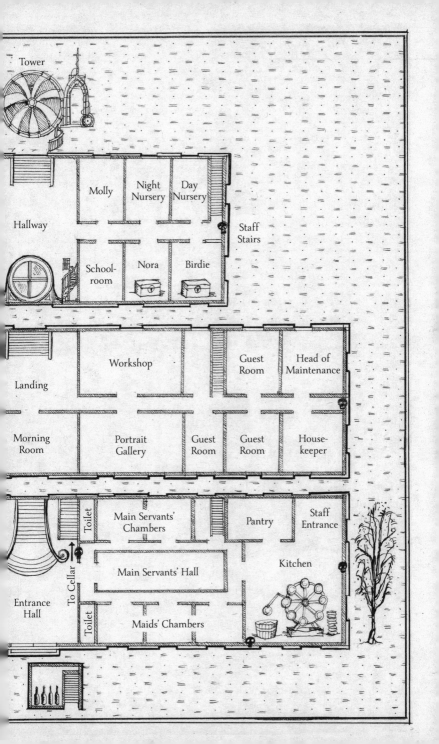

Tower

Hallway

Molly

Night
Nursery

Day
Nursery

Staff
Stairs

School-
room

Nora

Birdie

Landing

Workshop

Guest
Room

Head of
Maintenance

Morning
Room

Portrait
Gallery

Guest
Room

Guest
Room

House-
keeper

Toilet

Main Servants'
Chambers

Pantry

Staff
Entrance

To Cellar

Main Servants' Hall

Kitchen

Entrance
Hall

Toilet

Maids' Chambers

Prologue

February 1846

TERROR AT ARCHFALL MANOR!

Sighfeyre Isle, the tidal island that is home to the enigmatic and extravagantly wealthy Cauldwell family, has been cut off from the mainland for four days. Now that the storm has abated, it has been revealed that unspeakable horrors have unfolded within the Cauldwell ancestral home of Archfall Manor during this period of isolation. A number of bodies have reportedly been recovered, and foul play is suspected.

It is not the first time that the Cauldwell family name has been drenched in mystery – Mr Thomas Cauldwell's daughter, Mrs Caroline Temple, has been thrice widowed, and eighteen years ago the elder Cauldwell son, Edwin, disappeared. Although his body was never found, the family reported him dead. These incidents continue to cast a long shadow . . .

1

The day the debt collector came, I was making cinder toffee. The sky was solemn and fateful, shrouding another grim January morning. A grey and miserable daylight strained through the window as I stirred the sugar and the syrup into water in a heavy-bottomed pan. They combined, melting into a gooey, oozing and dangerously hot sludge. I stopped stirring and put my spoon on the worktop before reaching for the jar that contained the white powder, which created an effect that was almost magical when I sprinkled it in. I grabbed a little tool I'd fashioned myself from wire, designed to whip air into my mixtures, and I whisked quickly, beating the mixture as it bubbled, frothing and foaming and taking on a lighter hue, the sandy colour of the coastline in summer. It was transformed.

I always thought there was something about making sweets that was like being a conjuror – take these humble ingredients, combine and transform them, create a treat that provokes the sensation of delight. What is that if not magic?

Before I lifted the pan, I blew away a loose strand that had escaped my plait. My hair, copper-coloured and as thick and strong as wire, required wrestling into submission every morning, and even when it had been fastened it managed to irritate me no end. This was the part where I needed to be careful – my grip was tight, but the pan was heavy, and it would only take one second, one nudge, one slip. Most people don't realize the dangers of working with sugar: not only does it burn, it sticks. You try to wipe away the sugar and you take your skin with it, leaving you raw, revealing the layer beneath . . . I was still waiting for my blistered finger to heal after the previous week's splatter of lemon caramel.

The constant threat of scalding kept me focused, despite the rowdy noise from the busy street outside. Our tiny, ramshackle sweetshop was just a short walk down from the towering Durham Cathedral but being in such a prime location came with a hefty rent and, crammed in among all the other businesses jostling for space, I knew we were barely breaking even.

I began to decant the toffee mixture into trays. It was during this precarious operation, with the surge of sugar requiring all my concentration, that the bell to announce a customer chimed. The toffee was a swollen, puffy thing as it spread across the tray with a life of its own. It breathed in, creating pockets of air in its skin as it cascaded from the pan.

'One moment!' I called, shepherding the liquid with care, scraping the rest of the contents into the tin. Our customers often liked to browse, anyhow.

But this was no ordinary customer. He lifted the wooden hatch of the counter and slipped through, strolled into the kitchen as if he were in charge.

'You can't come back here,' I snapped. 'I'll be out to serve you when I'm finished.'

'I'm not here to rot my teeth,' he said, and his voice was as silky smooth as the centre of a violet cream. His tone, though, was as sharp as a sherbet lemon.

He had shoulder-length hair the colour of coal and a dusting of dark stubble over high and well-defined cheekbones. I couldn't help but envy him his thick tweed coat with its cape over the shoulders – the winter had been biting and showed little sign of relenting any time soon. Despite the warmth of his clothing, his eyes had shards of ice in them. The palest of blues.

He was blocking my way out, and my whole body tensed. A taut muscle in my neck started to twitch. I no longer felt merely irritated by the interruption, but deeply unsettled.

'If you're not here for confectionery, then you've walked into the wrong shop,' I said through gritted teeth, trying to sound braver than I felt.

'Oh, I'm not mistaken,' he said. A smile slid across his lips, which were thin and almost disappeared as they stretched. It was not a kind smile, and my skin started to prickle. He laughed, and it was a robust sound, the laugh of a man who settled down in a comfortable bed and slept every night with a full belly.

'What do you want then?' I snapped, placing my hands on my hips even though inside I was shrinking, like one of those birds who puff up their feathers as a defence. My nerves were frayed. 'I'm not interested in riddles. Can't you see I have enough to do?' I gestured wildly at the kitchen – it was full of the clutter of a morning spent crafting sweets.

'No riddles,' he said. 'I'm here to collect your debt. It's court-ordered now. Your landlord has had enough of waiting.'

My stomach sank. I knew that some months we had struggled when business was poor, but I didn't know Mam was in debt. My gut plummeted further when I thought of the money I'd been stealing from our shop's takings in return for late-night lessons in reading, writing and arithmetic from Josephine, a tutor at the boarding school. I was investing in my future, I'd told myself. But at what cost?

'So?' the debt collector asked. 'Do you have the money?'

'How much is it?'

I steeled myself to hear the answer, but no amount of preparation could have made the blow easier to receive. The sum was staggering, and, given the meagre profit we made at the shop, clearing it by selling sweets alone would be impossible.

'I don't . . . I . . .' The words stuck in my throat.

'I didn't think so. In that case, what do you have for me?' He appraised the row of pans, picked one up and weighed it in his hand as if to determine its worth like a piglet at market.

'You take that and we won't be able to pay the rent, let alone put anything towards the debt. How am I meant to make sweets without utensils?'

The man bared his teeth. 'I don't think you understand. You won't be making sweets here for much longer. This is the end of the road.' He pulled out a document from his pocket and slammed it on the worktop. 'One month to pay up. One month before your ma is hauled off to the debtors' prison, and the bailiffs take every last thing. I'm merely here to collect enough to keep you in business until then.'

I stared at the hand holding the paper. The fingers were bonded together by what looked at first glance like an elegant piece of jewellery, but bile rose in the back of my throat as I realized that the polished silver bar wasn't there for decorative purposes. The raised ridges were designed to turn his fist into a weapon.

'I'll check the cash drawer,' I said, defeated, trying not to think how we'd pay for food. 'Let me past.'

He moved, and I shuffled out from behind the worktop. I had a vision of clobbering him round the head with the cast-iron frying pan hanging on the wall, skewering him with the poker that stoked the fire, tipping the cinder toffee mixture all over him . . . But the pictures were momentary. Any bravery I'd felt had melted away for good.

I opened the drawer and surveyed the modest takings, minus what I'd already pocketed to give to Josephine for that evening's tutoring session. The regret was a damp lump inside me, like a failed pudding.

I counted out the coins and placed them on the counter. 'Take it then,' I said.

It was worse than if I'd been robbed in the street. I felt cowardly. But what else could I do? I was no match for him, unkempt in my apron stained by remnants of candies and pies of the past.

'Barely touches it,' he said, sneering at the offering. He snatched the coins up, anyhow, and raised his fingers to his brow in a mock salute. His pockets jingled as he opened the door to leave. A gust of freezing air pushed its way past him to raise gooseflesh on my arms. Then he turned and said nastily, 'I must say, I have been confused about this whole affair. Given her connection with them, why doesn't your mother just see if her wealthy friends the Cauldwells will pay up for her?'

I frowned, an uneasy feeling creeping down my back.

Sensing that his words had produced the desired effect on me, and smirking once more, the man finally decided to stop tormenting me. With a last nod, he turned and disappeared down the street, leaving me with the empty cash drawer and an embarrassment as hot as boiling sugar. My cheeks flushed, despite the chill. What he had said about the Cauldwells unsettled me deeply. That family were no *friends* of Mam. They were talked about all over town, but she always shuddered at the very mention of them ... Which, of course, made them fascinating to me.

The Cauldwell family were enigmatic, immensely wealthy and incredibly reclusive – they lived on a private tidal island called Sighfeyre Isle just off the coast. The patriarch of the family, Mr Thomas Cauldwell, was a famed inventor, like his father before him, but he was known for his reluctance to leave the island.

And somehow they'd been connected to my father. The last time Mam saw him, he was heading to Sighfeyre Isle – then he was never heard of again. That was as much as she had ever been willing to tell me, which naturally only fuelled my fascination with them further.

The lifelong dearth of information about my father had always left me feeling incomplete, in a way I knew Mam could never understand. Her upbringing was very simple and loving, although her parents had passed away within a year of each other, several years before I was born. I knew that grief plagued her daily – I was all she had left.

'The less you know about your father, the better,' she'd tell me. 'It's my job to keep you safe.'

That antagonized me more. That the Cauldwells were somehow linked to my father meant they had already determined so much of our fate – from the incomplete feeling never knowing him gave me to our current desperate financial situation.

I stewed on the debt collector's words for the rest of the morning until Mam returned from running errands, cursing the cost of ingredients. I was scrubbing the pans, an ache in my elbow and a tight crick in my neck. I'd been holding my shoulders up about my ears, and it took a concentrated effort to relax them, to roll them out like dough. There was still a lot of work to be done, so I buttoned my lip, thinking about when would be the right moment to ask Mam about what the man had said. I'd have to be careful – one wrong move and she'd shut me out, I knew it.

When our work for the day was done, I discarded my apron. Mam prepared a plate of crusty bread and heated a little pot of dripping, and, when she was done, I extinguished the candles and plunged the kitchen into darkness, leaving just one tiny stub, cupped in my hands, as a little paring knife of illumination. The stairs sighed beneath us as we ascended into the family rooms. The upper floor had creaky wooden floorboards and exhausted ceiling beams. There had always been a perception in the town that in order to run a shop you must have money. If only that were the truth. There was no pile of gold hidden away under our floorboards, only dust.

Mam's face was stern as we sat to share our meagre supper. 'You have that look about you. You're plotting.'

'I am not plotting,' I said, but of course I was.

I was desperately considering our options. Even before the visit from the debt collector, I had always tried to be one step ahead, somewhere in the future, chasing to keep up with my dreams. That was why I'd begun my lessons – I wanted to do something *more*. Although I'd never quite had the luxury of time to figure out what that something might be, I knew I'd need some sort of education to give myself a chance.

I looked at the sorry state of the room around us and wanted to cry. We worked so hard, but it still wasn't enough. Now Mam would have to do hard labour in the prison to pay off the debt, long and back-breaking hours that would make our days in the shop seem like a holiday. Families could live there too, allowed to pass in and out, so I would have a choice to make – try and fend for myself, homeless and with no prospects, or join Mam in prison.

Mam pressed again. She knew something was wrong, her eyes narrowing. 'What's happened?' she asked.

'A debt collector came to the shop today,' I said flatly.

Mam put her head in her hands. 'Oh, Helena. I'm sorry,' she said. 'I thought I could get on top of it . . . find a way to pay. But it's out of control.'

My heart sank. A tiny part of me had hoped it might all have been some terrible mistake. 'Mam, if we can't pay . . .'

She shook her head. 'I don't see how we can. It's just too much. I'm so sorry, Helena.'

'Don't be sorry,' I said, struggling with the guilt and my regret. 'I . . . I've been taking money from the cash drawer.'

'I know,' Mam said softly, simply.

Shame rushed to my face. 'You do?'

'You've been getting lessons from that girl at the school.' Mam arched an eyebrow. 'Do you think I'm completely oblivious to what goes on around here? You can't deceive me. I'm the one that raised you – by myself, I might add – and I didn't do that by being a fool.'

'Well, you did a good job of convincing me that I'd managed to keep it a secret,' I said with a tiny smile. I always thought I was skilled at reasoning, prided myself on my investigative ability. Seemed as though I'd inherited that from my mother.

'You know I only want good things for you, Helena,' Mam said. 'We would have ended up here whether you took that money for your lessons or not.'

A silence settled between us. There was something else I needed to ask her, and yet it felt explosive to do so. But I couldn't wait any longer.

'The debt collector said something odd when he left. He said you should ask your friends the Cauldwells for help.'

She froze as if I'd poured ice-cold water over her head.

'What did he mean?'

'Nothing,' she said. Too quickly, too firmly.

'But why would he –'

'I don't know, Helena. But I forbid you from speaking about them again. That family are dangerous. They – they're the reason your father is dead.'

2

I was stunned. I'd heard Mam's opaque warnings about the Cauldwell family so many times over the years, and she'd hinted that she thought they were behind my father's disappearance. But this was the first time she'd accused them of being implicated in his death.

I never met my father. He died when I was just a baby. It pained Mam deeply to talk about him, so when I was younger she'd only offered up tiny jewels of information now and then, and as I grew older I knew better than to ask about him. So the facts I'd gleaned about my father were limited: Mam had called him Ned; his eyes were the exact same shade of brown as mine; he'd had an extensive repertoire of hilarious anecdotes about a cat he'd had as a child; his favourite sweet was a violet cream; he was a watchmaker by trade.

Once, after I'd been pestering her for more information on him, Mam asked me, from what seemed like a place of hope, 'Surely you can't miss what you've never had?'

And I'd said, 'Yes. Yes, you can.' The fact he wasn't there changed every part of who I became.

Mam had never told me the specifics about how my father died. I'd always assumed that something had happened to him on his journey to Sighfeyre Isle – crossing the causeway that kept it isolated from the mainland was known to be perilous at times, so it seemed a fair guess. And I didn't heed Mam's warnings to leave the matter alone. Instead, I'd become utterly obsessed.

Over the years, I took the task as seriously as if I were a detective at Scotland Yard, devouring gossip and hearsay alongside weighty pamphlets about the Cauldwells' inventions. A few years before, I'd found a pamphlet stashed away among some old paperwork in the shop. It was written by Edwin Cauldwell, the elder son of the family. It was a complex treatise on a theory of time, full of theoretical arguments and odd diagrams, including a strange scratchy illustration of an archway. I'd shown it to Mam, asking whether it had belonged to my father, and she'd taken it away from me.

What little I learned continued to fascinate me. The Cauldwell family had historically been known for all manner of pioneering research and spectacular innovations, and had funded many more through the Cauldwell Institute of Invention, which had been led by the family for generations. Thomas Cauldwell, the current patriarch, was retaining leadership into his old age.

A widower in his seventies, Thomas had had three adult children. The elder son, Edwin, had died eighteen years before, and his younger son, Wilbur, was reputed to be as reclusive as his father. There was also a daughter – Caroline

Temple (née Cauldwell, latterly Richardson, latterly Burton) – who was best known for surviving three husbands. While the first had died tragically of tuberculosis, the other two, if the gossip in the papers were to be believed, had died in 'suspicious circumstances'.

Not that any of that was much help to me now. I tried to ask my mother for more information about what she'd meant by accusing the Cauldwells so directly, but, as I'd suspected she would, she refused to say any more. I knew better than to press her once she'd gone silent – but I couldn't sleep that night for thinking about what she might have meant.

The day after the debt collector came, I obtained a second-hand daily paper our neighbour, an ill-tempered milliner, had finished with. I pored over those pages until the tiny print began to swim, desperately seeking any kind of advertised opportunity that might help us to make some more money.

So, when my eyes alighted on the vacancy, it hit me with such force that I almost lost my balance and toppled off my chair: the Cauldwell family were seeking a governess to join their staff.

Caroline Temple was returning to her ancestral home, Archfall Manor, and was in need of a governess willing to reside on the tidal island to educate her daughter. I already knew that her third husband – the one whose name she bore – had died under unfortunate circumstances, but this time she was fleeing London after two decades. *Suspicious*,

I thought. The pay was very good – not sufficient to prevent the repossessions and Mam's incarceration, but enough that, after a couple of years' work, I might be able to turn our fortunes around.

It felt as though fate had reached out and tapped me on the shoulder. Not only was this a chance to save Mam, but I might – just might – be able to find out more about what happened to my father.

What other choice did I have than to apply?

That night, after Mam had surrendered to another exhausted slumber, I crept back downstairs and penned an impassioned letter of application by candlelight. I wrote about how I believed that the daughter of a family with such an incredible history of invention and innovation deserved a tailored and practical education, and how I intended to deliver this through a scheme of learning that followed the child's line of enquiry to retain engagement and focus. I based it on my own notions of education, on the way that I studied with Josephine. We alternated between gulping down scientific treatises and indulging in reading practice (my favourite novel was a modern romance about first impressions gone wrong – though I chose not to mention this fact).

That the ideas in my letter were rather outlandish for consideration by the societal elite did cross my mind as I arranged for its delivery. And yet, given what I had learned about the Cauldwell family, I reasoned they might be just the thing to make me stand out. I worked harder on that letter than I'd worked on anything in my life, knowing that it might be my only opportunity to gain access to the house, to gain access to the family, to gain access to the truth.

There was a necessary deception involved. My name didn't come with a glowing teaching reference – not like the one I knew Josephine had. So, with only a modicum of guilt, I took hers and signed my letter *Josephine Martin*.

Days passed, then weeks. We drew ever closer to the court-ordered deadline, and we were nowhere near repaying the debt. Mam seemed to grow thinner before my eyes as our belongings disappeared from around us. The debtors' prison loomed. And then . . . a letter.

Thick, textured parchment. Upon the front, the shop address elegantly inked. Fastening the back, a ruby-red wax seal, imprinted with a crest featuring a curling letter C. My fingers trembled. A response from Sighfeyre Isle – I hadn't dared to imagine it, and yet here it was in my hands. I tore it open immediately, thankful that Mam was out. I could barely read the letter enclosed, the excitement making my vision wobble and the words jump around on the page.

Mrs Caroline Temple was inviting me – me! – to a trial period at Archfall Manor where I would act as governess to her daughter, with a permanent role pending her approval. The thrill that rushed through me was dizzying, disorienting and spiked with anxiety. It was everything I could have hoped for, and now . . . it was real.

When I told Mam, I lied several times. I lied about the household, saying that I'd be working for a family in

Edinburgh, and I lied about how I'd got round my lack of experience, saying that Josephine had vouched for me and written a reference. There was something inscrutable in Mam's expression, and I was caught off guard by the strength of my own feelings. I was not ready to begin the painful process of detaching myself from her, from the one person who loved me – and through a lie I knew she'd be devastated by. The deceit twisted uncomfortably inside me.

But it needed to be done. For the money . . . And, more than that, for the thing she had sworn to keep from me. The truth.

I wrapped my arms round her so that she wouldn't see the tears brimming in my eyes.

'What an opportunity!' Mam's voice was full of pride. 'A governess. Imagine that!' She seemed struck through with grief, or relief, or some concoction of the two.

'I'm delighted,' I said.

It was a half-truth. There truly was a part of me that harboured excitement for what was about to unfold . . . But a dark trepidation also left me fearful because the warning still stood. For all my fascination with the Cauldwells, Mam believed them to be dangerous – and so far I had no evidence to the contrary.

'Always knew you were a bright one –' Mam planted a kiss on the top of my head – 'from the moment I held you. You looked right at me, as if we'd met before in another life. So sharp.'

I'd heard Mam tell this story many a time, polished over the years so that it became as smooth as a mint imperial rolling over her tongue. There were many anecdotes like this, where I said something interesting as a child, where I became proficient in a skill before my time, where I gave some indication that the brain ticking inside my skull had potential . . . The message was clear: I was clever. Special. Destined for something. Isn't it funny how the things that people tell you about who you are become the things you rest your identity in? Because if I was not everything that Mam believed me to be . . . then who was I?

I just didn't know. And I simply refused to accept that not knowing was my fate.

Mrs Caroline Temple had invited me to join them on the tenth of February – two weeks away – and so I made a tutoring appointment with Josephine as usual, but this time with corrupt intentions. Throughout the session, I waited for an opportune moment of distraction, which arrived when Josephine was interrupted by one of her charges and had to attend the dormitory where the boarders slept.

Uncertain how long I'd have, I swiftly began rummaging through her drawers, searching for the reference papers I knew I might be asked for when I arrived at Archfall Manor. They were neatly tucked away with a small purse filled with coins, and although there was the temptation to pocket these too while I was already committing a theft, I knew that any additional layering of guilt would be more than I could bear. I slipped the reference papers into my dress, and returned everything else as it had been.

*

About a week before I was due at Archfall Manor, the bailiffs descended on us. That morning, as I dragged myself off our ancient, sagging mattress, there was a horrible clatter that shook my very bones. I stumbled clumsily towards the stairs and listened to the cacophony of chaos. It was the sound of the upheaval of everything we owned.

I spotted three bailiffs traipsing in and out of the shop, brawny arms full of our belongings: saucepans, skillets, trays. These were the tools that Mam and I used every day to make the sweets. Some of these items of culinary equipment had been in our family for generations. They represented hours of work, years of dedication to the craft, decades of hope that this business would provide a good living for us and a legacy for the ones who came next.

And now anything that wasn't nailed down was being carted off.

I ran down to the kitchen where Mam had crumpled to her knees, her body wrapped round a small frying pan that we used when making pancakes on Shrove Tuesday. She looked up at me and saw that we were, momentarily, alone.

'They've sent for the constable,' Mam said. 'You know what that means.'

And I did know. If I didn't get out of there with haste, I'd likely be dragged away to the debtors' prison with her. I had to leave.

The bailiffs returned empty-handed and ready to grab more. I dashed up the stairs and crammed my paltry belongings into my satchel. My property did not amount to much – a shawl; my best dress, second-hand from the market but in excellent condition; my next-best, torn at the sleeve; my undergarments; the two books I owned, both gifts from Josephine on my eighteenth birthday, a Dickens and an Austen . . . and Josephine's stolen reference papers. I slung the satchel over my shoulder. Anxiety rose through my chest and lodged in the notch in my throat, making it hard to swallow.

I waited at the top of the stairs for the opportune moment to escape without my bag being searched for valuables. Mam was standing by the back door, had opened it for me in preparation. She gestured for me to come down, and wrapped me tightly in her arms. I could hear the thud of her heart, didn't want the embrace to end.

'Keep yourself safe,' she said. 'And write to me if you can. I don't know if I'll get letters in prison . . . but write them anyway.' I hated to think where she was going, how we would be apart.

'Of course I will. I love you.'

'I love you too.' She let go of me and forced a smile, but I could see the tears forming in her eyes. 'You're my brave girl. I'll miss you so much.'

The doubt had begun to creep in, to squeeze at my heart. I wasn't ready. I should have had another week to prepare, to say a real goodbye. We'd never spent a night apart in all our lives. I dreaded the thought of where she'd be by the time darkness fell.

'I'll work hard,' I said. 'And one day we'll be together again.'

A growling internal cruelty had started to rear its head. *You're not good enough. They'll see right through you and dismiss you immediately. You will never be worth anything.* I ushered the beast back into its cave with promises that it could berate me later, that it could keep me awake all night if it wished. But now I had to leave.

I hovered for a moment.

'Go.'

I told Mam I loved her again, my throat closing up and my eyes beginning to fill so that my vision started to swim. A clatter at the door signalled the return of the bailiffs, and so I slipped out into the alleyway. The back door slammed shut behind me.

I looked up at the shop, not knowing if I would ever set foot in it again, and a deep crack opened inside me. But I didn't have time to feel the tremors reverberating. I had to make myself scarce and there was only one place I could go.

With tears streaking my cheeks, I careered down the winding paths like a carriage with one wheel torn off. The harsh wind whipped me across the face as I ran. The cobbled streets of Durham were unforgiving, my feet in their thin shoes getting pummelled with every step as I hastened past the cluster of shops, weaving and dodging through crowds. I went as fast as I could, as though it might be possible to outrun the thoughts telling me I was worthless in this world, that it didn't matter how hard I tried, how hard I worked, I'd never be more than the girl from the sweetshop.

Sprinting past the River Wear, I hushed the echoing criticism in my mind and tried to focus on the task at hand.

I might never have been a governess before, but I was smart, I learned fast, and I wasn't afraid to take risks. I gritted my teeth. This post could just be the beginning for me.

It was only as I reached the corner before Harry's place that I smoothed down my skirts and slicked away the tears from my face. Even to my oldest friend, I would not show my devastation.

3

Harry Mirren was a coachman with a sweet tooth who worked for his father's transport service, and had been coming into the shop ever since we were children. Mam always had a theory that Harry was sweet on me too, and that one day I might have a realization about him – the sort of realization that ends in declarations of love and vows of commitment ... But I never saw him as anything other than a friend. He was somebody I could trust, though trust didn't come naturally to me, and it had taken years of practice, a slow, steady build. When we were younger, I'd sometimes make up secrets just to see if Harry could keep them. He always did.

When I arrived at the yard, Harry was wielding a paintbrush, tongue sticking out in concentration as he covered a scrape along the door of his coach. It looked as though the claws of a wild animal had ripped through it. He daubed the black paint on carefully.

'All the paint in the world couldn't make that coach look like new,' I said. I'd suppressed all my sorrow to present my usual nonchalant self to him. Harry started in surprise at the sound of my voice and turned to me, a spatter of black paint flecked across his cheek.

'Oh, you wound me,' he said, pretending the end of the paintbrush was a dagger about to pierce his heart.

I frowned. 'Looks like the coach is the wounded one.'

Harry turned serious for a moment. 'You may jest, but that's the work of a highwayman. Father was lucky to get away with his life.'

My mouth twisted in horror. 'That's not funny.'

'I'm not joking. Took every penny Father had on him. All his earnings from going to London and back, and you know that's a five-day round trip for him. So the coach is damaged, the horses are shattered and not a penny left for the trouble.'

'Harry, I . . . He's all right, though?'

'As right as can be, but I don't know how we're going to pay the rent this month.'

'You're lucky the horses weren't hurt.'

'I'll say – lots to be thankful for.' Harry snorted and blew his hair out of his eyes. It bounced to the rhythm of his breath, as soft and light as thistledown, and the colour of straw. 'Now then, what can I do for you, Trouble?'

'I need transport,' I said, and hurriedly added, 'I'll pay, of course.'

'You'll do no such thing. Where am I taking you?'

I cleared my throat. 'You must promise that you won't tell anyone. Not a single soul.'

'I swear it.' I never found trust a light or easy experience, but I knew I could rely on Harry.

'I'm going to take a governess position at Archfall Manor,' I said.

His eyebrows rose so high, they looked as if they were trying to escape his face completely. 'You're doing what?'

He knew that I'd become interested in the Cauldwell family, had even been a useful collector of memorabilia connected to the family given that he travelled further than me. But he believed it was just part of my studies with Josephine. I hadn't told him about the mysterious connection between the Cauldwells and my parents, that Mam considered them responsible for my father's death. I quickly explained about the advertisement, the letter, taking Josephine's reference, and the invitation to work for a trial period.

'You've been plotting all this for weeks then? You are unbelievable,' Harry breathed, and I got the sense there was a compliment buried in there, even if he couldn't understand the way I had kept this secret from him. He added, with a brief ripple of doubt in his eyes, 'I think there's something you should see first.'

He dashed into the house and brought out a little booklet, the likes of which I'd seen before. Sensational, nasty little stories, often called *penny bloods*. 'I saw this in town last week and had to get it for you.'

'*The Widow of Despair*?' I crinkled my nose. The rag was referring to Caroline Temple.

'You know she's been widowed three times now? One child from each husband, the youngest just a baby. People are starting to think she's cursed . . . or a murderess.'

'Surely you don't believe things like that,' I said.

'Well ...' Harry's brow was furrowed. 'I'm not sure about the curse idea, but people do get murdered, don't they?'

I took a deep breath. People did get murdered. Wasn't that what Mam had implied about my father? That the Cauldwell family were responsible? But she'd never called them murderers outright ... And the evidence against Mrs Temple must have been insubstantial in the cases of her husbands or she would have been arrested.

'Why the sudden rush?' Harry asked.

There was no point keeping it a secret, so I told him about Mam and the debt collector, and his cold eyes, and the chaos of the bailiffs and the threat of the debtors' prison.

'If I got caught up in the transfer to prison, they'd charge my keep to Mam's account. And if they decided that I was also liable for the debt, they could put me to work. Not that I'm afraid of hard work,' I added, 'but it becomes a trap, doesn't it? It becomes impossible to get out.'

Harry nodded. 'Your wages end up just covering your keep, and the debt never goes down.'

'Exactly,' I said, thinking again how hopeless it sounded, how lost Mam would be if my plan didn't work. 'And the salary at Archfall Manor is good.'

'I can see you're determined, and there's no stopping you once you are. Crossing to Sighfeyre Isle is only safe twice a day.' Harry was giving in, as I knew he would. 'It'll take us about an hour and a half to get even to the causeway, so the

27

earliest we'd arrive there is early evening. But I will take you, if you want me to.'

'I do. Thank you.'

Harry looked as if he were about to say more, as if something else were crossing behind those grey eyes of his.

'What?' I asked.

'You might be gone a long time,' he said.

'Maybe. It's not exactly something I can predict.'

'No.' He paused, pressed his lips together. I could almost see his thoughts dancing in circles. There was something he wanted to say, but he was fighting himself. 'I suppose you might be able to write to me?'

'I didn't know you could read,' I teased, but he went bright red.

'Well, I do a little. You wouldn't have to make it a novel.'

I squirmed – it was never my intention to embarrass him. This was how we had always jested with each other, an easy raillery that was never meant to be cruel. Harry was warm in all the ways I was cold; he was soft in all the ways I had created a hard shell round myself. But clearly this jab had struck too hard. I reached out and grabbed his hand, gave it a squeeze. 'Of course I'll write to you.'

He pulled his hand away, the flush in his cheeks spreading all the way to his ears. 'I'm sure you'll have plenty to keep you busy.'

'Undoubtedly. But I still will,' I said, although I couldn't really imagine how my hours would be filled when I arrived at Archfall Manor. Everything had begun to speed up, and I didn't feel ready. Mam called it plotting, the way I liked to be prepared for every eventuality, but to me it was more like what I imagined directing a play would be like. I wanted to set the scene, lay markers on the ground, and practise so that I might be ready for the unfolding when the live performance began. My rehearsal had been cut short, and I was going to have to rely more heavily on improvisation. It was almost time for the curtain to go up.

'We'll take Treasure,' Harry said. 'She's got a few days in her, and it's not as if there's a heavy load.' Treasure was a stocky horse, with thick strong legs and a beautiful chestnut-brown coat.

We set off at noon. I rode up front with Harry. There was a bounce and rhythm to the coach as Treasure trotted. Eventually, the city fell away into the countryside, and the sky seemed to expand in every direction. We were small beneath the rolling grey of the clouds, and the ominous thickening of the darkness in the sky.

Before long, we were the furthest I had ever been from home. I felt the string that tied me to Mam, to the shop, stretching taut inside me, tugging at my heart. I wondered what was happening to her. Had she been dragged off to prison? It made me feel sick to imagine. Our separation hurt like a clumsy kitchen knife slicing flesh.

I glanced sideways at Harry, to distract myself. I felt the urge to break the silence, the way a cat will sometimes push something fragile off a mantlepiece just to have done so.

'What are you thinking?'

His mouth twisted in a wry smile. 'You always ask me that,' he said. 'It causes whatever thoughts I had to freeze immediately and disappear. Then I look like a thoughtless fool with a mind full of air.'

'I just wondered if you were thinking about home. Does it not bother you to leave? Especially when you have to travel and stay away?' I asked, wrapping my shawl round me to fend off the bitterness of the wind that whistled past.

'Sometimes,' he said, and then fell back into silence.

This was an unsatisfactory answer. I wanted to know if this melancholy pang were fleeting, or if I would be forever wounded while I was away, like an injured animal.

'What do you usually think about when you're travelling then?'

Harry seemed utterly bemused, shaking his head with a little laugh. 'Why must someone always be thinking? Is it not enough just to breathe and to feel your chest fill with fresh air? You know your problem, Helena? You spend so long up here –' he tapped me on the side of my forehead – 'that you forget to be here,' and he slapped the seat we were sitting on.

My mind began to settle. Harry made everything seem simpler. Maybe I was thinking too much. But it was a momentary relief. A driving rain started to lash at us, and I shivered, though when Harry urged me to get in the carriage I refused. I wanted to see it all – all of the path that was leading me towards my new destiny.

Finally, we saw it.

Sighfeyre Isle was a surprisingly fragile-looking thing at first, poking up from the sea. The outline of Archfall Manor was a shadow against the grey sky, its central tower stretched up like the hand of a drowning man reaching for somebody to cling to. As we got closer, its hard lines and jagged rocks became clearer.

By the time Harry and I arrived at the coast, the tide was in, meaning there was no causeway path. We meandered through the small town, finding a public house that overlooked the sandy shoreline. We nursed the same drinks for hours, our clothes drying out in the warmth of the fire, as we waited for the moment of revelation when evening had begun to draw in . . . and, before our eyes, the way to Sighfeyre Isle appeared. The water receded, lapping back, retreating bit by bit to expose the causeway.

Where there'd been nothing but water, there was now a route. It happened so very fast, like the twinkling unveiling of the stars in the sky, or the release of rain earlier in the day. Nature showing us something that had been there all along, but merely hiding from sight, like a seasoned player revealing their hand in a game of cards.

'I never tire of seeing that,' the landlord said, appearing at our table and nodding out of the window. He was a rotund fellow with bulging eyes and a dark beard dashed through with grey.

'It's like something from a fairy tale,' I said, my voice breathy and awed. We all watched for a moment as the water continued to abate round the narrow, craggy pathway.

'Or a ghost story,' the landlord said. 'If it weren't for the deliveries, you'd think the family in that house had died a long time ago. Although there's a story that says even those that take provisions to and from the island don't ever see anyone living. Makes you think those deliveries are more like a sacrifice to whatever is really inside that old house.'

I found myself shivering, despite myself.

'So, where are you two headed?' the landlord asked. 'We've got a couple of rooms if you're needing a place for the night.'

'Thank you, but that's what we've been waiting for.' I gestured at the causeway.

The landlord looked startled. 'You're going to Archfall Manor?' He seemed utterly taken aback. 'I'm sorry, miss, I didn't mean to –'

I raised a hand to stop him. 'You didn't know. Thank you for your hospitality. You're an excellent storyteller. The rain has stopped, so we'll be on our way.' I stood and busied myself gathering up my now-dry shawl.

Harry cleared his throat. 'You're ready?' and I gave as convincing a nod as I could manage.

I sat up front with Harry again, and he geed Treasure into action, steering her downhill towards the coast. The air was full of a salty freshness that tingled the inside of my nostrils. The road wove down, slashing across the beach that stretched out on either side. When the tide was high, the road was abruptly cut off. But now that the water was low enough, a well-worn trail had been exposed, covered in tiny wet pools nestled atop the dips of the rocky surface. The causeway was a shimmering pathway, thin and straight, pointing like an arrow towards Sighfeyre Isle.

When we reached the edge of the sea, Harry brought Treasure to a halt. 'You're sure you're ready?'

I swallowed, pushing back the tightening of my throat. There was something fearful about the crashing of the nearby waves. It seemed as if they might swell and decide not to stop, that they'd end up engulfing us. But then I looked at the lights of the big house on the peak of Sighfeyre Isle. The whole place was glowing in the early-evening dusk, lit up as if oil cost no more than the mud on the bottom of your shoe. The house seemed alive.

And I remembered why I was there.

'I'm ready,' I said, and Harry encouraged Treasure once more with a click of his tongue and a flick of the reins.

We began our journey across the causeway, and my stomach turned. The sea seemed to me a tempestuous living thing. It would be so easy for it to take us. The way ahead was uneven, and the causeway was so narrow that there was barely enough room for the coach to fit. It wouldn't take much for Treasure to stumble, for us to plunge over the edge and be lost to the waves, but Harry was calm and steady beside me, and he guided his horse down the middle of the path carefully, allowing her to take her time.

I tried to focus on the manor growing closer, instead of the roaring of the sea echoing in my ears and the petrifying sight of the wind whipping the foamy waves into a frenzy. It occurred to me that this was the closest I had ever felt to nature, to death. It occurred to me too that my father had been here before me – had travelled this narrow path, come to this island, and never returned.

My shivering grew more intense.

And as we arrived at the other side of the causeway, I felt as though I were moving from one world into another, as though I were going to live with the fairies from the stories that Mam used to tell me as she melted a tiny taste of chocolate into warm milk for me before bed. Mam's imagination would twist the tales in ways I could never anticipate, but the ending would always be the same – a happy one, where the tricks of the fairies were exposed and bested, so that the human child could return home once more. I hoped that would be the case for me here too.

I breathed a sigh of relief as Treasure's hooves began to strike the surface of the island, and I looked over my shoulder to make sure that the sea was well and truly behind us. Turning back again, I could see that the big house was still a way ahead, but the windows glowed, almost seemed to throb against the darkness of the brickwork. Archfall Manor stretched three storeys high, a sprawling wing to the west and another to the east, and right at the centre was a jutting tower.

The biggest and brightest window of all was on the second floor, underneath the tower. Unlike the others, this was a great circular creation, split into four by intersecting timbers. It had the appearance of being the very heart of the building, and it gave me the strangest feeling. It was almost as if Archfall Manor were a living, breathing thing whose very soul resided in that central window. And above the window was the tower, topped by arches that made a crown.

A gasp of awe escaped from my mouth before I could help myself. I had never seen anything like it. It was worth braving the anger of the sea to get here. The house drew me in, like a fish on a reel.

'Don't tell me I've lost you forever,' Harry said as if reading my mind. 'This place has enchanted you already, and now you'll never come home.' He gave a small laugh, then suddenly made a strangled noise in the back of his throat. 'Whoa, Treasure!' he said, struggling with the reins.

We lurched to a stop, and I realized with horror that the solid surface of the road had descended into a thick, treacle-like mud. Treasure was struggling. Every time she lifted a hoof, there was an awful sucking noise. As she strained ahead, we pulled forward just a little, but not enough to shift the wheels of the carriage, and we rocked backwards again.

'We're stuck,' Harry said.

It was worse than that, I realized, looking over the side of the seat. We were sinking.

'What happened to the path?' I caught the panic in my own voice.

Harry ran his hands through his hair, his teeth gritted and his eyes wide. 'It was there, and then it wasn't. It felt solid. I couldn't see. It's so dark. I just –' He broke off and leaned forward in his seat, trying to get a better look at Treasure. The mud was halfway up her forelegs, and the more she struggled, the more the mire seemed determined to pull her in.

I stared again at the house – it was still too far away for anyone to hear us if we called. I considered clambering off the coach to try and make my way on foot, but surely I would be sucked down into the marshy bog as well. I had visions of us disappearing into the swamp, gurgling our final breaths as the sludge clogged our mouths, our noses ... We had arrived on Sighfeyre Isle, but the very ground seemed determined we would never make it to the house. It wanted to devour us, swallow us, and there would be nothing left to show we had ever been here.

4

I just needed to think. Could I leap from the coach to one side or the other, and hope to land on more solid ground? I peered out into the night again. We were utterly stranded in the ever-darkening mire. The brightly lit allure of Archfall Manor, closer than it had ever been, was still so far out of reach it pained me. We were lost in the darkness. If only someone at the house could see us . . .

Once the idea had occurred to me, I came alive with the urgency of it. We needed to create a light, a light bright enough to capture the attention of somebody who could come and help us. I slipped off my travelling shawl.

'Can you get on Treasure's back and cover her eyes?' I asked Harry.

He followed my gaze to the oil lamp suspended from a hook on the side of the coach. He hesitated, weighing the risks. He looked suspended in ice, his entire body completely frozen. Then he let out the breath he was holding in a great huff that steamed in the cold air. He galvanized himself into action, flinging one leg over the front of the barrier and then the other, speaking to Treasure in that gently coaxing voice again. Once he was firmly settled on her back, his hands covering her eyes, I opened the little window on the lamp and fed in the corner of my shawl. It caught alight, a tiny flickering flame at first.

The fire began to spread along the shawl, and so I lifted it, a blazing flag that couldn't fail to capture the attention of anyone glancing out of one of those many windows – so long as there was someone there to see it, of course. When the flames crept close enough to my fingers that I could feel the heat, I dropped the shawl into the mud, where it twisted and shrivelled as it burned to nothingness.

'All we can do now is hope that somebody saw.'

A brief moment of optimism lit in my chest. It was a smart idea, we had acted fast and, from what I could tell, Treasure had calmed and we didn't seem to be sinking any further. Harry released his hands from shielding Treasure's eyes and shuffled his way along her back.

When help arrived, perhaps twenty minutes later, although it felt a lot longer, it was also on horseback, but our rescuer knew where it was safe to step, the advantages of an insider.

'Who are you?' the rider called, authoritative and bold. He drew closer, and a pale lamp illuminated his features in flickers. Even so, I was startled to see that he was young, and handsome, with strong cheekbones and deep amber eyes.

'Please,' I said. 'Can you help us? The horse is stuck, maybe hurt.'

The rider's face creased with concern. 'What are you doing here? What are your names?'

I almost said Helena, almost fell at the first hurdle. The time had come to step into my new role, to hide my life behind a mask. I knew I would make fewer mistakes if I stuck as close as possible to truths rather than indulge the whims of fantasy, but even so I would need to stay alert to conceal my true identity.

'Josephine. Josephine Martin. And this is my good friend Harry Mirren.' Harry nodded his head in greeting, but I'd noticed him tense up when I had used the false name.

'Never heard of you,' the rider said.

'I'm the new governess.'

'I see.' He barely disguised his suspicion. He was defensive, proprietorial. 'The house isn't expecting you.'

'I know. I'm early, but I have brought my reference, and Mrs Caroline Temple offered me the post. I have her letter.'

The rider ground his teeth, deliberating, which only served to further define his jaw. A little muscle twitched in his cheek; our arrival was discomforting to him. 'You're lucky I saw your signal.'

'And who might you be?' I asked, trying to suppress the irritating flutter he inspired in my belly.

'Jasper Wright,' he replied. 'I work at the house. Maintenance.' He dropped off his horse and on to the spongy ground, seemingly knowing through instinct or experience where to land. 'We'd better get you inside.'

Then he was all practicality, unloading the wooden planks his horse had pulled on a little cart and creating walkways to bridge the distance between us. Harry followed Jasper's clear instructions, unhitching Treasure from the coach, while our rescuer set up a harness on his own horse which he then threw to loop round Treasure.

'The way the mud sucks you in out here,' Jasper called over the wind, 'you have to try and move horizontally. She mustn't lift her legs straight up. She'll just get stuck that way, as if she weighs more. But we'll get her out.'

I could see he was enjoying being the expert, his face lighting up as he outlined his plan. When he smiled, his cheeks scrunched up, revealing dimples that folded in, and his eyes crinkled at the edges. There was something irrepressibly radiant about him, in spite of his previously chilly demeanour.

'Your coach, however . . . we'll need to come back in the morning and see what we can salvage of it.'

Harry turned pale. The coach was his livelihood. I felt a stab of guilt for having ever put him at risk like this.

Jasper spotted this and instantly leaped in to provide reassurance. 'Don't worry. Nothing's unsalvageable in this house. We'll be able to get it fixed, but it might not be travel-worthy right away. My father and I, there's nothing we can't mend.' His smile now was wide and proud.

'Well,' I said, an edge to my voice that I didn't intend, 'aren't we lucky to have you?'

Jasper lifted his eyes to meet mine. 'I'd say you've got terrible luck,' he said. 'When we're expecting guests I always put down planks over this part, but it's still unusual to get as stuck as you have. Then again, this is the sort of thing that happens when you arrive somewhere unannounced. Be thankful you didn't trigger any of the traps.'

He sounded so sincere, I couldn't tell if he was joking, and suddenly was chilled with fear. He was right. Why had I thought I could simply turn up?

Because Mam and I are desperate, I thought, and sat up straighter.

Jasper pulled a timepiece from his pocket and consulted it. I only caught a fleeting look at the timepiece, but it appeared to be real gold, an heirloom perhaps, and it had all manner of extra hands and buttons I couldn't fathom the purpose of. I wondered if it were an invention of sorts – the kind the Cauldwells were famous for. But then why would one of their servants have such an item?

'I'll take you to the servants' entrance,' Jasper said, interrupting my thoughts. 'I'm sure we can work out what to do with you.'

He clambered back on to his horse and encouraged her to walk forward. Under Harry's careful guidance, Treasure lifted her leg, and Jasper's horse took all the weight. The sound of the sucking sludge peaked, before finally, mercifully, releasing Treasure from its hold. Inspecting her leg, Harry declared it unbroken, and got on her back.

Giddy with relief, I became more aware that the breeze was fierce, cutting right through the thin material of my dress. The air was tangy and salty and serrated with grit. Noticing my discomfort, Jasper jumped down and gestured for me to start moving towards the house.

'Wait, my bag is in the coach,' I said.

Jasper expertly stepped round to the back of it and

climbed up, avoiding the sinking sludge. He edged his way round the outside of the coach, spider-like, his feet never touching the ground, and opened the door. Reaching inside, he pulled out my sorry-looking satchel. 'Is this all?'

I flushed with embarrassment. 'Yes, thank you.'

He slung the satchel over his shoulder, and then guided me down, telling me exactly where to put my feet, his hand hovering in anticipation of my slipping. Solid ground had never felt so good. Once he was certain I was safely on the planks, Jasper put one booted foot in the stirrups and swung his leg over his horse. He tapped the space behind him. 'Hop up.'

'I . . . I don't know how.' I felt like a fish squirming on the end of a hook.

'Put your foot in the stirrup – that's right. Now take my hand.'

He reached down, and I grabbed his hand – a rough, working hand – and with his help lifted myself on to the back of the horse. I arranged myself side-saddle behind him, which I knew was the proper way for a lady, but it felt more than a little precarious. Perched on the horse's back, I was so very high up and flooded with giddiness again.

'It's a good job I didn't bring a heavy bag,' I joked, and Jasper laughed. It seemed as though he was warming to me. I glanced over my shoulder at Harry, who was watching us with what looked like apprehension creasing his features.

'Hold on,' Jasper said, and I tentatively placed my hands on his shoulders. Then he gave a quick kick, and the horse jolted forward. For a moment, I feared I might fall and gripped both my hands round his waist. I felt him tense slightly beneath my fingertips, the tiniest of movements that only served to draw my attention to his strength. He'd said he worked in maintenance – what did that mean? I found myself wondering how often our paths might cross.

The uneven lurching from side to side of the horse's gait was a peculiar sensation, the wind boxed me about the ears until they ached with the chill, and all around us was the great, wide, open marsh. In every direction, the sea swelled round the edges of the isle, tormented and angry. And, up ahead, Archfall Manor loomed over us.

The house had seemed like a bright, hopeful beacon when we had first arrived on the island, but as we drew closer I noticed some strange details and felt the back of my neck prickle with unease. At various locations across the brickwork, what looked like iron skulls with gaping, glassy eye sockets appeared to be built into the exterior wall.

'What are they?' I asked Jasper, pointing and wondering if I were simply mistaken in what I thought I was seeing.

'Ah, they're very clever,' Jasper said, and I could hear the admiration in his tone. 'They've been part of the house for a long time. The gazes of the faces are connected, so that you can see all through the house.'

That made me shudder – not just the fact that they were indeed skulls fastened to the walls, but also the idea that someone could be watching you without you realizing. It was an unsettling thought. Harry caught my eye as Jasper enthusiastically launched into a passionate oration about how the mechanics worked – all the angles and mirrors and glass perfectly arranged to make it possible. He looked as disquieted as I felt.

The stately main door was the grand entrance I'd always imagined, although finished, of course, with one of the glassy-eyed skulls. But instead of bringing us to the threshold, Jasper swept us round the east of the house. As I'd expected, there was a separate modest door for the servants to enter by, and a lean-to to shelter the horses from the worst of the weather before they went to the stables. As Jasper helped me down from the horse, Harry tied up Treasure.

And so it was that the very first time I entered Archfall Manor was through the staff entrance. I was struck then with the sense of having changed my fate irrevocably. Even if I wanted to turn back, it was too late now. Once I stepped through that door, nothing would be the same again. I prayed that I would find the fortune and the answers I craved.

5

The warmth of the kitchen flooded my bones instantly, and my body shivered gratefully. A great range emanated so much heat that even the stone-slab floor had soaked it up like a sponge. I was hit by a wall of steam and the hot, rich and comforting smell of slow-roasted meat. My mouth watered.

Every surface was covered in food – multiple courses prepared at varying stages of completion, ready to be timed to perfection. Soup bubbled, stuffed lobster rested, the range blasting heat was filled to bursting. My eye was drawn to a strange contraption that was washing plates autonomously. They were fastened to a great wheel that spun, dipping them into hot, soapy water, and a clockwork arm with a sponge then swiped across them. It seemed that the hallmarks of the Cauldwell reputation for inventing were everywhere.

At one of the great tabletops, a slender woman was working a dough. She paused to wipe sweat from her forehead with her apron, seeming breathless with exertion. The woman turned at the sound of our entry, and I noticed exhausted lines around her eyes as concern immediately creased her brow.

'Jasper!' The same amber eyes, the same sharp cheekbones, and a voice loaded with the unspoken language between parent and child. This must surely be his mother.

'Look what I found out in the mire, Ma,' said Jasper. 'A new member of staff, it seems ... and her ... transport provider.'

Harry stiffened beside me, bruised by the dismissive introduction.

'I'm the new governess,' I interjected. 'Josephine Martin.'

I reached out my hand, masquerading a calm I did not feel. This wasn't the moment to plunge into the fact that, technically, I wasn't invited, and technically I had been made a conditional offer of a position, and had not been appointed permanently.

'Teresa Wright,' she replied, brushing her floury hand across her apron and shaking mine. She maintained a still and steady expression, appraising me. 'We're not due a governess yet.'

'She's early,' Jasper said, before meeting my eye and giving a grin that turned my cheeks hot.

I reached into my satchel to recover the reference document, and thrust it into Teresa's hands, waiting while she perused it. It seemed to please her enough that she relaxed, just a little.

Jasper continued. 'You know we could use the help anyhow, Ma.'

'Don't I just. We have a skeleton staff,' Teresa explained, spotting my puzzled expression. 'Mr Cauldwell has long felt that staff are an unnecessary expense and a risk to his privacy and seclusion. When my husband and I moved here twenty-five years ago, it was already a very small team, but it's shrunk further over time.' Jasper had been born here, then.

'At the moment, it's just me and Pa on maintenance, and Ma in the kitchen and housekeeping,' Jasper interjected.

'No grooms? No gardeners?' Harry asked, shaking his head in disbelief.

'I look after the horses,' Jasper said, 'and do what I can in the grounds. It was fine when it was only Mr Cauldwell and Mr Wilbur to take care of, but now we've got a full house again, and we've not the staff to keep everything ticking over.'

I knew what he was referring to, of course, before Teresa explained to me. Mrs Caroline Temple, the Widow of Despair, had only recently returned to her father's home with three children in tow after the death of her latest husband. There was Nora, a year older than me, Birdie, eight years old, who was to be my ward, and the baby, Edmund, for whom Mrs Temple had brought a nursery nurse. It transpired that poor Molly, the nursery nurse, was taking care of the baby as well as setting about tasks like dressing Mrs Temple, Miss Nora and the children in the morning and preparing beds of an evening.

'Doesn't Mrs Temple have a lady's maid?' I asked.

'As I said, Mr Cauldwell prefers to keep staff to a minimum, so Mrs Temple only brought the nursery nurse,'

Teresa said firmly. 'It's taken him enough time to allow her to advertise for a governess.'

Although I sincerely wanted to probe and ask more about Mrs Temple's abrupt return to the house, I couldn't be too obvious in my questioning. But secretly I was snatching every crumb of information as if I were starving for lack of it. 'Well, I look forward to meeting Miss Birdie and beginning lessons.'

Jasper let out a strange little snort. Teresa shot a glare at him.

'What's so funny?' I asked.

He shook his head. 'Only someone who had never met Miss Birdie could anticipate her presence so eagerly. Haven't you wondered why the governess's post is vacant?'

'Well, I assumed because the previous governess was unable or unwilling to move to Archfall Manor,' I said, feeling a little irritable. 'Mrs Temple has been residing in London, has she not? Not every governess might want to relocate.' I hated this feeling of being on the back foot somehow. It was like peering through fog.

'Jasper.' Teresa's tone was stern. Clearly, she had a habit of discretion that her son was yet to gain.

'Right,' Jasper said, and I suppressed a sigh – perhaps Jasper would be easier to mine for information when his mother wasn't around to remind him of his loyalties to the family. 'No more talk about the family then.'

Teresa's frown deepened. 'I have no problem with a bit of talk among staff,' she said matter-of-factly, 'but I will not tolerate rumour under this roof. Speculation at the expense of our employers is beneath you.'

'I wasn't –' Jasper began.

Teresa raised her finger for silence. Harry and I met each other's eyes, both slightly amused at having to witness the telling-off.

'I only mean to prepare her.' Jasper glowered, and I could feel the embarrassment radiating from him. I was beginning to believe that he might be just the guide I needed to navigate the complexities of life on Sighfeyre Isle.

'So, what are we going to do with you, little governess?' Teresa tapped her chin, thinking aloud. She glanced up at a large brass clock on the furthest wall and tutted. Her lips moved as if she were having an internal conversation, debating the correct course of action – whether to hide me until morning or take me to meet the family now, even though they would soon be appearing for their evening meal.

Teresa huffed a sigh, clearly having made a decision. 'I think we must make you up a bed for the night, and you can be presented to Mrs Temple in the morning.' She turned to Harry. 'And you, will you be needing to stay tonight?'

'His coach is a bit the worse for wear, and his horse needs to rest,' Jasper said. 'He can take the spare bed in my room tonight, and then Pa and I can have a look at repairing the damage to the coach in the morning.'

'You think you can fix it?' Harry asked, leaking anxiety.

'Well, if I can't, Pa definitely can.' Jasper slapped a hand on Harry's shoulder. 'Although I can't promise you'll be ready to go tomorrow. Hope you don't have any urgent appointments.'

Sorry, I mouthed to Harry.

'Jasper, will you show Josephine to one of the empty maids' chambers? I'll bring you some sheets after supper.'

'Follow me,' he said, leading me out of the kitchen. As we left, I heard Teresa quizzing Harry on his plans for departure. Opening the first door on the left, Jasper revealed a modest dormitory with two unmade single iron-framed beds and a little basin.

'Is this . . . where I'll be staying?' I asked. I'd hoped that, as a governess, I would be housed with the family, not with the servants. I'd heard governesses often occupied an elevated role within the hierarchy of the house, and the thought of such a social promotion had filled me with excitement.

'I'd imagine so,' Jasper said, shrugging. 'Molly sleeps in the room next to the nursery right up on the second floor, so you'll be on your own in here.'

I fought to keep my disappointment hidden. Truthfully, I'd been hoping for soft bedspreads, plump pillows.

'As a newcomer at Archfall Manor, I suppose I will have to familiarize myself with the ways of the house quickly,' I ventured.

'I should say so. Strange ways here, that's for sure,' Jasper said with a chuckle. 'And the Cauldwells are very particular about how they like things done. We're only just getting used to it all being different with the arrival of Mrs Temple and her children.'

His hand was pushing the door open, and I was trying not to notice how his arm tensed, how his broad shoulders filled the doorway. For a fleeting moment, it crossed my mind how improper it would look if anyone saw Jasper and me, our eyes meeting across the room . . . And yet it felt unlikely we'd be interrupted by anyone. There really was only a handful of staff for a house of this size.

A strange, discomforting sensation drizzled through me as I walked into the room, like melted lemon sugar sliding through a hot cake. With dismay, I recognized the feeling: I was attracted to him. I'd felt that way before, years ago now, when I first met a lad who worked at the butcher's shop, who I nursed a secret infatuation with. He was crushed to death by a carriage before I ever made my feelings known, and I cried for a week . . . and had never felt that way about anyone else since. But now here it was, horribly inconvenient, ignited. I ought to have been focused on my plan – keeping my head down, earning some money, and perhaps finding out some snippets of information about what happened to my father – but my mind was suddenly flooded with the sort of thoughts that belonged in the fictional romance novel I'd been so entertained by.

'Well then,' I said, hovering in the middle of the room, waiting for Jasper to leave.

'Ah,' he said, realizing what I was waiting for and backing out of the doorway. 'Of course.' He shook his head at his own absent-mindedness, making the thick waves of his hair bounce, and let out a small laugh.

'What are you laughing at?' I asked.

A smile flickered across his lips like the flame of a candle. 'Only a thought.' He shook his head again.

Might his thought have had an echo of mine? Did something intangible flicker between us?

Then he suddenly turned pensive. 'I'm sure you're curious to meet the family, but there's a piece of wisdom I'd offer you for tomorrow. Something my pa has always said: follow their lead.'

'Follow their lead?'

That almost-smirk again. 'My pa, Gabriel Wright – he's head of maintenance, but the work he does for Mr Cauldwell with the inventions is what many would say is unique ... Pa always told me when I was growing up, if I wasn't sure how the Cauldwells wanted me to act, to follow their lead. They appreciate a little boldness.' He gave me an earnest and encouraging smile – his most true of the evening.

I took this opportunity to dig a little more. 'The inventions, is that the work that you do too?'

Now his eyes truly shimmered with excitement. The transformation in his features was immediate. 'Yes. Well, I'm learning,' he said. 'The skulls you saw are just the start of it.'

'I saw the contraption in the kitchen too,' I said. 'It's very clever. Must save your mother some time.'

Jasper beamed. 'One of Pa's. I'll show you more when you're settled in.'

He turned to go, but I wasn't quite done with him yet. 'What are you working on at the moment?' I asked.

'Mostly I've been learning about electromagnets,' he said. 'Mr Cauldwell went to a lecture held in London and hasn't stopped talking about the potential of them. I mean, you have to understand: the fact that he left the island to attend this lecture tells you just how important the theory is.'

'Electromagnets?' I was baffled by the word alone.

'It's complex ... but it's the idea that you can use magnets to induce a current across an electrical conductor. Electricity is such an incredible force, and there's so much we're still learning about it ... What I've been wondering is whether the power of it could be used to manipulate time. Speed it up, slow it down.'

I gawped. I didn't understand the scientific principles, and some of the words he'd used I couldn't even deduce the meaning of. But what he was describing, his idea about time ... it was impossible. Fantastical. I shook my head. 'You can't be serious.'

'You have no idea.' Jasper grinned. The dimple on the left was deeper than the one on the right. 'What we're trying to do here will change the world. It's like the archways at the top of the house – do you know what they were built for?' His eyes sparkled, and I was captivated, my heart puttering in my chest. Jasper's excitement was contagious – the exhilaration ran in little rivers of sensation across my skin.

'No,' I said, entranced, but I thought I knew a little already – I'd read Edwin Cauldwell's pamphlet. I realized there was something about Jasper that felt like meeting somebody I already knew, had known for a long time. When he spoke about the inventions – with wonder in his voice – I could tell he was dreaming of a bigger future for himself. He nurtured a deep aspiration. And that . . . that spoke to something right at my own core. 'Tell me.'

'Two decades ago, the elder Cauldwell son, Edwin, was working on a theory of time. He thought it existed in layers, and if you could create a powerful enough doorway, you could make a window between two layers. He was developing a prototype using an archway at the top of the manor, convinced that if he could harness lightning . . . Well, this new notion of electromagnets could change everything.'

I thought of Edwin's pamphlet, the one my father had kept about the theory of time. It was more than just an idea: it was something Edwin had been actively working on. And it sounded as if there had been recent scientific developments that would have made a huge difference to his work.

'He died, didn't he?' I asked. 'The older son, I mean.'

Jasper nodded. 'Eighteen years ago last month.'

I felt a sudden chill. Eighteen years ago, I was a tiny baby, and my father had already left my family to come to Sighfeyre Isle. He was connected with this work somehow, I was sure of it. I wanted to ask Jasper – *did Edwin work with a watchmaker? Did he commission someone to come to the island?* – but I knew that would surely only arouse suspicion.

'And his work hasn't been touched since then?' I asked instead – but immediately sensed this was probing excessively. A barrier rose behind Jasper's eyes. A wall that wasn't there before constructed in seconds.

'I think I've said too much,' he said.

'Not at all,' I said. 'I'm sorry – I'm just curious. I've never heard of such wondrous things before.'

'I forget sometimes,' he said, folding his arms across his chest.

'Forget what?'

'That some things belong to Sighfeyre Isle and some things don't.' Was he talking about the information he'd given me, about the archway? Or . . . was he talking about me? 'We don't usually have new people arriving from outside.'

'Wait. Have you ever left the island?'

Jasper shrugged. 'A handful of times, but it's never been an issue. It's not as if the town is much to get excited about,' he added quickly, but I sensed something brewing beneath. He couldn't meet my eyes any more. I was eager to regain the easy companionship we'd had just moments before. Before he'd considered he might have shattered some unspoken pact of secrecy and broken the spell. 'I need to go back and help Ma serve the dinner.'

He turned and left me alone with my thoughts, my mind buzzing like a hive. I tried to sift through everything I had learned. More than ever before, I had a sense that this place held clues. But it felt as though the secrets of Archfall Manor would be closely guarded.

*

After the family had finished their dinner – a lengthy affair – Jasper came back with a large bowl of hearty root vegetable soup for my supper. It was so creamy and perfectly spiced I couldn't help but shovel it into my mouth greedily, bursting with gratitude, and shortly feeling more satisfied and full than I had in weeks.

'You were hungry,' Jasper said, laughing.

'It is absolutely delicious,' I said. I wanted to ask him more about the archways, the theory of time, but just then, Teresa arrived, sheets bundled in her arms. She bustled into the room and set about making up a bed for me, giving Jasper a sharp look over her shoulder, a reminder of the correctness that seemed to have abandoned us, the fact that we'd forgotten it wasn't proper to be alone together. He gave me a little wave and disappeared down the corridor.

I shook my head slightly. I needed to forget Jasper and focus my attention on what I had come here to do. I wasn't going to earn the money needed to get Mam out of the debtors' prison overnight. I had plenty of time to uncover how the family were connected to mine – and clearly pressing the issue wouldn't get me there any faster.

When Teresa was finished, she reassured me that she would come for me first thing in the morning and asked if I needed anything before bed. I sheepishly gestured to my mud-soaked gown, flushing with embarrassment and explaining that I only had one other. She nodded in understanding, dipped out of the room and came back after a while with a pile of neatly folded gowns that Molly the nursery nurse had kindly offered to donate to me. I was surprised to learn they were apparently her oldest outfits, and spare at that. To me, they were beautiful and so much softer than anything else I'd ever worn. She'd even included a robe and a nightgown. I asked Teresa to please pass on my gratitude, but she assured me I would have the chance to thank Molly myself the next day.

When she finally left, and I was alone, I stripped down to my undergarments and pulled the nightgown over my head. When I climbed beneath the bedsheets, I found myself instantly soothed by the comfort of the bed. As much as my mind was whirring and attempting to plan my next steps for the morning, I found myself unravelling into sleep.

And yet there was something that couldn't stop wriggling around in my mind. Edwin Cauldwell had died the same year as my father had. Surely there was a connection between the two deaths? It was the nearest thing I had to a clue so far . . . I knew my father had been interested in his theories of time; he'd had a copy of that pamphlet after all. He'd been invited to come here. Maybe Edwin had been consulting him? Maybe he needed a watchmaker – that would fit, surely?

Edwin Cauldwell died believing his invention would facilitate time travel. Did his reckless experimenting hurt my father in the process?

I didn't believe in the fanciful concept of what he'd been investigating, but it seemed to me that the arches were the place to start looking for clues about my own past. At the very least, I would uncover more about the death of Edwin Cauldwell, which would be useful information for my assimilation into the household. But I might also be able to ascertain how – *if* – his death was connected to my father's. It was somewhere to begin.

6

I was muddled, in a state somewhere between slumber and waking, when a dreadful clattering roused me. There had been some haunting dream troubling me; I vaguely remembered the sensation of being lost within a labyrinth, the panicky feeling in my chest like a giant moth beating its wings, searching for light. I realized I was tangled in the sheets, which were damp and twisted round my legs, and I was so utterly disoriented, not remembering where I was. The night was dark, the sort of darkness that felt alive and crawled in front of my eyes.

As I came to my senses, I realized that the noise that had woken me was the wind thrashing away. I had never known a wind so violent – it seemed as though it had a personal grievance against the window, against the manor, against Sighfeyre Isle itself. As my eyes adjusted, I saw the window pane clinging to its frame desperately, and the shape of the draped curtain, an unfamiliar shadow. I hated the racing of my heart, and tried to rationalize my fear to myself. It was natural to feel this way. I was not at home. Home was many miles away, and . . . And it was empty. I was alone in a strange place, shocked out of sleep by the anger of the wind. Of course I felt fitful and disturbed.

But then the whispering began. It was odd; it seemed to be coming from the walls of the room itself. A sound like an endless trickle of water, a whisper, desperate and fast, but so muffled that I could not make out any individual words. It was like trying to eavesdrop on a conversation made for someone else's ear, and yet I had a sense that the whisper was meant for me. It sent a shudder down my back, inevitably making me think of ghosts. I'd heard of spirits calling through from another realm, and I ground my jaw down against the fear, though my teeth threatened to chatter right out of my mouth.

I forced myself to consider logic again – I had never tolerated notions of the supernatural before and did not intend to now. And yet – who could it be, talking at this hour? Everyone was sleeping, in rooms so far away it would be impossible for me to overhear them. Surely the whispering was just a figment of my imagination, my mind seizing upon the unsettled weather and conjuring the rest due to the strangeness of my surroundings, caught in the in-between world of waking and sleeping.

That is how I convinced myself that the whisper was something to be ignored. I pulled the sheets round me for comfort and muffled the noise with my pillow and my blanket. I did not want to listen to it.

Now I wonder how it might all have been different if I had tried harder to hear the solicitations of that whispering voice. Which of the horrors that unfolded on Sighfeyre Isle might have been prevented if I had listened, if I had understood?

But I was frightened, and I wanted to block out the sound. I struggled to fall asleep again – the way the shadows fell across the bed disturbed me; the empty bed opposite mine unsettled me; the room felt altogether too strange and unfamiliar. And every time I released the blanket from its muffling protection of my ears, the whisper continued to try to reach me.

Eventually, I became peaceful again and surrendered myself to sleep, only to be roused once more by the crying of the baby, a pained wail that echoed out from somewhere else in the house. The whisper was silenced by the sounds of life, and I told myself that indeed I had imagined or dreamed it in the first place, thankful for the respite and the intrusion, although I did not fall back into an easy sleep.

When morning finally broke, it took me a moment to realize I was at Archfall Manor, miles away from the sweetshop I'd always known. The truth settled with a twang inside, as if I were an instrument with a broken string. Waking up alone, and so unrested after the disturbed night, I was wracked with grief being away from Mam. It was as though my heart were a bowl of liquid caramel being scraped out for every last drop.

I dragged myself out of bed and splashed my face with cold water from the basin in the corner. I changed into one of the dresses from Molly – a dark navy creation with narrow sleeves and a lacy collar. I had to reach behind my head to button myself up, feeling as though I were playing pretend, acting out the role of a governess. I *was* pretending to be someone else, and I couldn't risk forgetting that.

I presented myself in the kitchen, where Teresa was preparing a large and extravagant breakfast – the smell of sizzling sausages made my mouth water – and she'd already arranged thick crusty bread, butter the bright yellow of daffodils and an array of cold meats. There was a platter of tiny, braided pastries, and a thick vat of porridge bubbled on the hob. Harry was ensconced in a corner, wolfing down a bread roll slathered with butter that seemed to be utterly delighting him. I had assumed this was food waiting to be taken to the dining room, but it seemed it was for us – or at least some of it.

'You ought to wait here after your breakfast,' Teresa said to me, 'and I'll present you to Mrs Temple when the family have eaten.' A ripple of nerves moved through me, the anticipation a raw sensation.

'You definitely want to wait until they've drunk their coffee,' Jasper said, strolling in. He wore an exhausted expression that suggested he'd slept about as well as I had.

'Enough of that, and help me, will you? Molly went to dress Mrs Temple a half-hour since, so they'll all be ready by now.'

I felt a pang of sympathy for Molly – up in the night soothing the baby, and then up at the crack of dawn to dress Mrs Temple, Miss Nora and Miss Birdie. The demands on the few staff here were extraordinary. Teresa had pulled together all the elements of what appeared to me a triumphant breakfast, prepared single-handedly, yet still maintaining her composure and her polished appearance. No wonder everyone had an exhausted look about them – it was too much for this small team to hold up the weight of such a house and such a family. It was a wonder they weren't all crushed to dust.

Jasper and Teresa balanced serving dishes up their arms. They bustled out of the kitchen and there was a calm left in their wake, the only sound the blip-blip-blipping of the bubbling porridge.

I went to Harry's side. 'Did you hear a noise last night? Like a . . . whispering?' I was eager for some confirmation that I hadn't entirely lost my mind.

'No,' he said, frowning. 'Do you mean the gale? It was pretty fierce. I don't have high hopes for the state of my coach.'

'You must be worried,' I said, disheartened he hadn't heard what I had. I sat next to him and tamed my hair into submission ready for my presentation to the family. 'I'm sorry, Harry.'

'Jasper seems confident they'll be able to put it right. But I tell you, I didn't sleep well, though,' he said. 'I was having strange dreams.'

'Dreams?'

'The walls were closing in on me . . . the room becoming smaller and smaller, and I was going to be crushed by them. It was as though the house were . . .' He trailed off and shook his head. 'It sounds foolish now the morning is here. I woke up in a terrible sweat.'

'That's horrible,' I said, and I wondered what the rest of his sentence was going to be. *As though the house were . . .* what?

He lowered his voice. 'Are you sure that you want to stay? Jasper and his mother seem welcoming enough, but . . . there's something about this place, Helena. It doesn't feel right. You don't have to go through with this, you know. You could –'

But Teresa and Jasper returned before he could finish, and before I had the chance to answer him. They set to work immediately again in a bustle of chatter, clearing and cleaning and setting off the spectacular contraption that sluiced the dishes.

'Will I go to Mrs Temple now?' I asked, aware that my nerves meant I was bordering on impatience.

'I'll take her,' Jasper said. 'And then I'll be back for you –' he pointed at Harry – 'to get that coach roadworthy!'

Harry gave him a wobbly smile that lacked conviction. If Jasper and his father weren't the miracle workers he claimed they were, the consequences didn't bear thinking about for Harry and his father. Guilt tore at me again, and I gave Harry a little nod. Then I followed Jasper out of the kitchen and finally, *finally*, like a culmination of my whole life until that moment, I went to meet the Cauldwell family.

7

As we emerged on to the pearlescent tiled floor of the main entrance hall, I struggled to contain a gasp. The light. There was so much of it! Light fuelled by oil and captured in orbs along walls that had been painted a delicate grey. A chandelier above us fractured the light into glinting shards. I had never seen light captured and *owned* that way – so excessively, so extravagantly. It was as though the Cauldwells had broken the sun into pieces and imprisoned it. The natural morning light from the windows was weak and strained by comparison, and the house would have seemed so gloomy without the glowing lamps.

I wanted it. I wanted to own light too. I thought with faint embarrassment of how Mam and I had eked out a tiny candle stub for weeks. A muddle of awe and envy fought inside me. Jasper watched my reaction, a smile flickering across his lips like a flame. His pride in this family and their house was almost as if they were his own. Perhaps one day I would feel that way too.

We walked past the centre of the entrance hall, which was dominated by an incredible marble staircase.

The stairs grew wider as they cascaded down in a way that made me think of a waterfall. The final step was an enormous curve. I found myself straightening up, becoming aware of my posture. The house demanded it.

'This place,' I murmured.

It was captivating, and I felt as though I had waited my whole life for it. I just needed to make sure that I earned it, that I proved myself worthy of a position. I had better get used to being part of the house. The sound of the sea crashing on the rocks outside reached us and reminded me how isolated we were on this tiny island. The persistent rolling of the waves was almost hypnotic.

'It is rather impressive,' Jasper conceded. 'I think you'll fit right in.'

I gave him a sideways look of scepticism. 'Because I'm so impressive?'

'You travelled to a tidal island in the beginnings of a storm and rode horseback for the first time in your life to get here,' he said. 'Oh, and you started a small fire to save your skin. I'd say you're a force to be reckoned with.'

The compliment ignited a glow in my chest, and I was rendered at a loss for words. He was so self-assured and free when he spoke – it was refreshing, and far from what I was used to. I was still grasping for a response when he touched my elbow gently, guiding me further across the entrance hall, to the western wing of the house.

'This way.'

'Anything I should know before meeting Mrs Temple?' I asked, considering how little I truly knew about my future employer ... I wanted to make the best possible first impression.

'She's very protective of her children,' he said. 'Despite having Molly, she insists on going in and out of the nursery herself all day. She's always been maternal, though. I remember when I was really little and she visited the isle, she'd secretly give me some rich toffee from the mainland.' His eyes glazed over at the memory, and even my mouth started to water at the thought.

'I know a recipe for toffee that would make your head spin,' I told him.

'I look forward to it.' He grinned deeply, and I desperately hoped I wasn't blushing.

Protective of her children. If I were to make a success of this, then Birdie must love me. Noted.

Just as we headed into the sprawling western-wing corridor, a striking figure as pale as a ghost appeared as if from nowhere. She wore a black gown with caped shoulders, tight sleeves and a full skirt, and her auburn hair was pinned up, smooth and sleek in a way that mine would never be.

Jasper bowed his head deferentially as he greeted her. 'Miss Nora,' he said.

The elder daughter. In all my research, she had remained a mysterious unknown, although from the timing of Mrs Temple's marriages, I calculated Nora must be about a year older than me.

'Jasper – who is this?' Nora asked. She took great strides towards us, and I took in her Cupid's-bow lips and long dark eyelashes. Her cheeks were pinched, more like an impoverished street urchin rather than having the plump roundness I would have expected in the granddaughter of one of the richest men in England. 'Are you becoming quite the cad? I don't see a chaperone.'

Nora was teasing, and she was delighting in it, an impish grin revealing her pointed eye teeth. 'How did you even manage to sneak her across the causeway? I love it, Jasper. I simply love it!'

'This is the new governess,' Jasper said, refusing to rise to her bait. 'Miss Josephine Martin.'

'New governess!' Nora rushed over to me and grabbed my hand, her perfectly cut fingernails leaving dainty half-moons in my palm as she forced my arm up and encouraged me to spin for her. I felt as though I might combust with embarrassment and anger at the indignity.

Nora appraised me further, and her strange playfulness was replaced with a severe, assessing gaze. 'My mother was most impressed with your letter, Miss Martin. She made me listen to her read it out over the breakfast table. Every damned word. It was quite something.'

'Thank you,' I said, although I wasn't entirely sure she had paid me a compliment.

Nora frowned. 'I thought we weren't expecting your arrival for another week. My sister will be most disappointed. I've been filling her days with mischief.' Her eyes were like twin flints sparking.

I mumbled something about personal circumstances having changed.

Jasper leaped in. 'She arrived last night. My mother thought it best to wait until morning to introduce her to the family.'

Nora raised one eyebrow in a perfect arch. 'I see. Well, I'll take you to meet my mother. I imagine she'll want to have a good look at you.'

Her voice was as fresh and crisp as the skin of an apple. But instead of taking me to her mother, Nora continued to stare at me, hard. She seemed so astute, I felt if anyone were to identify me as a fraud, it would be her. It would only take one slip of the tongue and Nora would certainly alight on it, like a magpie on a lost engagement ring.

'Best of luck,' Jasper said under his breath, but his smile was muted.

Finally, Nora gestured for me to follow her, and I glanced at Jasper over my shoulder, a lone figure in the stretching corridor.

'So, you're to bring my feral little sister into line, are you?' Nora asked as we walked.

'I hope to be able to give her a good education.' I wasn't sure what sort of response Nora wanted from me. Was she always so inquisitive, so provoking? It was wrong-footing me.

'She's a little fiery.' Nora said this with pride. 'Ate her last governess alive.'

'I'd probably taste quite bitter.'

It was supposed to be a joke, but the second it was out of my mouth I worried that I had overstepped. Nora burst into an easy laughter, but my relief was short-lived. Her tone swiftly turned sinister as she gave me an undisguised warning about her little sister.

'I'm afraid I'm not joking. Birdie tricked her, you see, and locked her in the basement of our London house. We didn't know she was down there, thought she'd run off. Only found her two days later, by which time she couldn't speak with the stress and the fear. In fact, I never heard her speak again; I was told they took her away to some kind of lunatic asylum in the end. I don't think Birdie means to be evil. She's so intelligent, you see. Perhaps you'll be able to get through to her.'

An involuntary gasp caught in my throat. Was Nora trying to terrify me? Was this some sort of test? It couldn't possibly be true, could it? I was attempting to regain my composure, ready for my introduction to Mrs Temple, when a great barking shout erupted from one of the rooms up ahead.

'It is *my time*, Father!' This yell was accompanied by an almighty thud, as if a table or a wall had been struck by an angry fist. The raging voice continued. 'Why must you insist on controlling everything? And how might you have felt had your father done the same to you? I will not have the opportunity to lead until I prise it from your cold, dead hands, will I?'

The conversation was obviously private and never meant to be witnessed or overheard. I felt keenly like an intruder.

I looked to Nora, who appeared unimpressed, even bored. When she spoke, it was in a disinterested drawl.

'My uncle, Mr Wilbur Cauldwell. He is . . . frustrated. My grandfather is head of an internationally renowned organization, the Cauldwell Institute of Invention. Mr Wilbur believes it is his turn now to assume leadership. Oh, and you must call him Mr Wilbur,' Nora added as an aside. 'My grandfather feels very strongly that he will be the only Mr Cauldwell in this house until he is dead. Which I think tells you everything you need to know about how Mr Wilbur feels.'

I was startled. His whole family addressing him as a child, although he must have been in his forties? It must have grieved him terribly to be lowered and humbled so.

Whatever Mr Cauldwell thought about his son's tirade, his response was quiet and controlled – not one jot of it trickled through the door as we walked past. But whatever he said whipped Wilbur into a greater fury, and his voice exploded once more.

'But Edwin is gone!'

'And don't you feel an ounce of responsibility for that?' This time, Mr Cauldwell's reply came through sharp and clear.

The door nearly swung off its hinges, smashing into the wall, as Wilbur burst through into the corridor, a snarl on his lips.

Nora and I leaped back, and I caught a glimpse of the room. The small figure of Mr Cauldwell was bent over a mantlepiece, a dying fire in the grate. He seemed neither surprised nor perturbed by his son's rage. Meanwhile, Wilbur stormed past us, eyes like lightning and steps like thunder. He was utterly committed to his rage, and, for a moment, I thought I had managed to avoid his attention – until he turned, and I was caught in the net of his glare. His gaze swept up and down over me as he scrutinized my presence in the hallway, one eyebrow cocked in curiosity. His head was square and blocky, like a tomcat's. Long whiskery sideburns added to the feline nature of his appearance, and his furious expression gave the impression of someone ready to fight, claws unsheathed.

'Who are you?' His voice was brusque, the tendons in his neck like thick ropes. The short question was laced with criticism, as though he were eager to expose me as a trespasser.

'I'm the new governess, sir,' I said. I dipped my eyes to the ground, as though I might be able to shrink back into the very wall itself.

'And you make a habit of lurking in corridors, do you? That's a good beginning.' There was a twitch in his left eye. His anger had been exposed, and he knew it.

'Oh, do control your temper, Uncle,' said Nora, her jaw set. It was the response I would have loved to give him. 'She's hardly lurking. I am taking her to meet Mother.'

'Is that so? Well, you'll soon learn your place,' Wilbur said, bringing his tone much lower than before.

I wasn't sure whether he was speaking to me, or Nora, or to both of us, but his words were broken glass, all spiked with threat. He turned and stalked away down the corridor. Nora took me by the arm, as if we were good friends taking a stroll out in the gardens, and steered me back on our path to find her mother.

The door creaked behind us, and Mr Cauldwell appeared. I allowed myself to take a look at him over my shoulder with as much subtlety as I could. I was struck again by his frailty – not what I had imagined of this leader of invention before I arrived. The legend of this family's patriarch had evoked a much larger man, but Mr Cauldwell was stooped and slim, and his shoulders seemed to bear an invisible weight. His hair followed a receding line, and what remained was thin and barely holding on. He looked like a haunted man, sagging eyes betraying difficulty sleeping. I thought the loss of his son hung across him like a cape. Here was a man who probably stayed awake, thinking about his eldest child, whose death had been reported, but whose body had never been recovered.

Mam's voice cut through my own thoughts, clear and ringing: *That family are dangerous . . . They're the reason your father is dead.*

And now I'd heard Mr Cauldwell ask his son if he felt responsible for the loss of one of their own. Two dead, that I knew of. Were these deaths accidental or . . . something worse?

My bravery was dissipating now that I had arrived. My tongue stuck to the roof of my mouth, and I felt sweat gathering uncomfortably beneath my arms, on my brow. But I knew I must steel myself. The Cauldwells were a secretive family, and there were hidden stitches I needed to unpick if I was ever going to understand them and adjust to my place in the household.

I had chosen this fate, and there was no turning back now.

8

As we walked, I tried to make a map of the house in my mind, building the enormous shape of it. Nora told me that her mother would be found in one of the reading rooms – one of them! – at this time of day, as she liked to spend her time immersed in literature as an escape from the tiresome reality of the isle. I counted the doors as we passed, trying to commit the floor plan to memory so I might find my way around by myself. Finally, Nora came to a halt at the end of the corridor and rapped the back of her knuckles against the door, which looked the same as all the others.

The door swung open with force, gripped by a woman who was a vision in black – she wore thick and elegantly embroidered skirts, glinting earrings and a necklace, both silver and clutching stones of jet, and atop her coiled raven hair there was a mourning cap like a crown. The Widow of Despair, Mrs Caroline Temple. She was a strikingly beautiful woman, and she was plump everywhere – cheeks, lips, waist. I noticed there were the beginnings of crow's feet and gentle lines across her forehead – perhaps caused by worry, I thought.

'I've brought your new governess,' Nora announced, as if I were a piece of post to be delivered.

'Governess?' Mrs Temple frowned, and looked at me for the first time. 'I'm not expecting a governess.'

I performed a small curtsey, keeping my eyes low. When I spoke, I did so slowly. 'My name is Josephine Martin, Mrs Temple. I know you're not expecting me just yet, but I am afraid some family circumstance has left me with no option but to come to you and request an early beginning to my employment.'

'"Family circumstance"?' Each word was crisply enunciated. 'I will be interested to hear more about that. My daughter and I certainly know what a challenge family circumstance can be.' The two of them met eyes, and I saw an understanding pass between them.

'I brought a reference,' I said, and rummaged in my pocket for the papers.

Mrs Temple reached out to receive them. Her hands were so smooth and delicate, the nails filed into perfect ovals. She had never truly needed to work. Mrs Temple scrutinized the reference papers, while Nora watched her face closely. My breath came shallow and uneasy, but she appeared impressed. When she got to the end, she folded the papers over and handed them back to me.

'So, Miss Martin. What brings you to Sighfeyre Isle earlier than we arranged, without sending word in advance? As you'll have seen, we are a small party here. I imagine your unexpected arrival has caused all manner of commotion in the kitchen.'

I cleared my throat, unsure how to proceed. If I were to tell the truth, what would happen? At best, I anticipated anger. At worst, the loss of all opportunity to learn the truth about what happened to Father, loss of the chance to save Mam from her fate in the prison.

The denial of myself made me feel uncomfortable. I had a false name, a false reference ... but perhaps the rest of my story need not be untrue.

I took a deep breath and I spoke from the heart. 'My mother has accumulated a terrible debt. My father is disappeared, believed dead. My family risk destitution without my success in this position. My mother is, right now, in the debtors' jail. I am her only hope of getting out.'

Mrs Temple's face twisted, captivated. She was looking at me as though I were a specimen in a jar. I was interesting to her. I could see the questions bubbling on her lips. She was wrestling with herself, wanting to probe further, and yet her manners and propriety were holding her back, seeing the way in which too much curiosity would be inappropriate.

'I see. Well, I am sorry to hear of your troubles. I suppose it might reassure you to know that I am able to release your pay on a weekly basis, if that is what you prefer.'

I did not want to appear too eager, but this was an incredible relief. That I might be able to send money to Mam in just a week was even better than I had been hoping for. The reminder of my purpose for being on the island at all put the horrible night into perspective. I could struggle through sleepless, haunted nights. I could survive this place to change our lives. I would. I had to.

'My children have also lost their fathers,' Mrs Temple added, as if this meant she could understand my circumstances.

Nora lowered her eyes to the ground, her expression inscrutable. I knew the children – Nora, Birdie and the baby, little Edmund – had been born to different fathers, all six feet under. In some ways, Mrs Temple was right. Each one of them had a father-shaped wound just like the one I bore. I wondered whether their grief felt in any way akin to mine. And what should I make of their mother, the widow? For all she wore the appropriate garments, the grief itself appeared subdued. She had told me of her husbands' deaths with cool detachment. Was it that she had a cold and callous heart, or just a well-protected one?

Unbidden, a darker thought came to mind. There had been awful accusations made about her in print. Was it possible that the woman standing in front of me was capable of terrible things? What if she *had* been behind her husbands' deaths?

When I'd been at home, I had felt that Archfall Manor was calling to me. It seemed my only hope for the truth, for a way to save Mam. But to arrive and see the darkness in the Cauldwell family was like taking a bite of a shiny apple and finding that the core was rotten. To imagine them had been one thing – to be presented with the reality, and to witness the messy, tangled-up threads of their connections with one another, was a different beast entirely. The enormity of what I'd done by coming here cascaded over me once more. There was suddenly a feeling, deep in my gut, that I had made a rash and terrible decision, that nothing good could come of being on this island.

Remember the money, I chanted in my mind. *Remember the money*. I was changing our lives. And I didn't have any other choice.

I might be in over my head, but there was no more time to think because I seemed to have passed some kind of test. Mrs Temple insisted I meet Birdie right away, and commence my trial period as her governess.

We left Nora, and Mrs Temple guided me back through the corridor of identical doors, smooth wooden panelling lining each wall – the antithesis of the crumbling stone of the sweetshop – up that spectacular staircase, up one floor and then up again. The circular window I had seen from the causeway allowed the gloomy grey efforts of the sun in, though the lamps in the sconces still blazed on. And then I spotted it . . . a little fracture in the opulence.

There was a strange alcove – a place where the lavish fixtures were absent, where the brick of the wall was exposed and a stone staircase appeared to wind its way up towards somewhere dark.

I wanted to explore up that staircase. The opening in the wall snagged my attention, and my eye kept catching on it, pulling my gaze back over my shoulder to get a final glimpse even as I tried to focus on following where Mrs Temple was leading me down the wing. The tower with the arches was up there, but why did it pull at me so intensely, loosening my attention like a thread? I knew with some certainty that I would have to investigate it – and as soon as possible.

We moved into a shorter corridor, and Mrs Temple paused for a moment outside one of the doors, with a hand resting against the wood. The room inside appeared to be quiet. I opened my mouth to ask how Birdie usually passed her time, but Mrs Temple raised a finger to warn me into silence. Her head was cocked so that her ear aligned with a particular groove in the carved flower pattern of the door. I peered at it closely – and realized it was a listening hole. I felt a flutter in my stomach once more. Were the family in the habit of spying on one another? Would they presume to spy on me?

After a moment more of listening, Mrs Temple yanked the door open without warning.

A small girl jolted upright from where she had been sitting at the foot of a single bed. I saw she had been drawing, her papers scattered over a great wooden chest at the end of the bed, her name etched upon it. She was skinny, with pointed elbows and cheekbones, dressed in the same black as her mother and sister. Indeed, she looked like a miniature doll version of her mother – dark hair, brown eyes, extremely expressive face.

'Mother, you really ought to knock.' She shot her mother such a murderous look, it seemed a wonder that Mrs Temple wasn't physically wounded.

'And give you a chance to hide your misdeeds, my dear? I think not. Now, Birdie – this is your new governess, Miss Martin. Miss Martin, meet my daughter Birdie.' Mrs Temple was smiling with forced politeness, though I could see the effort it was costing her.

'Pleased to meet you,' I said.

Birdie's chocolate-truffle eyes assessed me. She fiddled with the latch of the chest. I entered the room, and crouched down to her level. 'That's a remarkable toy chest,' I said. 'May I look inside?'

'It's not a toy chest,' Birdie replied witheringly. 'It's a treasure chest.' She pulled herself taller, as if to raise herself above me.

'I see. Well, you must keep your most precious things in there,' I said.

'Not really. Grandpa crafts them. We've all got one; it's nothing special.' Birdie kicked the chest, as if to show how little she cared. And yet I could see that beneath the bravado there was a desperate feeling. I recognized it, I thought. A clamouring to be the detached one, the clever one.

'I think it's beautiful,' I said. I looked at Mrs Temple. She was watching us interact, and her lips were turned up slightly at the edges. 'You're all very lucky to have been given such gifts.'

'They're not just *gifts*,' Birdie said. 'They are designed to be absolutely private. They're iron inside, so you couldn't break them open, not even with an axe. We all have our own key – just the one key – and you must always keep it on your person. Grandpa says that everyone must have something of their own that is for nobody else. How are you meant to create or be original or invent anything if you don't have a secret place to keep it? Not even Mother has seen inside our chests, and that's the same for everyone in the family. It's an important rule.'

'That's right,' Mrs Temple said. 'It's a tradition in our family.'

'How long is she staying?' Birdie abruptly turned to ask her mother, as if I were no longer there.

Mrs Temple looked at me. 'Well, it rather depends. Miss Martin's appointment is subject to a trial period.'

Birdie thought about this. 'I suppose we all have to hope that you're not as silly as Agnes. I'm sure you might have already heard, but she's in the asylum now.' Birdie smiled and gave a little shrug.

Now it was Mrs Temple's turn to give her daughter a deadly stare. An involuntary shiver slipped down my back, but I was grateful to have been forewarned on this matter by Nora and refused to let the little girl see any sign of weakness. Birdie was merely trying to unsettle me, and I would not let her.

I remembered Jasper's advice. *They appreciate a little boldness.*

'Well, from what your sister Miss Nora told me, you gave your last governess a terrible time of it,' I said. 'You ought to be careful Agnes doesn't escape and come to find you in the middle of the night.' I walked over to the window, framed with heavy-lined curtains, and tapped my knuckles against the glass as if assessing its strength.

Birdie appeared uncertain. 'That's not possible,' she said. 'Is it, Mother?'

She looked to her mother for reassurance, and I looked too, hoping that my assertive gamble had paid off. Mrs Temple's expression was satisfied. I understood that she was impressed at my handling of Birdie. Protective or not, she knew any governess of that child was going to require nerve, ingenuity and assertiveness.

'I suppose that depends on whether Agnes is still alive,' Mrs Temple said. 'You did frighten the girl half to death.'

I nodded. 'And I'd imagine a ghost would find it much easier to make it across the causeway,' I said, solemn as a pallbearer. 'As it happens, I have experience of ghosts,' I continued, planning to use the interaction to my advantage for as long as possible.

Birdie's eyebrows shot up. 'You do?'

'I do. The first thing we're going to need is some salt on this window.' I ran my finger along the sill.

Birdie adopted a stance full of bravado – hands on hips, chin jutted out defiantly – but I could tell she was interested by the way her eyes were following me. We were all startled by the sound of the baby breaking into an outraged wail elsewhere along the corridor. Mrs Temple's gaze darted to the door, and she turned towards it instinctively pulled by the cry of her infant.

'Well, it looks as though the two of you have begun a most constructive relationship. I shall leave you to it! You may begin your lessons next door in the schoolroom, and Mrs Wright will bring you lunch at twelve.' Mrs Temple was talking quickly now, in a rush as the crying heightened. Although Molly the nursery nurse was surely soothing baby Edmund, it seemed as though his mother couldn't bear to stay away. 'Lessons should continue until five p.m., after which I should imagine your assistance would be appreciated by the household staff in the completion of their before-dinner chores.'

'Of course,' I murmured, and with that Mrs Temple left the room.

Once Birdie and I had performed an invented ritual of protection at her bedroom window, the rest of the morning passed quickly in the schoolroom, which was arranged with a wooden desk and two chairs, a slate with chalk, a stack of paper, and a pot filled with pencils and a little knife to whittle them with.

I began by taking notes from Birdie on the way her previous education had unfolded – mostly learning her arithmetic by rote and recitation in the morning, then reading practice after lunch, followed by some basic needlework or a little piano. When I had assessed as far as possible the level she was at and found it mercifully below the level I had got to with Josephine in my own learning – a matter previously of real concern for me – I asked her to produce a piece of her best writing on a topic of her choice. This freedom captivated her until lunchtime, when Teresa brought two trays with cucumber sandwiches, jam biscuits and a plum each.

'I've heard that jam biscuits are good for the brain,' Teresa said with a smile, giving Birdie a gentle nudge. Birdie shrugged, unimpressed at the attempt to win her favour, and I saw Teresa's face fall a little.

'I'm surprised you've heard much of anything, being stuck on this tiny island all the time,' Birdie said, and I spluttered awkwardly, shocked by her rudeness.

'Thank you for our lunch, Mrs Wright.' I was keen to move things swiftly on, had been hoping to ingratiate myself with Teresa, not witness her being humiliated, and by a child as well. 'I'm always grateful for a jam biscuit, although I have some doubts as to the veracity of the claim that they benefit learning.' I smiled so she would know I meant this in a friendly way, but her face was flushing, and she seemed to want to get out of the room as quickly as possible.

I considered whether to chastise Birdie, to let her know how rude I thought she'd been, but larger than my outrage was my need for her to like me. My trial period depended upon it. And so I said nothing, wondering if that made me weak or just desperate.

While eating, Birdie commented, 'I never had a governess that let me choose any part of what I was to learn. I like that you did that.'

'I'm glad you enjoyed it. And what have you chosen to write about?' I asked her.

'It's a story,' she confessed in a whisper.

'A story?' I was a little surprised at this. I had thought she might select a topic she'd had the opportunity to learn about and present everything she knew. But this was an act of creativity.

'It's an adventure story about a girl who learns to sail a boat and travels far away to discover the creatures that live in the sea. She meets a mermaid living on a rock who gives her three riddles to solve.'

'What an imagination you have!' I said.

'And then the mermaid rips her flesh from her bones, and eats her all up.'

Birdie meant to shock me, I'm sure, and I was annoyed at how well it had worked. Fairy tales for children are often ghoulish, but I found the casual slaughter of her main character a little unsettling. I had to carefully manage my facial expression to mask how perturbed I was.

After we'd eaten, I encouraged Birdie to select a book from her own collection. She returned with a volume of *Grimms' Fairy Tales*.

'One of my inspirations,' she said with a broad smile that showed one of her incisor teeth was missing, waiting for the adult one to emerge. I instructed Birdie to read aloud to me and this whiled away the time very nicely until Mrs Temple arrived at five to see how we had been getting on.

'Have you had a good day?' Mrs Temple asked, and I was ready for the glow of Birdie's praise.

Birdie shrugged with disinterest. 'We will have to see how all the other days go.'

I swallowed my disappointment at this review. But then, I supposed, what should I have expected? Birdie was far from a straightforward charge, and clearly it was going to take time to earn even a little of her trust. I needed to be patient. And keep my head down in the meantime.

9

When I finally returned to the kitchen in the servants' quarters, Teresa stood in the centre of the room, her eyes quickly skimming across each of the dishes she'd prepared for that evening, like an artist appraising their masterpiece. Beside her, waiting for direction, stood a girl about my age, with red curls on top of her head, who quickly introduced herself as Molly. I spotted that the shoulder of her dress was damp, no doubt from the baby spitting up. Harry and Jasper were sitting in the corner together, already appearing like firm friends as they talked about their preferred methods for grooming a horse with a tempestuous disposition.

'Can I help you serve tonight?' I asked, and Teresa smiled at me gratefully, handing me an apron, a ladle and directing me to the soup. When I had spooned out enough portions of the delicate seafood broth, we began the walk down the long corridor to the dining room.

'Was your last household like this?' Molly asked me under her breath. 'I've never experienced anything like it. Imagine owning a big house like this and not even having a footman to help wait at the table! Mrs Temple kept a proper household staff when we were in London, you know, before Mr Temple . . .'

'No,' I said with a swift shake of the head. It reassured me to know I wasn't the only one for whom Sighfeyre Isle had not matched expectations, who felt out of their depth. 'I've never been in a household like this.'

I hadn't anticipated serving the family, although perhaps there might be advantages. I would be helpful, unassuming and seek any opportunity to listen closely. Inside the dining room, the family were sitting in grim silence at a long mahogany table. Mrs Temple was already pouring a glass of red wine for herself. Nora caught my eye and smiled; she was keeping Birdie occupied with some sort of game created with a piece of elastic wrapped round their hands, twisting and turning it into different shapes.

Mr Cauldwell sat at the head of the table, resting his chin in his hand and looking somewhere into the distance as though he were dining alone, not in the presence of his family. It was as if he were made of machinery himself, cogs turning internally.

As I moved round the table, there was the tinkling of a fork against a glass, which made everyone sit a little straighter and look towards the head of the table. Mr Cauldwell cleared his throat. 'I wish to speak to you all about the future. You all know that I am . . . slowing down. To my eternal frustration.' He gave a low chuckle that Mrs Temple politely echoed, although her expression seemed a little strained.

Teresa served Mr Cauldwell and Mrs Temple, and Molly served Nora and Birdie. When I set the final bowl in front of Wilbur he barely acknowledged it, his frown deepening with every passing second so that his face reminded me of a gathering storm. It was our job to remain invisible, make it feel as though the soup magically appeared before them. I was eager to hear more, but had finished my business at the table and so reluctantly stepped away, listening to Mr Cauldwell continue.

'I wish to inform you all that I am going to be taking a step back from the Institute in the next few months. I am finding myself less and less capable of completing my work.'

I made my way to the door, hanging back to let Teresa and Molly go ahead of me and taking the opportunity to glance at Wilbur. His eyebrows had shot up as he struggled to suppress what looked like hope. This was what they had been arguing about earlier – perhaps Mr Cauldwell had reconsidered his position. Perhaps he was finally ready to hand over leadership to his son. I lingered in the doorway.

'When I step down, a vacancy will be created, and it is my duty to nominate my replacement. As you know, this has typically been passed down through the Cauldwell line to the firstborn son. In the absence of my firstborn son –' he raised his eyes to the ceiling and paused for a second – 'I will be hosting a competition on this island in a month's time. I intend to invite the most brilliant inventors of the day to take part, so that I might fund their next project and select my replacement as leader of the Institute.'

Once again, I was stunned by this family and their complicated machinations. To decide your own son was not worthy of inheritance was one thing . . . to announce it so publicly was quite another.

Wilbur's eyes were bulging, his jaw was clenched and a tiny muscle jumped in his cheek. It was beyond an insult – it was the theft of his birthright. I decided not to stay and witness the strength of his reaction.

I slipped away, hoping that my attempts to listen hadn't been noticed. My hands were shaking a little, the tension in the room affecting me, and I had a terrible feeling in the pit of my stomach. Might Wilbur not be able to *earn* his position if he entered the competition? What would it mean for the house to host an event of that scale? Would I be expected to wait on guests hand and foot? And then another thought crossed my mind – perhaps Jasper could enter? Might it be his opportunity to ascend from his current station? I decided I would share what I'd overheard with him when the moment was right.

Back in the warmth of the kitchen, the staff and Harry had gathered by the range, talking among themselves. Even though there was a large servants' hall with benches and tables, I had observed that they preferred to congregate in the kitchen instead, perched on stools. I noticed right away that Molly could barely take her eyes off Jasper, her face aglow and rosy.

Beside them, a giant of a man was holding court about how he'd fixed the spokes of the back wheel of Harry's coach with a new tool he'd invented, which sounded like a cross between a hammer and a knife. He had sandy-coloured hair touched with grey at the temples, and wore exhausted garb: a collarless shirt and patched waistcoat, and stomping work boots. The long and the short of his boasting was that Harry would be leaving at the next safe crossing time, first thing in the morning.

'There is more I could have done to improve that old coach, if you'd only felt brave enough to let me try.' The man laughed as Harry looked sheepish. 'I've got a prototype somewhere of a new motorized –'

'Enough of this,' Teresa said, exasperated. 'Will you all make yourselves useful or get out from under my feet? If you must discuss it, find somewhere else. Oh, and Josephine – this is my husband, Gabriel.'

Gabriel turned to me and nodded, and I returned the gesture.

Teresa immediately busied herself once more, ensuring that the next course was ready to be taken to the table. Jasper stood up and relieved her of the burden of a large platter, planting an affectionate kiss on the top of her head. I took the next platter and followed him into the entrance hall.

'I've been catching up with Harry today. He says you've known each other a long time,' Jasper said.

'We have,' I replied. 'He's my oldest friend.'

'He made me promise to be kind to you.' He glanced over his shoulder, and his expression was like that of a court jester, full of mischief.

'Oh, I can assure you that won't be necessary. You're welcome to be absolutely neutral to me,' I said jokingly in return.

'It must be nice to have such a long-standing friend,' Jasper said wistfully, and it dawned on me how lonely he must have been growing up on this island, with no children his own age to play with. Perhaps that was why he was trying to be friendly now. 'I imagine you'll miss him.'

'I will. But I'll write to him,' I said, not ready to betray the nerves that were already building in me at the thought that, once Harry was gone, my decision was wholly made. I would be staying on this isolated island, in this strange house with its disturbing noises at night and this fractured family. I just had to hold on to the reasons why I came: I needed to free my mother, and somewhere in this house was a truth I was desperate to uncover.

Returning to the dining room, I was apprehensive, but I needn't have been – the atmosphere there now had shifted and was almost surprisingly jovial. That seemed to be thanks to the fact that Wilbur no longer sat at the table – I could only assume he had stormed off. Instead, Mrs Temple was entertaining Mr Cauldwell and Nora with an anecdote that seemed to involve some Institute members she had been invited to dine with when she had been in London. I was struck by her easy charm – she was witty and expressive, and she cast a spell of levity over her family. Even Mr Cauldwell's face had brightened as he regarded her with what looked like fondness.

Birdie watched me intently as I laid my platter down at the centre of the table. Her lips were moving as she fixed me with her stare, and although I couldn't make out what she was saying, it made me think of chanted curses. My hands grew clumsy under her inspection, and to my dismay I dropped the serving tongs with a terrible clatter. This made Birdie smile in a self-satisfied way that caused a rage to swell inside me. She wanted me to fail, and now I was making an utter fool of myself.

Seeming to sense what had happened, Nora muttered something under her breath to Birdie, who huffed as if scolded. I met Nora's eyes, and she gave me a sympathetic smile. I returned it gratefully. She was a strange young woman, no doubt, but I needed all the allies I could get.

It seemed Nora wasn't done with me either. When the evening meal was eventually complete an hour or so later, Nora caught me by the sleeve as I helped to clear the final plates. My stomach grumbled in complaint – the whole five-course affair had taken several hours, and I was keen to get back to the kitchen for my own dinner.

'I'd like to speak to you,' she said, and what else could I do but nod? I hung back after Mr Cauldwell and Mrs Temple had departed the room, and Molly had collected Birdie to prepare her for bed.

'You mustn't let Birdie unsettle you,' Nora said firmly. 'This is what she does. She's very good at it.'

I wasn't quite sure what to say in response – I knew it wouldn't be right to criticize Birdie to anyone in the family, but Nora was making all the normal boundaries seem hazy.

She wasn't speaking to me like staff, and she seemed to be inviting my criticism. Was it a test of some kind? It was confusing, and at a time when I was still trying to find my position in the house, she was making it even harder to determine how I should act, what my role was supposed to be.

'I'm sure she will settle when we get to know each other,' I said, erring on the side of graciousness.

'Perhaps,' Nora said. She hummed a little tune, and then looked as though she had been struck by an idea. 'Has anyone given you a full tour of the house yet?'

I shook my head. 'I've been piecing it together bit by bit.'

She stood quickly, all purpose, the layers of her dress rustling as they fell into position. 'Well, you must let me be your guide!' There was an endearing eagerness about her offer. I wondered whether she was also very lonely. If she had been raised in London, the isolation of Archfall must have felt acute.

I tried to ignore my grumbling stomach, and made an attempt at matching her enthusiasm, although I would have preferred to retire to the warmth of the kitchen and take advantage of my last night of Harry's companionship. This opportunity was exciting, of course, the chance to learn more about the house, the unusual contraptions that lined its halls, and perhaps even the family if I kept my wits about me, but for all her attempts at friendliness Nora herself exhausted and unnerved me.

She gripped my hand. 'Come with me.' It was an order, not a request, the tone of her voice shifting. An assertion of her dominance, of her position above me. She couldn't seem to decide if she wanted to be my friend or my superior. Obediently, I followed her out into the corridor, where we immediately came upon Jasper.

'I was looking for you,' he said. His eyes took in Nora's tight grip on my hand, and he seemed puzzled by it. 'You must be famished. Won't you come and have your supper?'

'Miss Nora is going to give me a tour of the house,' I said, hoping my tone conveyed gratitude to her, instead of the desperation I felt to follow Jasper, partake of supper.

'Oh, come now,' Jasper said. 'Miss Nora, you must wait until morning. The poor girl hasn't eaten in hours.' As if to emphasize his point, the grandfather clock in the entrance hall struck the lateness of the hour.

Nora let go of my hand as if it were burning her. 'Of course,' she said, her cheeks turning a little pink. 'I didn't think.'

Once again, I felt disoriented. Jasper spoke to Nora as if he were the one in charge, not her. My head was spinning with the shifting rules of this strange house, and its even stranger dynamics.

'I'd love to have a tour in the morning,' I said appeasingly. 'Perhaps Birdie could help too, if you would care to meet us in the schoolroom?'

Nora turned cold then. Her eyes narrowed, her body stiffened, and she took a step away from me. 'Enjoy your supper.' Her voice was harder than it had been before, and a cymbal of regret clanged inside me. Clearly I'd made the wrong choice, slighted her – though who could guess how deeply she was wounded.

She stalked off down the corridor, and Jasper shook his head, letting out a steady stream of breath. When Nora was out of sight, he murmured, 'She is an oddity.'

'What do you mean?' I had felt it too, of course, but I wanted to know what Jasper meant by it.

Jasper considered my question. 'When she first got here, she seemed so interested in everything, always asking questions, always poking into every room. Now, she mostly just floats through the place like a spectre, haunting the reading rooms, the music room, the portrait gallery. Sometimes she lurks near the entrance to the servants' quarters, as if she's just desperate to bring about a situation where she has someone to talk to.'

'I should have gone with her,' I said, regret sticking in my throat, like choking on the rough stone of a peach. I certainly didn't want to make her into an enemy.

'Plenty of time to learn your way round this place,' Jasper said, missing the point, whether intentionally or not I couldn't tell. He was so secure in his position at Archfall, it didn't seem to matter much what Nora thought of him.

We headed back to the kitchen, the residual heat from the evening's food preparations lingering to wrap round us like a blanket. Harry was nowhere to be seen, and Teresa told me he had retired for the night.

'He looked so exhausted, I sent him to bed,' she said. 'You can't be travelling when you're already weary.' Although I knew she was right, and Harry had been worn out from his disturbed night, I couldn't help but feel a little disappointed not to have the chance to spend this last evening in his reassuring company.

Teresa spooned out a bowl of broth for me, with a thick hunk of bread slathered in butter, and I greedily gulped it. This was the best part of the day. In the kitchen, during that precious hour, my senses were overloaded with the rich, full smells, the warmth soaking my skin like a hot bath, a simple supper to fill my stomach, and the busy clatter of Teresa clearing away to drown out my negative thoughts. Molly was seeing to the baby, and Gabriel apparently still had errands to attend to elsewhere in the house, but Jasper stayed to keep me company, and the glow of him, his easy laughter, was a soothing balm at the end of the day. It was strange, the immediate affinity I felt with him, and yet I couldn't help but embrace it, distraction though it was.

'I want to taste some of that toffee you were talking about,' he said with a grin.

'Toffee?' Teresa asked, overhearing.

'I turn out a pretty good batch,' I said, despite myself. 'My mam and I used to make sweets together all the time.' I made it sound as though this were a pastime in our kitchen at home, not our trade. I wanted to be known by these people, but only to a certain extent. Thinking of Mam twinged like an injured nerve.

'You'll have to show us,' Teresa said approvingly. 'Mr Cauldwell has always had a sweet tooth. He regularly places an order with a confectioner on the mainland.'

'If you've got enough sugar, there's not much I can't make,' I said. Sugar was the basis of everything in the confectionery world.

'Oh, we've got sugar,' Jasper said.

I felt like there was a challenge brewing, and it lit a fire inside me. I listed the ingredients I would need, and Jasper eagerly sought them out from the pantry – simple things, easily to hand in a wealthy household like this. Teresa pretended to show mild disapproval and looked up at the clock, tutting, but when I asked if they were serious about me giving a demonstration then and there, she appeared more interested than annoyed. Jasper looked at her, seeking permission, and she shrugged her shoulders.

'There are worse things you could be doing with these night-time hours,' she said. 'And I'm certain Mr Cauldwell will be delighted when there's fresh toffee to be had in the morning. I think he'll be rather impressed.'

So she perched on a stool, eager to learn, although I knew she must be tired and that her presence was more to act as chaperone, to give Jasper and me the opportunity to get to know each other without straying into the territory of inappropriateness. Between the three of us there was an ease as I started to measure out the sugar and syrup. As I stirred, I told Jasper and Teresa how these were the techniques that Mam had taught me when I was little, and when I grew older I began to understand how I could use the ingredients to create my own recipes.

'It's like Pa and me,' Jasper said. 'When I was little, he showed me how to take things apart and put them back together again. Inventing is just the next logical step after that. If you know how something works, you can figure out how to make it work differently.'

'Exactly,' I said.

Jasper hovered at my elbow as I worked. 'Can I take a turn?' He had a wide-eyed enthusiasm I'd rarely seen in anyone my own age – as though he hadn't grown so exhausted that his sense of wonder had been crushed.

'Roll up your sleeves then.'

He followed my instructions with a grin. When I handed him the spoon, his arm brushed against mine and my skin tingled pleasingly. I snatched a glance at Teresa, who cleared her throat. She'd noticed our closeness. I took a step to the side, creating a bit of distance.

It was the first moment since I'd arrived that I truly felt maybe I could belong here on Sighfeyre Isle, could find a way to stay comfortably. But then, when we were finished and had left the tray to set until morning, the night truly began, and alone in my room it wasn't long before all my fears came rushing back.

10

That night, the whisper troubled me again. I had collapsed into bed, weary from the fullness of the day and my disrupted sleep the night before, and gratefully dissolved between the bedsheets. My mind was blessedly empty as I slept, dreamless and untroubled. But the comfort didn't last.

Helena . . .

I was dragged into consciousness by the sound of my name reverberating in my mind, as though somebody had been crouching right by my bed, hissing directly into my ear. Caught in the blur between night and morning, I struggled against my twisted sheets, a cold sweat beading on my forehead. The incessant whispering persisted, insidious and grasping for my attention.

I scrambled up to sitting, fixing my gaze on the walls – were they closing in on me, like in Harry's terrible dream? The darkness throbbed, and my ear kept catching on the insistent sound. More nonsensical thoughts intruded. It felt as though a part of the house itself were reaching for me, stretching through the corridors, seeping from the walls, to get to me. A strange notion, I knew it. But I couldn't push it from my mind.

I held my head in my hands as though I could physically settle my fevered thoughts. Houses were not sentient; they did not wake their inhabitants or torture them in the night with sinister sounds that made them question their sanity. I was delirious with tiredness, that was all. This was just part of settling in, of being in an unfamiliar place. Still, I felt certain the sound couldn't just be a person whispering in the room next door – there was a spaciousness to it. It seemed to fill the room, to press in on me from all directions, from every wall. Shapeless, formless sounds. Not words. Just an indistinct murmuring.

And yet I couldn't forget that I'd heard my name. My true name. The name that nobody at Archfall Manor knew. It had sounded so real, but it was an impossibility.

And so my mind flailed about, trying to find a logical explanation. The wind, caught in pipes, gusting through the walls? Mr Cauldwell had set up all sorts of intricate connections throughout the house – I had seen them: the listening hole, the watching skulls. Perhaps it was related to one of those.

I wrestled against the whispering, my head shoved beneath the pillow to block it out.

I felt as though I had finally succumbed to a deeper sleep when I was disturbed by a rough knocking on my door.

'One moment!' I called.

Morning. It was morning again, weak light pressing through the gap in the curtains. I threw on one of the outfits that Molly had donated to me – a white blouse paired with a dark grey skirt. I was fastening the buttons at my throat when Harry called through the door.

'Last chance to say goodbye! Jasper says I'll miss the chance of crossing if I don't get going.'

My throat constricted at the thought of him leaving. He was an anchor in this strange and unfamiliar place. I neglected the final button, a tiny, fiddly thing, and raced to the door. Harry looked miserable, grey circles beneath his eyes. Immediately, he took my hand roughly between his.

'Come with me,' he said, his voice low and his breath coming out fast and bothered. 'Please, you can't stay here.'

'What are you talking about?' I frowned. 'Harry, we've been through this . . .'

'I can't leave you here. I don't . . . I don't think it's safe.' His eyes were wild and fearful. 'I know it sounds like . . . superstition. But there's something wrong with this house.' Harry shook his head. 'I had that dream again last night, and I woke up by the bedroom door, Jasper rousing me. I'd been sleepwalking, was trying to force my way out of the door. That's never happened to me before.'

I looked at him, hardening my expression. I couldn't let any doubts creep in, even though I knew there was something unsettling about the house, even though I was frightened too.

'It sounds like you're *worrying*,' I said. I wriggled my hand free from his tight grasp. 'But I will be fine. And I think you're forgetting that I don't have a choice any more. I can't come with you. I need this job.'

My voice cracked, and I hated the weakness of it. I couldn't let him talk me out of staying. What else was there for me to go to? Even if I could bear to leave all my questions unanswered, the life I'd left behind was already gone. This job was my only chance to make enough money to help Mam.

'I . . . I have to go,' he said slowly, beginning to accept that I wouldn't be coming with him.

'I know,' I said.

Harry hesitated, began to open his mouth as if the words were halfway out, and then stopped.

'What?' I pressed.

'I think you can trust Jasper,' he said carefully. 'I don't like leaving you here, but I think you can rely on him. We got to chatting a little in our room both nights, and as far as I'm concerned he seems reasonable, and generous, and kind. And you're going to need that here.'

'Right,' I said, trying to ignore the fact that I wanted to melt into his shoulder and beg him to stay with me so that I didn't have to learn to trust anybody new. Instead, I resisted and trod my well-worn path of self-reliance. 'But, Harry, I don't need to trust anyone here. I don't need to rely on anyone but myself. I can manage this. I promise.'

He smiled, but it didn't reach his eyes. 'I hope you're right. I'll look out for your letter.'

'I hope you get a better night's sleep tonight,' I said, not allowing myself to say anything maudlin or sentimental. 'And, Harry . . . thank you.'

Then, with a final nod, he was gone.

I saw him leave the grounds from my window. The sky was as grey as the sea, and the causeway was a thin, shimmering pathway. I watched him go until even the horse and the coach were just tiny specks, and moments after that, as if perfectly timed, the water began to rise, swallowing up the route once again, as if it had never been there. I felt heavy with the loss of him, and surprised at the speed with which loneliness engulfed me, arriving as though we had a prior appointment. Yet I had no time to dwell on those sensations because my lessons with Birdie were due to begin.

When I arrived at the schoolroom, an envelope addressed to me had been pinned to the door. I took it down and checked the room but it was unoccupied. I knocked at Birdie's bedroom door too, and when there was no reply I pushed it open. Her bed was made up neatly, but there was no sign of Birdie. I knew that she was playing a game with me even before I opened the envelope. Inside, she'd folded up a piece of paper with a challenge upon it:

You're new to this house and you've so much to find.
Follow my clues if you're that way inclined.
To learn about our family, go beyond the horses –
Twenty paces, a gate and all of our losses.

It was a clever little ditty she'd invented, and the half-rhyme at the end jolted me the way I was certain she had meant it to. Birdie had crafted every word of the invitation to entice me into a game; I recognized the beginnings of a hunt. She wanted me to follow her. It reminded me of a little dog that had belonged to the butcher's boy, who would drop a stick at your feet and prance off, looking back to check whether you were going to throw it for him, dancing about on his toes, coming a little closer once more to see whether you were going to play. Though I rather suspected that this particular dog would bite.

Of course, I could have taken the envelope and its missive straight to Mrs Temple, let her know that Birdie was absconding from lessons, and perhaps it would have been wise to – but I was intrigued, and I felt that perhaps the game could be a way for us to form a bond, for me to learn what it was that made her tick. Birdie had undeniably put effort into the writing of the clue and, remembering her fondness for fairy tales, it seemed the least I could do was follow the breadcrumb trail she'd left.

The wind was up, but there was only a light spattering of rain as I headed out of the servants' door, the kitchen mercifully quiet, with no one about who might question what I was doing.

I went past the lean-to and made my way towards the stables, treading carefully and pulling my shawl tight against the biting chill. The breeze was fierce, cutting through the material of my blouse, and above me the dark sky groaned. Before long, there would be a great release of rain that I hoped to avoid. From the outside of the house, it was easy to forget that the bewildering labyrinth of rooms was all contained within the two long wings that stretched out symmetrically in either direction. There was a simplicity to the façade that the inside denied.

I turned my back on the lonely building that sprawled across Sighfeyre Isle possessively, its single tower stretched up like a warning signal, a hand telling visitors to stop. In every direction, the marshy ground was desolate, and beyond it the sea swelled round the edges of the isle, tormented and angered by the wind. I wondered if the island felt any different in the summer, more hospitable and welcoming. It seemed to me that the manor wanted us locked up tightly inside, away from the wildness.

I marched on past the stables, counting out my twenty paces as directed by the clue, and saw the gate ahead of me, wrought iron twisted into intricate swirls. This was where Birdie had wanted me to come, and it took only a moment of drawing closer for me to realize what she meant by 'losses'. The clue had brought me to a graveyard. I unlatched the gate and went through it, taking in the quiet, unassuming headstones, weathered and aged. It looked as though little care had been taken over the preservation of the stones, several of which were damaged and crumbling, and one of which had collapsed completely.

The graves themselves were overgrown with weeds – no floral displays for the ancestors of the Cauldwell family – and it was clear that no money had been spent on this small plot of land. There was no peace here, just the endless roar of the sea and the wind. It seemed to me that these relatives had not been laid to rest, but had instead been eaten up by the ground, placed in the earth like a sacrifice to the appetite of the island.

I read the more recent names, recognized a few from my research into the family – Louis Percival Cauldwell, the previous patriarch; and the present Mr Cauldwell's late wife Mary, 'beloved mother of Edwin, Caroline and Wilbur'.

What did Birdie mean by bringing me here? Was it just her ghoulish nature, trying to unsettle me further? If so, it wouldn't work on me. Once someone was dead, their body was nothing to fear. I didn't believe that the ghosts of the Cauldwell family were lingering in this place – no, if there were any phantoms lurking, I was certain they were inside the very walls of the manor, whispering in the night.

A little further along the row, I spotted a white envelope fluttering in the wind. It had been tied round one of the stones with a piece of string and had grown a little damp, was limp in my hands when I ripped the note free from inside. A different sort of puzzle had been written out in Birdie's neat handwriting. It was an equation, two in fact, the twin strings of numbers arranged over two rows. Each one had additional operations added in to complicate matters.

When I looked at them, they began to squiggle and squirm in front of my eyes. It made me feel rather silly for in the lesson I'd delivered the previous day I'd set a rather simple task for her – the writing out in words of what had felt to me impressively large numbers. Her skills were obviously more advanced than she'd revealed.

I clutched the paper close to my chest and headed indoors to puzzle out her equations by the range in the kitchen, where my bones could warm through once more.

I grabbed a stubby pencil and set to work. At the end of my puzzling, I was left with two numbers – a one and a five – and while I was certain my calculations were correct, I wasn't entirely sure what my next steps should be. I presumed that Birdie intended this clue to take me somewhere else within the house. If so, I wondered how the numbers could connect to the rooms. If I was numbering them, how should I go about it? By storey first, I determined, and so I headed up to the first floor – if it were all a dead end, then I would have to think again. But when I emerged on to the landing, I spotted that the first door on the western side had been labelled with a number one.

Seeing that neat number fastened to the doorknob gave me such a thrill – despite myself, I was enjoying Birdie's little game. She was a clever thing, and she wanted me to know it. I dared to hope that this might be a step in the direction of us growing closer – or at least respecting one another. I started imagining myself setting a similar challenge for her the next day, as I counted the doors down the wing.

From what I knew about the layout of the house, these rooms consisted of family bedrooms mostly. I was now beginning to wish that I had taken up Nora's offer of a tour. At least then I might have known what I was walking into. When I arrived at the fifth door, I pushed it open and was startled by the ringing of a bell. It was an ugly sound, a heavy clang that made me startle in fright. The room that lay before me was a bedroom that had clearly been unoccupied for many years – the thick layers of dust confirmed that nobody resided in here.

I spotted Birdie's next clue immediately – laid on the pillow of the grand four-poster was an envelope. I darted for it quickly – the clanging of the bell had unnerved me, and I wanted to be out of the room and moving on. Strange how this unoccupied bedroom gave me more of a chill than the graveyard had done. It, unlike others in the house, felt dead. There was no other way to explain it – nothing felt alive in here. Moreover, I sensed the room did not want me to come in, as fanciful as that sounded.

Snatching the envelope, I realized an odd trinket lay beneath it: a bracelet, its silver beads tarnished with time, woven together with string. No, wait – with *hair*. Dark hair, thick as twine, weaving the beads together. I dropped it in distaste.

It must be a memento mori, I realized: a reminder of somebody lost. I took another look round the room, which revealed all sorts of unfinished business: on the bedside table was a half-completed cross stitch of what appeared to be the façade of Archfall Manor; on the dresser a discarded shawl that had not been put away properly; a little plate that matched the rest of the set in the kitchen, a handful of crumbs upon it, no doubt as hard as pebbles now. The room had been left exactly the way its occupier had last had it, with the addition of the memento-mori bracelet and, I cursed under my breath, Birdie's clue.

I turned to leave as hastily as I could, close to screwing up the envelope in anger, and came face to face with Mr Cauldwell.

'You shouldn't be in here,' he said. His voice was measured, but something trembled beneath the surface calm.

A horrid panic began to rise in my chest – would he dismiss me from the household, presuming me a spy or, worse, a thief? I had no doubt this was what Birdie had been hoping to achieve with her elaborate game. She knew the bell would alert her grandfather to my presence in a room that was, very clearly, not meant to be disturbed.

I began grovelling. 'I'm so terribly sorry.' I wished I could dissolve. 'I got myself lost. It's very clear that this room was not meant to be disturbed, and I offer you my sincerest apology.'

'This room belonged to my late wife. Nobody comes in here,' Mr Cauldwell said.

He wasn't looking at me; he was peering over my shoulder, taking in the emptiness of the room. Once more, I was struck by how haunted he seemed. His skin was loose over his cheeks, wrinkled and creasing, and his eyes had a filmy glaze about them.

'Now get out.' His voice was full of darkness, an undisguised anger simmering.

'Yes, sir.' I couldn't stop my voice from shaking as I exited the room, my head bowed as I dipped past him. The sound of the door closing behind us was firm and final, and I cast frantically about for another excuse or a more fulsome apology. 'I would have never –'

'What is this?' He snatched the envelope out of my hands as nimbly as a bird nipping a worm from the ground. The note inside was unsheathed in seconds. As his eyes scanned over the clue inside, my mouth turned dry as sand, all the liquid in my body seeming to seep out of my hands. 'Well?'

'Miss Birdie created this sort of . . . game. With clues to follow.'

He fixed me with a stare over the top of the paper. 'The cellar,' he said dryly. 'You access it through the little door by the bottom of the staircase in the main entrance hall.'

Then he crumpled the clue in his fist and turned on his heel, leaving me in stunned silence.

11

The door to the cellar would easily go unnoticed unless you'd been directed to it. It blended in almost perfectly with the panelling of the walls and had a small latch that released the door with a flick of my thumb. Birdie might have been hoping I'd be distracted by this stage for longer, buying her an additional hour or so of freedom while I untangled her riddles, traipsing across the house like a fool ... Had she even been anticipating I would make it this far, or had the hope been that I would be dismissed on the spot for trespassing into her late grandmother's room?

I could have questioned her motives unendingly, but what I knew was that I would not let her win this game. Whatever her aims, she wasn't going to succeed in besting me. She had underestimated me, underestimated my determination, underestimated the desperation that drove me. I needed this job, I needed every penny it would provide, and I wasn't about to give up. It was almost an obsession.

The little door opened straight on to a tight, crumbling staircase and I nearly stumbled as I passed through, leaving it open behind me so that the light might reach round me, making my descent possible. My heart began to race, and I felt as though I could lose my balance at any moment and tumble down the stairs. I pressed my hand against the wall and, on each step, brought my foot carefully forward to drop down. Every so often, there was a little nook in the wall, and I examined each one for a clue.

I got to the bottom, on even ground at last, but I was as unsteady as if I were on a boat. The narrow shard of light from the doorway did little to illuminate my surroundings, although I could make out the shape of rows and rows of dusty shelves containing glass bottle after glass bottle. No envelope could be seen at first glance, and that was when I started to become suspicious, backing up and turning to the staircase once more, a bad feeling curdling inside my stomach, realizing too late my predicament as I remembered the trap Birdie had laid for her last governess. It was the same, it was a trick, and I heard her cruel little laugh at the top of the stairs, saw her shadow in the doorway.

As she slammed it shut, I was plunged into complete darkness, cursing myself for my own stupidity. I had walked right into her trap, so consumed in my overthinking that I'd missed the obvious threat in front of me. I had been too flustered from the encounter with Mr Cauldwell and the risk to my position, too determined that I wouldn't be bested by Birdie's riddles, too eager in my efforts to see this as an opportunity to gain some respect. I was an idiot.

My eyes strained to adjust to the dark, throbbing in my head. I could barely see in front of my own face, but an irrational urgency clanged through me like an alarm, my body scrambling up the stairs, propelled by the fear that tore through me.

I had been adamant that Birdie would not outwit me, but now, trapped in the pitch-blackness, I was a vulnerable creature, the dark encroaching on my sensibilities. In my panic and distress, I became clumsy, unable to see where I was planting my feet, and they escaped from beneath me. My arms flailed as I fell, landing with a harsh jolt that sent a jarring pain up to my elbows, and my chin bashed against the steps. I was undone, splayed across the steps, and I gathered myself up, all my determination dented by the fall. Blood ran down my neck from the graze on my chin as, gripping the wall, I pulled myself back to my feet and limped up to the top of the stairs.

'Birdie!' I called, pressing my face against the coarse wood, knowing it was hopeless. I hammered my fists against the door as hard as I could, the side of my hands aching with the force.

Useless. Of course she wasn't going to answer, and there was nobody else to hear me. I would only be heard if somebody were passing, and it could be hours before someone happened to walk through the entrance hall. I wouldn't be able to make a noise endlessly . . . I sank down again, perched on the top step, and held my head in my hands.

I thought of the horror story of Birdie's last governess, trapped for two days, unable to speak at the end of her ordeal. How long would it take to lose your mind in darkness, tormented by hunger and thirst? Not to mention a whispering voice, one that seemed determined to infiltrate my thoughts and disrupt my sense of reality . . .

The house breathed around me. The dark seemed to swell, to shift and move. I dreaded to think how my distress might build if I were subjected to Birdie's cruel confinement any longer – but in fact it was only moments later that the door blessedly opened, and I was bathed in the relief of daylight.

Nora stood before me, holding out her hand to help me up.

'She was watching you through the skulls,' she said, pointing at the nearest one, its gaping eye sockets all glass. 'The problem being she was so delighted with herself and her little plan that she didn't notice I was watching her the whole time too. I've sent her up to her bedroom.'

'Thank you. I'm grateful – truly. Why would she do such a hateful thing?' I said bitterly.

I was shaking with anger, all the fear melting away in the heat of my rage. All notion of the appropriateness of my words disappeared, all boundaries forgotten. 'There is something wrong with that child.' The words were like hot spits of molten sugar from my mouth, searing and painful.

Nora flinched as though the words had been directed at her. I realized my error right away and wished I could cram all the words back into my mouth, even as tears of frustration pricked at my eyes. A fierceness passed through her features as if she were a cat protecting a litter of kittens. Nora was happy to release her own venomous criticisms of her sister, but for anyone else to do so was a personal affront – she now looked less pleased at having rescued me.

I began to correct myself, once more concerned for my future in the household. I had to wrestle my emotions into submission. 'I didn't mean –'

But Nora interrupted me. 'Don't you think I've thought the same thing about her?' she said. 'Don't you think I look at this family and sense that there is something wrong with us all? Sometimes I think Death himself sits on my shoulder, waiting to see what our family will do next.'

Her words sent a shiver down my spine, and for a second I wanted to press her about the whispering voice – did she hear it too? Did she sense that something was moving within the house? But I couldn't find the words, couldn't bear to reveal any of these thoughts.

'I ought to go to Birdie,' I said, though the idea of attempting to resume our lessons filled me with trepidation.

'You don't give up, do you?' Nora's stare pinned me to the wall.

'No,' I replied. This job was going to take an iron will and a constant focus. 'And I won't.'

After the incident in the cellar, I forced my anger at Birdie to one side, although it cost me to do so – more than anything I wanted to scream at her for her cruelty, for her manipulation. But I knew that wouldn't achieve what I needed it to . . . Instead, my approach the next day was to stress that I had underestimated her strengths in arithmetic, was impressed by her puzzles, and that we could channel her energies appropriately.

When I wasn't teaching, I was completing chores,

scrubbing the floor in the kitchen for Teresa until my elbows ached and my knees felt raw, serving meals to the family, settling into the routine of the household. Even the eerie whispering at night had begun to feel repetitive, a strange quirk to be disregarded and blocked out.

But the house was not content to be ignored.

On my fifth night at Archfall Manor, I was already half anticipating that the whispers would reach for me, but I could not have imagined the horror of the nightmarish noise that woke me. A grinding, nerve-shredding sound of metal on metal that set my teeth on edge and sent a shudder down my spine. It seemed to come from the heart of the house itself, grasping at me, piercing through the corridors. It sliced through me so viscerally I was certain I must be bleeding into the bed, and I froze, my hands in the air defensively. That noise was nothing I had ever heard before, like metal come alive and shrieking in pain, or if machinery were sentient, screaming . . . And it hurt. My muscles were tense everywhere, an involuntary clenching all through my body in response. The noise peaked in intensity so that it was almost unbearable.

As abruptly as it began, the dreadful sound ended. In the dark, all I could hear was the rasp of my own fast breathing and the thud of my heart, which had leaped into my throat and felt stuck there. Despite my desperation to be rational, this time I was certain the sound was supernatural. Not a dream, not created inside my head, but not of this world either.

I was losing my mind.

It was the distress of metallic parts, screaming as they were bent into something new. It had sounded as though every invention in the manor were crying out. Pain and sorrow leaking from the very walls of my room, the house itself lamenting in the night.

I wanted to imagine it was an inventor, up late into the night. The screech of metal, the bending of physical matter. One of the inhabitants of Archfall, honing their abilities and ideas. But my body knew differently. This sound was meant for me.

And, in the absence of it, the whispering began. The house wanted me to *listen*.

I slipped from the bed and padded across to the wall. It was cold to the touch, and I pressed my ear against it. This added not a jot of clarity to the whisper, horribly eerie and unnerving.

And so I waited. And waited, the dark creeping along my shoulders, down my neck, round my bare feet. 'What are you trying to tell me?' I whispered back into the wall.

Then there was a word, more clearly enunciated.

Arches.

I jolted away from the wall as if it had burned me, my body immediately tensing. What the whispering voice had said felt like a call, like a command, like a summons. Weren't the arches at the top of the house central to everything? To the structure of the building, to the mystery of the past, to the hopes of the future . . .

I shuddered and sought out the robe I'd been given and pulled it tight about me. There was no hesitation – I'd had enough of this house's torments and riddles. I crept from my bedroom and haunted the corridors of Archfall Manor like a ghost, flitting through the kitchen and up the back stairs, drawn past the separate bedrooms where Teresa and Gabriel slept as housekeeper and head of maintenance rather than sharing as man and wife, then through another door and into a part of the east wing that held the guest rooms and the portrait gallery, where suddenly every fixture in the place oozed wealth.

Padding softly along the velvet carpet that stretched the length of it, I ran my fingers over the smooth wooden wall panelling. Emerging through yet another door, the landing lay ahead of me, split by the great marble staircase heading up and down, linking the three floors. An iron skull on the wall opposite me fixed me with its glassy eyes. Surely everyone was sunk too deep into their own sleep to be watching me? Into the depths of the house I went, into the belly of the house.

I knew where I was heading. Up yet another floor, on to the next landing as if I were going towards the schoolroom. It had stuck out like a splinter in a thumb the first time I'd seen it. The alcove, a wound in the wall, where the ancient steps snaked up in darkness, winding towards the highest point of Archfall Manor.

At the top, I would find the arches. Deep inside me, I also felt a certainty that I would find some of the answers I'd been so desperately craving.

I hovered at the bottom of the steps, which curved round and round in the darkness. A shiver of inevitability rippled down my spine. I wasn't frightened in that moment, even though I had been before, even though a logical part of my brain told me that I *should* be, that everything about being here was wrong. In the middle of the night, barefoot, in a house whose night noises were capable of causing me physical pain, inhabited by a family I'd been warned were dangerous, that seemed to be followed around by death . . .

And yet. The only thing I felt was that this was fated. I was calm. I had never believed in the concept before, had always held tight to the notion that I alone was responsible for my destiny. And yet. And yet.

I was always going to end up taking the first step of that staircase. And the next. And the next. I fell into a hypnotic rhythm of climbing, my legs burning with the exertion and my chest bursting as I grew breathless.

The stairs were never-ending, and I started to feel like a character in a fairy tale. I tried not to think about the fact that bad things happen to deceitful people in such stories. Abruptly, I was faced with a towering door made of iron. It had a keyhole, but most crucially of all it had no handle. It would only open when the key was inside the lock, its weight sufficient to pull open the door.

I paused, breathed out my disappointment. In that moment, I could no longer remember what I had been expecting. Of course an invention of this importance would be locked away. I pressed my palm flat against the door. A heartbeat seemed to move beneath my fingers, as though they were pressed against a chest. It felt . . . hot. Thrumming with energy. *Alive*.

I gasped and snatched my hand away. A spreading warmth moved through me – from my hand up through the rest of my arm. The strangeness of it unnerved me so deeply that I thought I might have turned to brittle sugar, that I might shatter at the slightest nudge.

The arches were out there. The late Edwin Cauldwell's invention was out there. And I knew that somehow it was all connected to my father. The house knew it too. The house had woken me in the middle of the night. The house was alive, was excited that I had listened to its call, had come to investigate.

These thoughts compelled me and terrified me – was it a type of hysteria to think this way? Was I succumbing to madness? A very quiet voice in my head told me to run, to run away from Archfall Manor and never come back. I did not listen to it. It was drowned out by the certainty that this was why I had come. Hadn't I felt drawn to this place?

I might have stayed by the door all night, transfixed and obsessed with finding a way to the other side. But I knew that would take time and patience. There would come a moment, I was sure of it, when the door would be open, and the house would let me know.

I couldn't have prepared for what the house would show me next.

I traced my steps back down the curving stairs to the landing on the second floor, where shadows hung like cobwebs, and the moon was bright and round through the colossal circular window. My whole body was trembling, not from the cold, but as though every part of me had been shaken by the sensation of touching the door, sensing the presence of the house.

The quiet of the night was disrupted by the sudden squall of baby Edmund. Molly mustn't see me as she roused herself to attend to him in the nursery. I raced down the next flight of stairs, and emerged at the top of the great marble staircase that widened into the main entrance hall. I grasped hold of the wooden pillar at the top as I spotted him. A dark smudge against the tiles. My heart leaped into my throat as I struggled to truly take in the horror in front of me. Crumpled and broken on the gleaming tiles, one hand outstretched, was a body. The body of Mr Cauldwell.

His hair was all flyaway from his fall, his neck at a strange angle to the side, his eyes staring, his mouth open just the slightest amount in a twist of surprise. Blood pooled beneath his head. He was so completely still that it was like looking at a portrait of the man. He seemed smaller somehow, the essence of him gone. He was, quite definitely, dead.

It appeared to have been a terribly unfortunate accident. A fall. The horror of it swept through me like a great wave, and a deep sickness settled in the pit of my stomach.

I froze. I needed to tell someone. But how could I? How could I explain that I was wandering the corridors in the middle of the night? No. I couldn't tell *anyone*.

The seconds that followed seemed to stretch out, elongated by indecision. There was a little shiver that ran like something alive – a spider or a beetle perhaps – down my back. I crept down the stairs and saw that around his neck a thin golden chain that might have been tucked inside his shirt was dangling loose, and looped through it was an intricate iron key. The key had caught my eye, and now I found I couldn't look away from it. I was glued to the spot, a marzipan figure fixed in place on a cake.

Take it.

Was it the whisper that spoke to me, or just the darkest part of my own mind? I couldn't tell, but once the thought had pushed its way into my mind I could not shake it. I needed to take the key, even though I did not want to. My fingers trembled; they felt as if they did not belong to me any more. I knelt quickly, unfastened the chain from Mr Cauldwell's neck and slipped the key, even heavier than I expected, into my pocket. It was a moment of madness. But the whole house seemed to sigh when I snatched it.

I stepped over the body, and as quickly and quietly as I could returned to the staff quarters and tucked myself away in my room. I turned the key over in my hands, examining it. The bit appeared to be a simple three-pronged design. With the chance to inspect it a little closer, I noticed that the bow of the key had an intricate design contained within its circle, the iron twisted into the letter T. For his given name Thomas? And the detail of the letter T had hinges. I pressed them with my fingertips, and they did in fact move, would make a different shape for a different lock.

It was very clever. Mr Cauldwell might have been a belligerent and divisive figure within his family, not to mention hugely privileged, but he had proved over and over that he was resourceful and innovative too. We are all made up of light and dark.

I thought, with regret, with a sick stomach, about the moment I had taken the key from where it hung around his neck, so very broken. I flinched, thinking about how dreadfully it would have hurt, how terrifying it must have been to fall. His end was so awful, so distressing, and nobody else knew.

That I had the key felt essential to everything. Why? Why had I taken it? An awful guilt oozed through my chest at the memory. I had felt compelled to the moment the notion had been seeded in my mind. The whisper seemed to have such a pull over me now that I'd begun to listen to it. *Arches*, it said, and I went. *Take it*, it said, and I had. The house, its walls – there was something living inside. I'd felt the thud of its heart. And that alive something had plans for me.

What was the key even for? What part of the puzzle might it be locking away?

I pulled the blankets up tight round my neck, but they did not warm me. The cold was rooted in my chest, icy tendrils creeping throughout my insides, taking hold. The strange whisper was quiet for once, and yet I stayed awake all through the night, the image of Mr Cauldwell's body etched on my mind, as I waited, waited for morning to come and his body to be found.

12

They found him first thing, of course. I intended to stay in my room until the last possible moment, but Jasper came knocking on my door. He looked so flustered, his face pained with the shock.

'Mr Cauldwell is dead.'

'Dead?' I hoped my voice didn't betray me. I couldn't tell him that I already knew, that I had found him first.

He told me that Mr Cauldwell had had a nasty fall in the night, and that Mrs Temple had taken to her bed in grief and shock after having found his body. He didn't say it out loud, but what moved between us was the knowledge of the bodies Mrs Temple had found before, of the reputation that followed her around, of the stories that had been written about her. The loss that circled her like a raven.

'It's awful, of course, but it sounds like an accident,' I said, trying to comfort him. There was nothing to suggest foul play, nothing that might bring the reporters to Mrs Temple's door once again.

The memory of the body resurfaced in my mind. I hoped that nobody would realize that something had been taken from Mr Cauldwell, that nobody knew of the chain he'd been wearing around his neck, suspiciously gone.

In the kitchen, there was a sombre feeling draped over the unfolding of the day. Teresa had already changed into a black gown for mourning, and she handed Jasper a black armband to roll over his shirtsleeve. They'd done this before, observed mourning rituals for the late Mrs Cauldwell, and perhaps Edwin as well.

Teresa turned to me. 'Have you something black?'

'I have a dress I can give her,' Molly said from her quiet perch on a stool by the range. She was pushing a spoonful of porridge round her bowl and looked vaguely sick. 'Mrs Temple provided me with a couple of black working gowns after the incident in London. I just . . . I can't believe it. She hasn't even finished her mourning period for Mr Temple. We left one place haunted by death . . . It's enough to make you believe this family is cursed.'

'Don't you say that word again,' Teresa said crossly, pointing a finger at Molly. 'We'll have none of that nonsense, thank you.'

Molly's mouth seemed to shrivel up at the chastisement, and we all remained in a horribly uneasy silence until Gabriel burst into the room. He was carrying a bucket filled with rust-coloured water that he sloshed down the sink. Molly flinched next to me.

'I've taken care of the stairs,' Gabriel announced to Teresa, and my stomach rolled, thinking of the blood circling its way down the drain. He soaped his hands. 'Mr Cauldwell is laid out in his bedroom. We need a doctor's certificate arranging. And we'll need that solicitor too, Mr Harris.'

His words hung in the air. A solicitor would handle the last will and testament of Mr Cauldwell – reveal whether he had put his wishes in writing. What would it mean if Mr Cauldwell had documented his preference to halt the traditional line of succession for his role within the Institute? Did that preference extend to the house and everything inside too? What would happen to the family in that instance? My insides went cold – what would happen to us, the staff?

'Will you go to the mainland?' Teresa sounded concerned.

'Somebody has to,' Gabriel said matter-of-factly. He seemed so collected, so wholly confident in his role within this tragedy. 'I'll cross at low tide this evening.' He dried his clean hands on his trousers and folded his arms across his broad chest.

Jasper suddenly seemed alert and interested. 'You're leaving the island?'

'Before you ask – don't,' Gabriel said, his voice a firm and dismissive growl. 'The answer is no. I'll go alone by horse so I don't have to ready a carriage.'

Jasper seemed to shrink away. He had been hoping to go too. How many times had that request been refused? When I'd asked him once if he minded leaving the island so infrequently, he'd attempted to minimize how much he cared – but I got the sense he cared a great deal indeed.

Every one of us in the kitchen stayed silent. Molly took my hand and led me up to her room on the second floor to find a black gown for the day, and I quickly changed. We were all expected to continue with our duties, as though there had been no event larger than a shattered plate. I was to teach as usual, despite the tragedy, so I trudged my way to the schoolroom, dreading my lessons with Birdie.

'I suppose I must spend my whole life dressed in black,' she said with a sigh.

I bowed my head. 'I'm terribly sorry about your grandfather.'

'Are you?' Birdie asked. 'Or is that just what you're supposed to say?'

I thought about his body, lifeless at the bottom of the stairs. 'Somebody that was here isn't with us any more. Someone who brought something utterly unique to this world has gone. Of course that's something to be sorry about.'

Birdie stared at me. 'I'd like to go to the library,' she said. 'I thought about including it in that tour I planned for you.' She smirked. Had I earned a grudging respect through my doggedness, my refusal to be terrified by her?

'I'd love to see it,' I said with as much sweetness as I could muster.

Birdie led the way. As we walked, I thought about the key I'd stolen from Mr Cauldwell, and wondered what it unlocked.

Birdie pushed open a door and gestured for me to follow her, leading me into a room whose entire left wall was lined with books from ceiling to floor. Fixed near the door was a contraption that looked almost like a grandfather clock, set back into the shelving. Instead of numbers around the face, there were words relating to the books themselves – *Tragic*, *Comic*, *Romantic*, *Horrific*, *Historic*, and more – and an arm with a claw-like attachment.

'What is that?' I asked.

'It's a little tool that helps you find the kind of book that you want – you select from these themes, and then it'll bring you something suitable. It seems to know what you're looking for.'

'How does it work?'

Birdie shrugged. 'Somebody must have devised a plan for it and calculated how to fit all the pieces together and then . . . found a way to make it work.'

I watched her closely as she turned the dial – *Medical* – and gestured at the claw-like attachment that sprang into action. It whizzed along the shelves until it landed upon a book, selected it and returned it to her. A guide to anatomy.

'But how . . . how does it know?'

'Know what?'

'Choosing a book, on a particular theme . . . that's something only a human could do. How does it know?'

Birdie just shrugged again, seemingly completely accepting of this extraordinary feat and quite amused by my bafflement. She began flicking through the pages of her anatomy guide. I knew she couldn't give me a more satisfactory answer about the nature of the invention, but it continued to occupy my mind. The inventor had used their genius to create a new contraption, but there was a leap into sentience that should not have been possible for the cogs and metal arm alone to achieve ... Was it an extension of the life force that I increasingly felt sure was inside the house, that allowed this strange invention to do something which should have been impossible?

'I was thinking about Grandfather falling,' Birdie said, ripping me out of my contemplation.

She was full of morbid questions. What injuries had he sustained? What was it that had killed him exactly, the blow to the head? The impact on his neck? The shock to his heart? She was almost like a tiny, gruesome undertaker, seemingly emotionally unaffected by the death of her grandfather, but fascinated instead. I had no answers for her, and suggested perhaps we turn our attention to some arithmetic, but on and on the questions came. Could he have been unwell before, to have taken a fall so unexpectedly on stairs so familiar? Had I considered that somebody might have pushed him?

'Pushed him?'

'You never know,' Birdie said with another shrug. 'It's just sensible to consider these questions. When my stepfather died, the police asked all sorts of questions about how it happened.'

I demurred – but once again felt startled by this peculiar girl, and her even more peculiar family.

At the evening low tide, Gabriel Wright left the island with a strict set of instructions from Mr Wilbur on engaging a solicitor to come and read the will, and the doctor who, Teresa informed me, acted as the registrar for the area to record events, and would be able to provide the death certificate and collect the body. Wilbur had inevitably stepped forth to fill his father's shoes, though we were all yet to discover what that might mean for the rest of us.

We all waited for Gabriel's return as though we were holding our breath. Knowing there was a dead body lying in a bedroom made the atmosphere feel tense and crushing, as though the air were being sucked out of the house.

That night, we served dinner to the family, all dressed in black. It was a sombre affair. Barely a word passed between them. Wilbur, above all, seemed rigid with stress, and I imagined he was waiting to see if his father's notions about the competition regarding his inheritance would indeed be detailed in the will, or if he would, after all, inherit the house, the responsibility, the money and the gravitas of his role within the Institute.

Mrs Temple's eyes were red and swollen, and she kept biting the corner of her mouth, making it sore. Birdie seemed nonplussed by the tension in the room, eagerly digging in when I served her plate, but Nora had Wilbur fixed with an unpleasant glare as though he'd displeased her somehow.

Nobody seemed to want to talk much in the kitchen either. Although I was burning with questions about how the running of the household would be affected, given that the head of the house had passed away, I kept these to myself. I did not want to appear ghoulish and overly practical in the immediate throes of grief. It would be best to wait for Gabriel's return the following day, and then begin to piece everything together.

I retired to my room earlier than on previous nights and dug out the key from its hiding place beneath my pillow. A thought occurred to me – the whispering voice had directed me to the arches, then it had urged me to take the key. Was there a connection there? Did the key belong to the lock of the iron door?

I wondered what it would feel like to come face to face with the arch that I was certain would give me some clue about what happened to my father. Was the house responding to this desire in me? Was it leading the way? I would have to wait for the cover of night to investigate once more, and time stretched out agonizingly ahead of me as I waited for the rest of the house to quieten down into sleep a little after midnight.

I returned to the foot of the twisting stone staircase clutching the key, my hand wrapped round it in the pocket of my dress. As I crept up each step, anticipation coursed through me. There was a rising excitement now, a strange sense of certainty that quivered in my fingertips. Was this what the whispering voice had been trying to guide me to all along?

I allowed myself to imagine the key slipping into the lock, releasing the door to let me inspect the arch for myself. I even nurtured a tiny flicker of belief in it, that I might find it, remarkable, functional, a window through time ... Because this was a place where invention seemed to have a life of its own. And if the house were alive, if it had woken me and whispered to me and showed me Mr Cauldwell at the bottom of the stairs before anyone else so that I might be the one to take this key, as if it *wanted* me to take the key and unlock this door . . . then why shouldn't the other incredible possibility be true? Why shouldn't Edwin Cauldwell's window through time be real?

These were the thoughts of night-time – when a life force seemed to pulse through Archfall Manor, where nudges and pulls guided me, and a strange whisper strained to reach my ear.

I arrived at the top of the stairs, wrestling with a thrilling fear. I placed my hand against the door and felt that beating thrum again, the heart of the house. Then I pushed the key into the lock . . . and it would not turn. I tried it multiple ways, taking the key out and moving its hinges to create different shapes. Nothing made any difference. It just didn't work.

Eventually, tired and disappointed, I returned to my bed, unable to shake the feeling that I had done something wrong, that I hadn't been smart enough to figure it out. I was so *exhausted*.

The disappointment was crushing. I had arrived on Sighfeyre Isle full of hope for my future – hope that I might finally find some answers about my father. Instead, I had been met with a locked door, haunted nights and sheer exhaustion, and come face to face with death. Everything about Archfall Manor felt rotten and wrong, but I was trapped inside it, like a spider underneath a glass.

13

The next day, I lived according to the routine laid out for me, as we all waited for Gabriel to return with the doctor and the solicitor. There was a certainty and inevitability to the rhythms of the house – I woke in the morning and served the breakfast with Teresa. After breakfast, I set about Birdie's schedule – morning lessons, a pause to eat, afternoon lessons – and she left me even more on edge than the days before. More testing boundaries, more unsettling comments about death, more looks that made me feel she was peering right *inside* me somehow, trying to see the blood and bone beneath my skin.

I left the schoolroom with a shudder. Nora was hovering in the corridor, giving me the distinctly unsettling impression that she had been waiting for me.

'My deepest condolences,' I said. The words felt like stones thrown into a pond – arcing through the air, dropping heavily, submerged.

'Thank you,' Nora said with an appreciative smile. She looked unsteady and her hands were trembling.

'I know that's what you're supposed to say, but I truly mean it,' I added, thinking about Birdie's dismissiveness of my condolences. There was something fragile about Nora. I wondered whether anyone had thought to ask her how she might be feeling.

'You don't need to be too sorry,' she said. 'He could be rather awful at times.'

'We are all made up of light and dark.'

I hadn't meant to say it out loud, but the thought had been echoing in my mind since the night Mr Cauldwell died.

Nora smiled. 'That's true.'

I thought perhaps I should leave, but she looked at me expectantly. It was as if she were hoping I might say something else, but instead the uncomfortable silence swelled between us. I wondered again whether she was feeling lonely. It wasn't as though she had any friends in the house – her siblings were so much younger, and there seemed to be no affection between her and Molly. Nora seemed to jest easily at Jasper's expense, but the two passed each other in the house only intermittently, more like different plants growing in the same garden whose leaves might brush only by chance. Perhaps I was the closest thing she could find to somebody to confide in.

'Sometimes you get what you ask for, but not in the way you think,' Nora said. 'My grandfather had this notion that I'd be married off to whoever won his little inventing competition. At least that ought to be forgotten about now.'

'Competition?' I asked, perhaps a little too lightly.

Nora narrowed her eyes at me. 'Don't pretend you

weren't listening. I saw you. I was watching you the other night at dinner. You were taking it all in.'

I lowered my eyes, the shame creeping all across my cheeks, even as I willed it to stop. 'He wanted to hold an inventing competition to identify a suitable replacement for his role within the Institute upon his stepping down,' I murmured, confirming that I'd been listening. There seemed no point in denying it.

'Invention is in the blood of this family,' she said. 'But do you think I've been given the opportunity to explore my potential? Do you think I might have been permitted to enter?'

'Would you have wanted to?' I asked, amazed at this revelation.

She didn't answer my question. 'To my grandfather, my only value was as an additional prize to solidify his legacy.'

'The fact that you didn't want your grandfather to marry you off doesn't make you responsible for the terrible thing that's happened to him,' I said. 'I know you might feel like you wished it, but that doesn't mean anything.'

'Do you believe in predestination?' Nora asked, sounding uncertain, as if the matter were something she'd been turning over in her mind for a long time.

'I'm not sure,' I said. The question made me pause. 'Do you mean the idea that everything that's going to happen is set in stone?'

It wasn't a notion I'd ever considered, in truth. I'd always been so busy and working so hard that I hadn't had the time or space to turn over such existential questions. But I felt now like I'd been confronted with many of these during my short time at Archfall.

'Yes, that's mostly it. The idea that life is all mapped out ahead of us,' she said. 'That it was always going to unfold this way. Do you believe in that?'

I found that an answer wasn't forthcoming. I had felt, at the bottom of the staircase leading up to the big iron door, that I was fated to be there. That I was meant to find, and take, Mr Cauldwell's key. That the whispers in this house were guiding me to a future I couldn't yet fathom . . .

Had Nora been reading her uncle Edwin's theories of time? His notions certainly seemed to lean towards a view that all time – past and present – was already connected. His essay had proposed that time existed in layers in which we could create windows. That was what the arch was meant to be – a window on the layers. I wondered if my father had believed it too. If you took the argument to its logical conclusion, then you would be able to look forward and backwards. Which would mean that all time, everything that has happened and everything that is going to happen, already existed, its layers already formed.

Whether it was true or not, all depended on whether the arch worked. It was dizzying to consider, and it made me feel utterly overwhelmed.

Nora was staring at me as I moved my mouth like a fish out of water. I was desperate to convey the depth of my ruminations, but even to mention an interest in the work of Edwin Cauldwell was to reveal more about myself than would be wise.

'I'm not convinced that we can ever know for sure,' I said. 'Maybe somebody will unravel that mystery someday, or maybe it will be revealed to us after we die, but I don't think you or I will ever know with certainty in our lifetime.'

'No,' said Nora. A tiny smile flickered across her lips. 'Perhaps not.'

The evenings had quickly become my favourite time of day in Archfall Manor. I assisted Teresa with the dinner preparation, finding it was physical enough to take my mind off everything that unsettled me so deeply. The repetitive nature of chopping and stirring freed me.

Having had no sign of him that morning, we thought that Gabriel would return at low tide that evening, but Jasper trudged into the kitchen, despondent. He had been watching for his father at the window of the morning room where Mrs Temple sometimes sat to take tea overlooking the causeway.

'Not back yet,' he said, his shoulders hunched and tension in his forehead.

There was a brief rap at the door, and Teresa and Jasper exchanged a look. It wasn't usual for anybody to do that. Teresa went to the door and opened it in one swift motion. I saw her posture immediately shift.

'Miss Nora, what can I do for you?'

I paused, my knife in the air, the onion beneath rolling. The sting of it had caught my eyes and I blinked away the fierceness of it.

'My uncle has requested that all staff report to the drawing room.'

The order was delivered briskly and without elaboration. If Nora knew what the summons was for, she didn't give any indication. The guilty part of me that took the key twisted inside, and my mind began to race away with a scene where we were all searched and our rooms stripped. My mouth went dry.

'Of course,' Teresa responded, and with flapping hands that betrayed her anxiety she gestured for Jasper and me to follow her.

In the drawing room, Wilbur was pacing, pinching the bridge of his nose. Molly was already waiting for us, her back to the fireplace, hands neatly clasped. When Teresa joined her and assumed the same position, I copied their stance, hoping it didn't appear as unnatural as it felt.

'Thank you for attending this meeting of the household staff,' Wilbur said. 'I won't take too much of your time, as I'm certain you have much that you ought to be getting on with.'

Teresa stiffened next to me, the implied criticism not passing her by.

'Following the death of my father, with immediate effect, I will be assuming his role in this household. Since the loss of my brother eighteen years ago, I am my father's heir in every respect, and as such I will be making any future decisions about the running of this house. With that in mind, I will be advertising for a proper housekeeper and butler to coordinate staff activity. Over the next few weeks,

I intend to give this house a full complement of staff befitting its size, in preparation for hosting the Cauldwell Institute of Invention for a celebration.'

I felt Teresa stir beside me again, no doubt at the mention of a 'proper' housekeeper. But my mind had caught on 'celebration'. A celebration of what? His father had just died. It was so presumptuous – that he should take over the running of the house and the Institute and celebrate the fact, when he knew that Mr Cauldwell's intentions before he died had been very different. Wilbur must have been hoping that his father never had a chance to solidify this wish in writing.

'With all due respect, Mr Wilbur,' Teresa said, clearing her throat, 'do you think we ought to wait until Gabriel has returned from the mainland with the last will and testament –'

Wilbur interrupted, his voice bordering on a shout. 'Do not use that childish name for me again. You will refer to me as Mr Cauldwell, as befits the head of the house,' he barked.

'Yes, Mr Cauldwell,' Teresa said evenly.

He looked at her, an awful sneer crossing his face. 'You might also wish to reflect on your own weak efforts at maintaining the standards of this house during your tenure as the most senior member of staff here. A new housekeeper should acquaint you with what is expected. You are indeed fortunate that my sister speaks so fondly of your little pastries that she insists I absolutely must retain you.' He laughed cruelly, dismissively.

That Teresa was able to maintain her composure beneath the force of his punishing tirade stunned me. She didn't even flinch as he verbally stamped on her, dismissing the years of skill and experience she brought to Archfall Manor. That the house was not a crumbling wreck was only down to the unwavering dedication and commitment of Teresa and Gabriel, and the rest of us knew it, even if Wilbur could not see.

'Now, all of you – get back to work.'

Teresa immediately set about preparing the dinner. While she'd remained calm in the drawing room, once we entered the kitchen it was clear that she was seething. She clattered and bashed around the kitchen, blowing air out of her mouth every so often like an agitated horse. Jasper and I quietly moved around her, as though one wrong word from either of us might cause her to erupt. She handed us both the finished results of her cooking efforts, and did not join us to deliver the meal to the family.

'My pa is going to be absolutely furious when he hears about this,' Jasper murmured.

'But what can he do about it?' I asked. 'He's just going to have to accept the changes.'

'We'll see about that.'

I glanced at him sideways. 'What do you mean?'

But we were nearly at the dining room, and Jasper just shook his head, a little smile playing across his lips.

Later, as we were clearing everything away in the kitchen, and we had a moment where his mother disappeared into the pantry, Jasper's hand closed round mine, and my stomach swooped involuntarily.

'I want to show you something,' he whispered. 'Pretend you're going to bed and then, when my mother has retired upstairs to her room, come back here. I'll be waiting.'

'What do you want to show me?' I whispered back.

'The inventing room.' He reached into his pocket and gave me a glimpse of a large ring of keys. Excitement crackled inside me. 'With my father gone, I'm responsible for locking up the house.'

'I . . . I can't. I want to, but what if we're seen?'

What would people think, what might they assume, if they found Jasper and me alone together in the night? And yet the temptation was so great. I might not get another chance to see this inventing room. What if there were something inside that belonged to my father, the watchmaker, evidence of his time here and what happened to him?

'Nobody will be up then,' Jasper said. 'Do you trust me?'

Before I had a chance to reply, Teresa emerged from the pantry, and I sprang away from Jasper, busying my hands by removing the plates from the spinning invention that had saved us the job of washing them. When they were all stacked and ready for the next day, I made a noise about retiring to my room, wishing Teresa and Jasper goodnight.

I wasn't sure how long to wait, wasn't sure if he'd still be there after I'd seemed so dismissive and hesitant . . . But I'd decided I *would* trust Jasper. The minutes crawled by before I decided I could sneak back out again and return to the kitchen.

'I hoped you'd come,' he said, swinging the great loop of

keys around on his finger. His face was lit by the dying embers of the fire, his eyes shining. 'Are you ready?'

'Absolutely,' I replied.

He handed me a tall, thin candle, kept one for himself, and then took my hand in his. We went through the great house together to the second floor and a room filled with the paraphernalia of invention. There were several long wooden tables piled high with tools of their craft: cogs, copper wires, springs, bits and pieces of various metals, magnets both small and large, saws, turnscrews. It reminded me of my kitchen back at home somehow.

He sifted through the drawers and pulled out a simple little mechanical timer. 'I made this when I was ten,' Jasper said with nostalgic pride in his voice. He demonstrated how it worked, winding the hand to a minute, and, when he released it, it ticked down a full sixty seconds, heralding its conclusion with a little ringing bell. 'Better than an hourglass?'

'Most definitely.' I couldn't resist smiling as I imagined a young Jasper with his first invention.

'I always thought I might do something else with it,' he said pensively. 'You could attach it to . . . . Well, I never figured it out.'

'Too preoccupied with theories of time.'

'And other things.' He was standing close enough that I could smell the peppermint sweet that was clacking against his teeth.

'Maybe you could have entered Mr Cauldwell's competition if it had ever come to pass.'

'Competition?' Jasper asked, frowning.

'He was planning to hold an inventing competition to identify the heir to his role within the Institute. He was stepping down.'

'He wasn't going to pass it down to his son?'

I shook my head. 'Who knows what will happen now, though. It all depends whether he had those wishes recorded anywhere.'

Jasper suddenly became distracted, as though his thoughts had taken him elsewhere. 'You mustn't tell anyone I brought you here,' he said. 'Mr Cauldwell was always so protective over everything in this room.'

'Do you think Mr Wil–' I stopped, corrected myself. 'Do you think the new Mr Cauldwell will feel the same?'

'It might not be up to him,' Jasper said. 'Some of this stuff rightly belongs to Pa. He's never been just like staff. He was Mr Cauldwell's oldest friend. Look, here's something Pa made.'

He opened a large drawer and pulled out a small device that looked a bit like a pocket watch, except with the addition of a little window in the centre that seemed to be able to state, with precision, the weather conditions. I'd seen barometers before and was not hugely impressed at first glance. It must have shown on my face because Jasper began explaining, demonstrating.

'You change the time,' he said, twiddling one of the knobs on the side of the glass dial, 'and it tells you what the weather will be like at that moment. It can predict what's coming, up to a month in advance.'

I narrowed my eyes. 'And is it accurate?'

'To the minute.' He beamed with pride.

'Impossible,' I said.

Jasper crossed his arms, and the fabric of his shirt seemed to sigh over the strength of them. 'Maybe you don't have a big enough imagination for this,' he said, teasing.

'I have an imagination!' I protested. 'But if this weather predictor is so accurate, why can't you buy one on every street corner?'

'That is what I wanted to share with you,' he said. 'On this island, we have long been making impossible things possible. The devices we make . . . when we're here, it's like magic sometimes. When we take them off the island, that doesn't always . . . translate. Inventions can do incredible things here that we can't recreate away from Sighfeyre. So we diversify, keep things simple. We produce less ambitious tools so the Cauldwell reputation for inventing isn't lost, so the family make their money . . . But the real magic happens here. The new Mr Cauldwell wants to remember that the family legacy is about much more than an institute or the financial gain from inventions.'

Jasper hesitated. His eyes were the colour of gingerbread. 'You think I'm insane.'

I shook my head. I was remembering the book-selecting device in the library, the pulsing of the door to the arches, the whispering voice that lived within the walls of the house.

'Do you . . . do you think there's something supernatural about it all?' I asked, tension bunching in my shoulders as I made myself vulnerable.

Jasper eyed me. 'I didn't have you down as someone who believed in ghosts, Josephine.'

I blushed, but, before I could say anything else, Jasper went on. 'I don't know exactly. There's an energy here that seems to be unique,' he said. 'But beyond that ... who knows?'

I didn't respond immediately. 'Let me see that.' I reached out for the timer. It was easy to work. I shifted the dial forward, selecting a time several hours in the future, and pressed in the knob. 'Intense storm?'

That didn't sound good. I'd heard about Sighfeyre Isle being cut off from the mainland, sometimes for weeks at a time. I assumed everything would be in order to keep us all fed in such a situation, but I didn't feel entirely comfortable with the idea. The rising winds and roaring waves had been enough to unnerve me when I first arrived on the island. A full-blown storm would be terrifying.

Jasper's expression changed, but not in the way I expected. No concern. It almost seemed like he was excited. The anticipation of it all mingled inside me – a fear and a thrill, both at the same time. It was the same way I felt about Jasper. When I looked at him, it was like trying to resist an inevitability, like trying to resist the gathering storm that threatened to rip across the island. Twin storms. And both would leave everything changed.

14

I was in the schoolroom the next morning with Birdie and Mrs Temple when the storm hit. I had intended to resume lessons firmly with Birdie, but Mrs Temple was already there, the pair of them watching at the window. I joined them to see what they were looking at.

Clouds rolled across the sky, casting everything into a deep shadow, and the rain poured, plump droplets leaping like frogs as they hit the mire outside. It was so dark that it might as well have been night although the morning was yet upon us.

In the distance, it was possible to pick out a group beginning to make their way along the causeway. Gabriel Wright on his horse, followed by two carriages. The first carriage was all black, with a thick plume of black feathers dampened by the rain – I wondered if this was the doctor. Mr Cauldwell's corpse wrapped in blankets and laid out in a bedroom, I had been trying to push from my mind. The second carriage, grey, drawn by a beautiful dappled mare and distinguished from the other by a glinting gold ornament on the roof, I assumed belonged to the lawyer.

The three of them progressed over the causeway, trundling along the precarious path, and the sight of them all forming a parade reminded me of the travelling circus that had come to Durham the year before. Those circus carriages were bright and vivid, painted in reds and yellows, but the black and the grey of this procession almost disappeared against the backdrop of the sea and the rocks.

The rumbles of thunder began. They rattled the very bones inside me.

'Is it dangerous to cross?' I asked Mrs Temple.

It didn't look as though the surface of the causeway had had sufficient time for the water to recede fully – but then, with the weather conditions being what they were, it seemed this was as good as it was likely to get, especially if the visitors were hoping to leave again swiftly before the crossing closed.

'Yes,' Mrs Temple said crisply. She had stiffened beside me.

Birdie looked breathless with excitement at the danger. 'They must be very brave to try when it's like that.'

'The crossing will only get worse if the weather keeps on this way. The last time I remember a storm like this, we were cut off from the mainland for a week,' Mrs Temple muttered.

I focused my eyes on the procession again. The carriages looked so flimsy against the unbridled anger of the sea, and Gabriel, on his horse, seemed completely exposed to the elements. The waters had been whipped into a frenzy by the wind – the pair of them were feeding each other's fury like a couple in an argument. The travellers were caught in the middle of the conflict. The horses struggled onwards, pushing against the force of the wind, their hooves fighting for purchase on the wet ground.

Unlike my own arrival, this one had been prepared for. Wooden boards had been laid out by Jasper so the horses would not have to strain against the sucking mud.

Then an intense fear clutched at my throat – a wave was rising. It was a monstrous creature, alive and surging, with its eyes firmly fixed on the group.

Gabriel spotted it first, and kicked his horse sharply, spurring it into a gallop, making a desperate bid for land. When he made it on to the boards and the safety of the island, Mrs Temple's shoulders visibly dropped with relief. The driver of the black carriage whipped his horses, causing the carriage to rattle and sway, a dead weight that prevented them from reaching Gabriel's speed.

Even though we could see what was coming, we at the window were powerless to do anything but stare helplessly. Each of us was struck by anticipatory horror at what was about to transpire. All Birdie's excitement had dissipated; she might have been a ghoulish little thing, but this was too much even for her. Mrs Temple was watching stoically.

For myself, all I could do was witness the inevitable, echoes of my conversation with Nora about predestination circling my mind. The thrum of my heartbeat cantered faster. I had a sense that this was the island defending itself, that the strange force that ebbed through the place did not take kindly to the intrusion posed by these outsiders.

The great wave opened wide like a mouth, and swallowed both the carriages.

For a moment, it was as though we had all been immersed beneath the waters. The room held its breath. The three of us were glassy-eyed at the window, as though staring might change the outcome, but nothing emerged from the chopping waves. The carriages, the horses, the passengers . . . all dashed against the rocks of the causeway and sunk.

'Are they dead, Mother?' Birdie asked.

I expected some words of comfort from her mother, but was shocked by her reply.

'What do you think?' Mrs Temple asked steadily. 'Evaluate the evidence and draw a conclusion.'

How could she possibly respond in such a measured fashion? Then I remembered. Death was not a strange and abstract concept to her, the way it was to me. My only experience of losing someone – Father – was from before I was able to form memory, and the whole event was shrouded in such mystery that all my thoughts on the matter were carved from imagination alone. But Caroline had lost three husbands, seen their lifeless bodies, discovered her father's body only two days earlier. She was training her daughter to think in a detached and emotionless way, as if she were a police constable in training . . . She was teaching her daughter to survive.

'Well, a person might have broken their neck during the crash. Or if they were knocked unconscious then that would have stopped them being able to attempt to break out of the carriage and, as it filled with water, they would have drowned. But even if they managed to escape their carriage, the waters are so strong they probably would have struggled to get to the surface, and ultimately drowned. Worst of all, if they did reach the surface, we haven't seen anyone make their way up the side of the causeway, and I doubt we'd be able to get anyone to them in time now. Even if they're not dead right this moment, then they soon will be.' Birdie paused for breath, and her eyes sought her mother's approval.

'Exactly,' Mrs Temple said.

'Shouldn't we send someone out there? Just in case?' I hated how frantic I sounded.

Mrs Temple looked as though I had thrown cold water in her face, woken her from a dream. 'I don't think so,' she said, shaking her head as if casting away the imaginary droplets. 'You have just witnessed how dangerous the causeway can be. I think, though, that I ought to go and see Gabriel.'

'May I come with you, Mother?' Birdie asked, clutching at her skirts and for once seeming younger than her years.

Mrs Temple hesitated, wrestling with her maternal instinct to keep Birdie close. 'No, no. There will be much to discuss . . .' She trailed off.

There would have been significant meetings in the course of the day if everyone had managed the crossing safely – the completion of funeral arrangements, the reading of Mr Cauldwell's will, the removal of the body. Gabriel would also soon learn about Wilbur's contentious proclamation of the previous evening, and I imagined that would require some discussion too.

'Well, I don't intend to stay here!' Birdie said in an eruption of fury. She stormed out of the room, slamming the door with all her might, the room itself seeming to tremble in response to her rage.

Mrs Temple closed her eyes and winced at the noise. She raised her hand to silence me, although I wasn't about to speak. 'You had best leave her be,' she said.

I nodded obediently, wishing I could fade into the walls. There was a peculiar churning sensation in my stomach, a lurching desire for my own home.

Mrs Temple swept out of the room with brisk efficiency, leaving me alone. My teeth began to chatter, a shiver that felt almost like a fever ripping through me. My mind was full of horrid images that pushed and writhed their way behind my eyes. If it wasn't Mr Cauldwell's still face, it was the carriages being swallowed by the sea, repeating and repeating and repeating.

I left the schoolroom in a hot burst of energy, needing to move my body physically to shift the thoughts away. As I was heading out on to the landing, I saw a glimpse of somebody darting up the snaking staircase in the alcove. They moved in such a way that aroused suspicion – and all I had caught sight of was an ankle, the heel of a black boot. Whoever it was, they were on their way up to the arches.

I dithered at the bottom of the stairs, wondering whether to follow. It seemed as though this might be my only chance to see the top of the tower for myself . . . And yet how would

I be received by the person waiting for me up there? Who would it be? Somebody using the distraction of the chaos on the causeway to come up here unobserved ... Their reaction to me finding them was unlikely to be positive.

Ultimately, I could not resist my own curiosity, and I would deal with the consequences later. This locked door had haunted me, had plagued my thoughts. The whispering ghoul of night-time had spoken to me, and it had led me to the arches at the top of those stairs, behind that great iron door.

I marched up the stairs as if I were following a summons, my breath hitching a little at my pace, my feet familiar with the unevenness of those worn and aged steps.

My heart felt like a stopped clock when I saw that the door was slightly ajar. The wind whistled through the gap. I knew if I shrank away, took the cowardly path, that I would not find this door conveniently open another time.

I gently pushed the door, turning the narrow gap into a great big yawn.

The beastly rain splattered so heavily it obscured my view, but I could make out seven arches round the edge of the tower's roof. The sky was as dark as if it were night-time, and the wind howled around as though it were tangled in the arches, like a fox trapped in a snare.

One of the arches had been dramatically altered. Although it was of the same rough stone as all of the others, some sort of clockwork device, the cogs rusted red through age, was fixed to the base, and coils of wire looped and wound up to a point at the very top of the arch where a brave, or foolish, figure was precariously balanced on a ladder, arms raised high to perform some kind of operation on a pointed spire.

As lightning forked across the sky, I began to fear for that person – broad-shouldered, strong legs braced against the ladder so that quick hands could perform their delicate procedure. When the head turned to reach for something from a bag whose handle was hung over the top of the ladder, I recognized the face immediately.

Jasper.

15

I watched him working, wondering at his skill. He was fast and focused, utterly immersed in what he was doing. It was only as he put his hand in his bag that he spotted me. The look that crossed his face shifted quickly from fear at first, no doubt at being discovered, to bemusement when he realized it was me.

'You're rather lost,' he called, his voice just reaching me before the thunder growled. I was suddenly aware of how drenched I was. The borrowed dress clung to my skin as if trying to persuade me to get it out of this rain.

'I could say the same about you.'

He shook his head, unable to hear me over the endless torrent.

'I could say the same about you!' I shouted, louder. I was certain that Jasper wasn't meant to be up at the arches any more than I was.

He clambered down from the ladder and bridged the gap between us. He, too, was soaked through, and his proximity to me flooded my brain at a moment when I most wanted to clutch on to rational thought. 'I knew you had your own inventing aspirations, but Edwin Cauldwell's arch? Does anyone else know about this?'

I took my time, each word landing like a piece deliberately placed on a draughtboard. His work on the arch was evidence of his calculated, persistent breaking of whatever household rule barred him from the tower.

His eyes narrowed as I spoke, the cogs and springs of invention whirring inside his mind. 'No, they don't,' he said, a rueful smile on his face. We were both somewhere we shouldn't be.

'What are you doing up here?' I asked.

'I wanted to try some of the new ideas from the research I've been reading about electromagnetism, harness the power of the lightning. It's been a long time since we've had a storm as powerful as this one. I finally have my father's keys . . . And the energy – the energy of the house – always seems stronger when there's a storm. It couldn't be more perfect.'

'This storm nearly killed your father,' I said, and Jasper's easy smile was wiped off his face. I kept talking quickly, to reassure him. 'He made the crossing, but the people he was travelling with didn't. The sea swallowed them.'

'No!' His face went slack with horror.

Then, in the moment of silence between us, the wind brushed against me, and the whisper began in my ear.

Listen.

The whisper pushed its way into my mind, and before I knew what I was doing I started moving involuntarily towards the arch. My feet seemed directed, pushed. A bolt of lightning brightened the sky. It reached down, like a pointed finger, and converged with the spire at the highest point of the modified arch. The entirety of the arch lit up, hurting my eyes with the contrast in the darkness of the storm. I was utterly entranced by it, and felt myself drawing nearer, pushing past Jasper, who almost faded away with the rest of my surroundings.

I saw that the inside of the arch shimmered – it was as though a glossy film had been flung up to coat the space. It reminded me of leaving a pan of liquid syrup to cool, a firm crystallized layer congealing on the top, opaque and cloudy. Something moved beneath the surface – shadows rolling – and although it was murky and impenetrable at first, the scene began to become clearer, more transparent. The view was familiar. It was the grand staircase from the entrance hall of Archfall Manor.

A fizzing sensation began to spread through my insides. How could this be possible? The staircase downstairs, reproduced perfectly at the top of the tower. The filmy covering was all that separated me from being able to take a step out of the rain and into the entrance hall.

My amazement swiftly turned to horror when I saw Mr Cauldwell at the top of the stairs. He took the first step, and his foot caught on something that shone, a fine thread at ankle height, and then he was falling, tumbling, his body breaking on the marble as my heart plunged into my toes. I was looking into the past, at the scene of Thomas's death, re-enacted in front of me.

And yet this time I had seen something that I hadn't

before. His fall had been engineered. At the top of the staircase, there was a metal object screwed into the bannister, about the size of a shilling. Curled round it was a thin wire. If you were to pull that out, it would create a tightrope across the top of the stair, near invisible.

What did it mean? Someone placed a device there to make a hazard that would immediately coil back into its casing like a snail into a shell. We had all believed it was an accident so readily. But somebody in this house knew differently. Mr Cauldwell had fallen to his death, and somebody planned it that way.

If I could just look a little closer . . . But then I felt myself sliding, as though I were losing my grip on the moment I was living in – I was in-between somehow. The rain no longer pattered on my brow, the wind no longer whisked my dress like meringue. I felt as though I could cross into the other room, the other time, and pluck the device from the stair as evidence. My body took on a strange weightlessness, and I reached out my hands for something to grip on to, for something solid. And then I lost my sight. Even though my eyes were open, I couldn't see. I blinked, and there was only nothingness. I couldn't feel the ground beneath my feet any more. A racing fear galloped through me. I was lurching forward; I was lost.

Then I was yanked back by strong arms, swept up and cradled to a broad chest, but there was a pain that flashed through my head, and once more I could feel the rain on my face. I opened my eyes, and there was Jasper, his amber eyes staring into mine and filled with terror.

'It worked, didn't it?' he said. He was panicked, but there was a thrill to his words too.

I couldn't answer him. I thought I was frightened by my experience, but he seemed worse; his breathing was heavy and fast, and he held me tightly as he scooped me up and carried me down the staircase.

My mind was muddled and my brain felt exhausted, as though I had been awake for days on end with no rest. The image of blood pooling beneath Mr Cauldwell's head refused to disperse, stubbornly resisting my efforts to cast it away. Jasper took me to the inventing room, unlocking it with his father's great loop of keys. He sat me gently on the edge of one of the long tables. My legs hung down, and he leaned in, examining me for injury.

'It was as if you were taken into a trance. It was . . . it was as if someone were dragging you to the edge of the roof. I thought you were going to pitch yourself through the arch and off the tower.'

I shuddered at the thought. Was that what it had looked like? That I was about to fling myself from the roof? I thought with horror about what might have happened if I had been alone . . .

Jasper ran his hands through his hair, wild and drenched. He looked at me intently, studying my face as though I were a broken invention he'd popped on the table to be fixed, the solution eluding him.

'Did you . . . did you see what happened through the arch?' I asked.

'I knew it! I knew something happened. But I didn't see anything myself.'

'The lightning struck the top of it, and then it utterly transformed,' I said, feeling exasperated at my own inadequacy to explain what I saw, what I experienced. 'It became like a window . . . It showed me the grand staircase in the entrance hall. And Mr Cauldwell . . . I saw him fall and then he was dead at the bottom of the stairs again.'

I heard Jasper's breath catch in his throat. 'You saw the past.'

'You didn't?' I asked, the urgency in me building.

'No, Josephine. I just saw you and the way you . . . changed.'

I froze at the unfamiliarity of the name. I wanted to hear him say *Helena* so badly.

'The arch. That's what it's meant to do, isn't it? Create a window through time?'

'Well, yes . . . but I can't believe it,' Jasper said, flummoxed. 'It's never worked before.'

'But you must have believed it could. Otherwise, what were you doing up there?'

'Well, I hoped,' he said, and I could see that hope was brimming so near to the surface it threatened to spill out of him.

Jasper looked so alive, it was as if the lightning had entered his body and illuminated him from within. Wasn't it that light I'd been drawn to the first time we met? When he looked at me, I didn't feel so cold or hopeless.

'This is ... this is unbelievable. It's everything I've been working towards for so long. Everything Edwin Cauldwell was working towards. What he died for.'

I knew what I'd seen, and I knew it was real, but a part of me felt deeply unsettled. If the invention had really worked, then why didn't Jasper see it too? Could it be the whole event was some hysterical invention of my mind, flung into a frenzy from the stress of my time on the island and my terrible sleeplessness? Or was there truth in it? There was only one way to know for certain.

A chilled droplet ran from the nape of my neck all the way down my spine. We had to return to the entrance hall and inspect the bannister of the staircase. If any sign of the strange little device were there, it would prove two things. Firstly, Edwin Cauldwell's theory of time was true, and the power of this place had created a window into the past through the invention he'd been working on. Secondly, someone in the house had made that strange little invention and placed it at a moment when Thomas Cauldwell would take the stairs. Which meant somebody in Archfall Manor had wanted him dead, intended for him to fall, and chose the moment when they knew he'd be coming down the stairs alone. There was a murderer in this house, and we were all trapped here with them.

16

'When I was looking into the past, I saw something,' I said hesitantly. It was one thing to tell Jasper that I had seen the past – he was already predisposed to believing in the fantastical inventions in this house – but it was another thing entirely to tell him that what I'd seen pointed to Mr Cauldwell's death being intentional, not an accident after all. I described the device to Jasper, watching his expression for any change. He listened intently, his face frozen and thoughtful. 'Do you understand what that means?' I asked. 'If the archway worked, and what I saw was real, then somebody in this house is a murderer.'

'We have to go. We have to see if there's any sign of it,' he said.

He was right – how else would I be able to know which horrifying set of circumstances was true? Either I was mad, or somebody in the house was a murderer. I struggled off the table and almost lost my balance, my body feeling strange and heavy.

'Just take a second,' Jasper said, his hands steadying me. A trembling shiver ripped through me. 'You don't seem very well,' he said, and what looked like genuine concern crossed his features. He bit his lip, seemingly unsure of what to do with me.

I thought of Birdie's previous governess in the asylum, and fear ran rampant through me – I knew what the Cauldwell family were willing to do if they considered me to be of unsound mind.

'I just need to get out of these wet clothes and into something dry so I can warm up again,' I said, trying to sound more assertive than I felt.

He reached over and touched my forehead with the back of his hand. His skin was cool. 'You're feverish,' he said. 'My ma will know what to do with you.'

'Please, just take me to my room,' I snapped, and he backed away from me, hands up in surrender.

'Of course,' he said. 'If you insist.'

Just as I followed him out of the room, though, he stopped abruptly, and I stumbled, trying to prevent myself from crashing straight into his back. Sounds of a bitter dispute came echoing along the corridor. I peered round Jasper and saw Wilbur and Gabriel standing very close to each other. Both men had their fists clenched. Wilbur, startled no doubt by the sound of the inventing room door opening, turned and noticed the pair of us hovering. The mere sight of us seemed to completely inflame him, a rage I'd never seen before swallowing up his features. Gabriel followed his gaze, and when he saw us too, the expression he wore was a mixture of disappointment and anger. The skin on my arms began to prickle with the tension.

Wilbur leaned very close to Gabriel and muttered something in his ear that turned him as stiff as a board. Then he stalked off in the opposite direction as Gabriel came lurching towards us.

'You fool,' Gabriel said to Jasper, his voice low and firm and rumbling like machinery. 'You're not supposed to be in that room without my supervision. Have you any idea what you've done?'

'I'm sorry, Pa,' Jasper said meekly. 'I just –'

'Enough!' Gabriel erupted. His face was full of fury.

Not for the first time in this household, I wished I could make myself invisible. It was no good wishing – Gabriel glanced at me and his face twisted.

'Your mother said you'd lost your head over this governess, couldn't talk about anything else. You might have ruined everything, showing off to her. Do you understand that? Everything I've carefully . . .' He caught himself, stopped.

Carefully what? Whatever he'd been about to say, he'd got a tight grip upon his anger now and was wrestling it into submission before he said something he regretted.

'I got a little lost,' I said, finding my voice, 'and took unwell. Jasper merely happened to hear me and was finding me a place to rest. He has been perfectly proper and discreet.'

'Then I'll not ask why the pair of you are soaked to the skin.' Gabriel's hand twisted into a fist, his fingers tensing as though it were a struggle to stop himself from lashing out. 'Jasper, think of everything I've worked for. Now, return my keys and get out of my sight.'

'Yes, sir,' Jasper said, utterly crestfallen. His voice was shaking. He reached into his pocket and returned the loop of keys, took me by the wrist and led me back to the staff quarters. When we were out of earshot of his father, he spoke again. 'You don't need to defend me. My pa will find any reason to remind me of the ways I'm failing him.'

'I'm sorry,' I whispered. 'What do you think they were arguing about?'

Jasper pinched the bridge of his nose. 'My pa has always taken a lot of responsibility for the late Mr Cauldwell's work and inventions.'

'And?'

'I don't know. Before he left for the mainland, he took some of old Mr Cauldwell's journals and locked them away.'

'Why would he do that?'

'Protection,' Jasper said. 'He said there are things that Mr Cauldwell had promised to him.'

'And he thought it would come out in the will.' I tried to disguise the suspicion in my voice.

'I suppose so,' Jasper said, rubbing the back of his neck. 'I mean, Pa worked with Mr Cauldwell all his life. Not just *for* him – really *with* him. They were truly friends. It was always Mr Cauldwell's name in the research journals, or on the patents, but my pa was just as much a part of the work.'

He said all of this so innocently. It was as though the implications hadn't filtered through his mind yet. He so wholly believed the best in people that he didn't even seem to realize that he'd just outlined a possible reason for his own father wanting Mr Cauldwell dead. How long could anyone realistically live with someone else taking all the credit for their work? The thought gave me a strange knot of dread, twine tangled up in my innards.

We arrived at the main landing, and I stopped at the top of the grand staircase that was central to everything. I halted Jasper with my hand and bent down to inspect the bottom of the bannister, running my hands over the polished wood.

And I found it. A perfect hole, bored into the wood like the path of a worm munching into an apple. Right in the place where I'd seen the little device in the window through time at the arch. I pointed wordlessly, and Jasper visibly tensed when he saw it.

It wasn't firm evidence, not by any stretch of the imagination. It was like many things since I'd arrived at Archfall Manor – a truth I knew deeply somehow, but could not prove. Thomas Cauldwell's death was not an accident. Another inventor found a way to dispatch him. Whoever had done it was still in the house somewhere.

Alongside the discomfort was a flowing relief. What I had seen at the top of the tower was not a figment of my sleep-deprived mind, was not a sign of my deterioration into madness. It really had actually *worked*. The arch had given me a window into the past. It was fantastical, the stuff of stories ... and yet somehow, impossibly, it was real. I looked up at Jasper. 'We have to talk about this.'

'You're shivering,' Jasper said, touching my elbow and helping me to stand. He was right – my skin was sensitive and chilled. 'Please, get changed into something warm and we can discuss this later.'

Alone in my room, I dried my hair with a towel and stripped off the sopping-wet clothes. A sick feeling swirled in the pit of my stomach. Apart from the wonder and awe I felt at what I'd experienced, I couldn't shake the pressing matter of what the arch had revealed to me. There was a murderer at Archfall Manor, and we were all trapped together in the eye of a terrible storm, cut off from the mainland for – how long?

I felt undeniably unsafe. How could I know who to trust? Whoever had planted the device for Mr Cauldwell to trip on was an inventor, so there were very few people I could rule out definitely – only Molly the nursery nurse had no inventing skill, and Teresa seemed to prefer the routine of her household management more than any of the contraptions that made her life a little easier here and there.

But any one of the Cauldwell family – and yes, I even considered Birdie among them – could be guilty. They had all grown up in a family where invention was considered normal and encouraged. Death followed Mrs Temple through every part of her life, and she had already endured scrutiny since her latest husband died. Would she really have come back here to kill her father, having faced suspicion from the authorities so recently? It seemed unlikely. And what would her motive have been?

Wilbur, though, was another matter entirely. I'd heard him arguing with his father my first full day at the house. His nasty sneer reverberated in my mind: *I will not have the opportunity to lead until I prise it from your cold, dead hands, will I?*

It was later that evening that Mr Cauldwell had announced his plans to retire from his role in the Institute of Invention, and that this would not automatically go to Wilbur, the way it had historically passed from father to son, according to family lore. Now, that, *that* felt like a motive for murder. The murderer had struck the following night – perhaps it was Wilbur, attempting to prevent his father's plans from coming to fruition.

That would have made it a crime committed in anger, a furious response following the snub and the embarrassment Wilbur had been subjected to, a desperate endeavour to preserve the things he believed he was due.

But my thoughts came round again to the little device. That suggested a greater premeditation. A tiny contraption had been made, in advance, with the intention of making Mr Cauldwell's death appear to everyone as an accident.

I unwillingly thought of Jasper.

There was no reason I could fathom for him being willing – or able – to *murder* Mr Cauldwell. I couldn't believe that. There was no part of Jasper that seemed capable of malicious intent or hurting anyone or anything.

His pa on the other hand … I thought of Gabriel's furious features and began to add up the evidence. Gabriel Wright believed he was due to inherit something from

Mr Cauldwell . . . intellectual property rights perhaps, or even a financial reward for his hard work. If he feared this was under threat as a result of Mr Cauldwell's new plans, would he have killed him? It was Gabriel who went to fetch the lawyer, Gabriel who would have known the storm was coming, Gabriel who said . . . I wracked my brains to remember exactly what he had said to Jasper – *think of everything I've worked for*. Was this murder, designed to look like an accident, the culmination of those efforts to secure a better life for himself, for his family?

Wilbur or Gabriel. The pair of them seemed equally unmoved by the death of Mr Cauldwell – only moved to anger, that is, directed it seemed at each other. And yet both of them had lost somebody terribly important: a father, albeit one who'd had a fractured relationship with his remaining son; an employer, one who kept his head of maintenance much closer than staff would usually be.

It was puzzling. Somewhere along the way I had become clinical in my approach, in a way that only an outsider could be, but inside, deep in among the tangled knots of enquiry that I longed to unravel, there was a little creature ensnared, a trembling fear that I could not shake.

Whoever murdered Mr Cauldwell was motivated by the inventions, by the legacy and the power of them. And there was one invention, above all, that had long dominated the thoughts of the household. The arches, and the window through time. And it had worked for me . . . My own sense of safety was capsized by the thought of what might happen if anyone else were to discover this truth. If the murderer cared about the inventions above all else, I had to guard my secret as though my life depended on it – because maybe it did. I felt certain of only one thing: whichever way I moved, whichever way I turned, Archfall Manor had sunk its claws into me, and I would never be the same when the storm lifted.

17

I desperately wished to speak to Jasper further about the whole extraordinary matter, but when I returned to the kitchen Molly already had him cornered. I tried not to make it obvious I was eavesdropping on their conversation, as when I'd arrived Molly had angled her body away from me. Instead, I busied myself collecting bowls for the thick noodle broth Teresa had made.

'When there's a storm, we're really to be trapped here until it ends?' Molly was asking, her pale blue eyes widening. It had been easy to forget, being a newcomer myself to the island, that Molly had only had a little more time than me to adjust to the strangeness of Archfall Manor.

Jasper nodded, his expression grim.

'But I usually send some money back to my parents with the weekly delivery.'

I didn't miss the rising panic in Molly's tone, her words strangled by it. Her family must be as dependent on her wages as my own. I'd also been hoping to find a way to make sure that my first pay made its way to Mam, and so I was snared by Molly's fears, catching them like a cold.

I tried not to think of the conditions Mam might be experiencing in prison, cast thoughts of her to one side only for more frightening ones to surge. If we were cut off from the mainland, what would happen to Mr Cauldwell's body? What would happen to us, trapped with the murderer stalking round the house? And, worst of all, what would happen if the house and the island never *wanted* to let us go? That last thought was irrational, I knew it, but there was no abating the rising fear that crashed over me in time with the rhythm of the waves outside.

'It's usually just a few days,' Jasper said, trying to sound reassuring. 'Maybe up to a week.' He was measured, unruffled. He'd been through this before – although certainly without a dead body and a flickering window through time revealing murder . . .

'What about food? If it goes on too long, won't we starve?' Molly was becoming more shrill, her fears leaking out. The house felt like it was closing in on all of us, squeezing us between its walls.

Jasper put his hands on her shoulders, comforting her. 'You don't need to be scared,' he said. 'We're very self-sufficient here. We have store cupboards with all the essential things we need to get us through, even if it does get down to vegetable broth and my mother's simplest loaf. And Josephine here can make some pretty spectacular things out of nothing but sugar, I've heard.' He turned to me, pulling me into the conversation, expecting me to be encouraging and supportive.

But I couldn't match his easy comfort. I was still thinking

about the dead body lying upstairs and the horror on the causeway. 'Shouldn't we alert someone about the carriages? About those poor people? Don't we need help?'

A gruff voice answered me. 'What we need is to keep our heads.' It was Gabriel, filling the room with his presence. Teresa followed him in. 'There's nothing we can do to help them. Whether the authorities are informed now or later doesn't change what's happened.'

'They're definitely dead then?' Molly asked.

Gabriel grimaced. 'I heard the sound of those carriages against the rocks,' he said, bringing his hand to his temple. 'You don't survive something like that.'

'We can't even get a message out?' I asked. Surely there had to be some way to let people know what had happened. Gabriel just shook his head. 'Or . . . I don't know, get help from a boat?'

Gabriel huffed. 'Not even the bravest fishermen will be out in weather like this. When the storm is over and the causeway opens back up, we'll be able to let the appropriate people know what happened,' he said. 'We'll have the death certificate completed for the late Mr Cauldwell and arrange a proper burial. Right now, his body lies in his room, and none of us need go in there. In the meantime, we all have jobs to do. From what Teresa tells me, the presumptive head of this house has expectations of us, and if he's intending to make staffing changes, then each one of us needs to remember the importance of keeping him happy. Understood?'

In those few sentences, he was authoritative and firm,

and oddly reassuring too. Gabriel was far more of a leader than Wilbur had been. I did not miss the word *presumptive* and everything that it implied.

'Dinner,' Teresa said, pointing at the clock.

'Right,' Jasper said. He flicked his eyes to the tureens. 'Josephine and I will take these.'

Was he as eager as I was to grab a moment alone together, to begin to unravel what had happened to us up at the arches?

Molly was visibly unhappy, but I couldn't work out why until she spoke again, her voice smooth and even. She tugged at Jasper's sleeve to turn him back towards her. 'Will we play cards tonight after supper, the way we used to?'

'Oh,' Jasper said, sounding taken aback. 'I don't think so tonight, no.' His response was dismissive, a little cold even.

Molly froze, and that's when I realized what I was witnessing – an ending . . . of something. I could guess well enough what, my mind filling in some blanks. Jasper had lived his entire life on Sighfeyre Isle. The arrival of Molly must have felt like an expansion of his world, and perhaps there had been a brief romance, but it certainly seemed over now.

I refused to dwell on it inordinately, not when my own world had crashed into the realm of the supernatural and the horrifying. I slopped the rich broth into the tureen I was holding and headed out of the room, glad to leave the discomfort of the situation behind. Jasper immediately caught up to me in the corridor.

'When we were at the top of the staircase before, you saw a notch in the bannister, didn't you?' I asked, keeping my voice hushed. He nodded, concentration crinkling his brow. 'That matches what I saw in the arch – Mr Cauldwell tripped over a wire, and when it was triggered it wound back into a little device screwed into the bannister.'

'So you really think somebody engineered Mr Cauldwell's fall to look like an accident?'

'I do,' I said firmly. 'I'm telling you. Up there ... it showed me a moment from the past. The device was there. Somebody in this house killed Mr Cauldwell.'

'But who, who would do that?' Jasper seemed horrified at the idea.

'Somebody who would benefit from his inheritance?' I suggested pointedly.

Jasper noted my tone, and looked deflated and anxious and impatient all at once, as if his emotions had been stirred together.

'Right,' he said with an edge to his voice. 'Well, you can scratch my pa off your list of suspects because he would never. You've got to believe me. He might be a bit brusque, but he's one of the gentlest people you could ever meet. He's just ... under a lot of stress.'

Gabriel hadn't seemed particularly gentle – not when he was shouting at Jasper and not when he was reminding us in the kitchen of the precariousness of our jobs under Wilbur's reign. For Jasper's sake, I wanted to say something reassuring, but the fact was I couldn't rule Gabriel out. We didn't know where he was when the device was placed;

he had the technical knowledge to create such a device; and he had a clear motive.

'Well, we need to go back to the arch then,' I said. 'We need to somehow get hold of the keys again.'

'That won't be necessary,' Jasper said. He reached into his pocket, and revealed that he had fashioned duplicates of the keys he knew he'd need if he wanted to continue his work on the arch. 'It was the first thing I did when Pa left me with them.'

'That's brilliant,' I said. 'We can use them to go back up there and try to uncover more.'

'I suppose you're right – though I still can't believe it,' Jasper said, his voice filled with awe. 'To think, Josephine – we have an invention that can see through time on our hands!'

'And I thought you said it was I who didn't have enough imagination for this,' I replied, meeting his eye with a smile.

'I just don't understand why *I* couldn't see anything. Why would it work for you and not for me?' There was no disappointment or jealousy in him, just a rabid curiosity.

'We have to run experiments,' I said. 'Try again. We need to work together. You're the one who understands the arch and how it is made.' My mind was buzzing like a beehive.

'Only when you feel ready,' Jasper said. 'It might be dangerous. We don't know what we're dealing with exactly.'

I wanted to argue with him, to tell him that – danger or not – it was the only way to understand this incredible tool properly, and hesitancy wouldn't get us anywhere, but we'd reached the dining room, and both of us instinctively straightened up, lifted our chins and pinned our gaze forward.

Jasper went ahead and began serving Wilbur, while I took a bowl to Mrs Temple. The pair of them seemed unaware of our presence at all, so intensely were they exchanging sour looks.

'I told you, I can't find it,' Wilbur was saying. His skin had gone a strange shade of grey. 'Wherever the old man kept it, it's not in his study or his bedroom.'

Mrs Temple was chewing at the corner of her lip, looking less certain than I'd ever seen her. Her eyes drifted to a blank space somewhere over Wilbur's shoulder, as if she could see something that wasn't there. It seemed as though she might burst into tears at any moment. 'You've looked . . . I mean you've checked *him*.'

'Father himself, you mean?' Wilbur asked. 'Yes. I'm not going in there again, though. Look, I can only think he hid it in an invention somewhere.'

I wanted to stay longer to listen, but I had finished serving, and Jasper had already gone, so there was no reason for me to be hovering there. I began to take the long route round the table, but Nora fixed me with a stare. She knew. She knew I was listening. I quickened my pace.

'Excuse me,' I heard Nora say behind me, then the scrape of her chair and the patter of her footsteps. I kept walking, eyes fixed straight ahead. The dining-room door closed with a click and then Nora's voice followed me down the corridor. 'I know you were listening again!' she called.

I stopped. My heart began to pulse a little faster. 'I didn't mean to listen, Miss Nora,' I said, but we both knew that was a lie. Nora raised an eyebrow and bridged the distance between us.

'Stop being so deferential.' Nora crossed her arms over her chest. She let out a huge sigh. 'Don't you think I'm dying to have someone to talk to about all of this? I'm trapped here just like you.'

I blinked, surprised. 'You ... want to talk about it with me? You wouldn't rather speak to your family?'

Nora snorted. 'My uncle is even worse than my grandfather. He told me this evening that he thought the one good idea Grandfather had had was marrying me off to an inventor to secure our family's legacy. Can you believe him! So I'm trapped after all. And Mother ... well, she's ... sensitive. Do you know what the pair of them are looking for?'

I suspected I did. 'I'd assume a copy of the last will and testament,' I replied.

Wilbur would want to secure his future as quickly as possible. Not just to solidify his role as head of the household, but to finally have free rein over the family fortune, both the one that sat heavily in his father's accounts and the one that was still to be made from the inventions. There was also the matter of Mr Cauldwell's leadership of the Institute, the role that Wilbur had been clamouring for.

'Wrong,' Nora said. She was enjoying this. 'They're looking for a key. They want to open my grandfather's chest.'

So that was it. Something slotted into place in my mind. What was it Birdie had told me? Every member of the Cauldwell family had a chest, a place to keep their secrets. She had told me that the chests were unbreakable, each one designed to be opened by a single key – their privacy allegedly inviolable.

'They want to open it? Would they really do that, without his permission?'

'Of course they would. How could anyone resist?' Nora said. 'Now maybe they'll find a copy of his will in there, and I'm sure that Wilbur's hoping it's an old version, before the competition notion struck my grandfather ... But it's more than that. Whatever is inside that box will be whatever my grandfather considered more valuable and private than anything else. An invention prototype perhaps, or a family heirloom. Either way, something my uncle and mother will want to get their hands on. The only problem is they can't find his key.'

My heart scuttered. They wanted to open Mr Cauldwell's box of secrets, and they couldn't find the key. They believed it was something he'd carry on his person ... and they were right. But they wouldn't find it there.

Because I had it.

18

After dinner, Jasper and I stayed up late in the kitchen, talking secretly again once everyone had gone to bed and keeping our voices low so that we would not be discovered. We were deliberating over a plan for heading up to the arches again.

'I don't know that we should,' Jasper said. 'You looked as though you were going to pitch yourself through the arch and off the edge. And that . . . that's what happened to Edwin.'

When I was up there, I did feel compelled to cross over into the vision in the arch. Was it all just an illusion? A sign of my faltering grip on reality? Would I have just . . . fallen? A cold horror poured into me, pooling in my toes and rising through me, filling me with a chill. The thought of Edwin Cauldwell falling and falling, and the thought that it might have happened to me too.

But I was certain that what existed through the arches was more tangible than that.

'How much do you know about what happened?' I asked. It was the part of the Cauldwell family story I had been desperate to hear since my arrival on the island.

'A little. The way my pa tells it, Edwin had been off on a research trip for nearly two years, and when he unexpectedly came home, without even sending word of his arrival, everyone was taken aback. They all knew he'd been working on the archway before he left, had been trying to do something with clockwork, but getting nowhere.'

Clockwork. Presumably this was when he crossed paths with my father.

'Was that why he went to the mainland? To look for a watchmaker? Somebody who was an expert in clockwork?' My voice sounded as if it belonged to somebody else. I was certain that hidden somewhere within this story would be the key to understanding what had happened to my father too. Thinking about him was like a hot knife through butter, my insides dissolving, but I had to ask the question.

'Maybe,' Jasper said. 'Apparently, Edwin was much like his father, always open to hearing the ideas of others.'

That would explain why Edwin had left the island, why he had returned with my father. He'd been looking for a watchmaker, somebody whose work would be the missing piece of the puzzle – Edwin's theories, the house's power, my father's skills.

'And did he come back here with a watchmaker?' I could hear the desperation in my voice. Jasper looked confused.

'I don't . . . No, I don't remember Pa telling me anything about a watchmaker.'

My heart plummeted. Before coming to Archfall, I'd thought, optimistically, that there would be some clue to what happened to my father, something I could begin to solve.

I didn't realize how hard it would be, when the doors I wanted to open were locked and the questions I wanted to ask blocked by the need to keep my secret. My father was not part of the story that had been handed down, yet I still had a strong sense that he was in among it somewhere. This family, and the people who served them, were deeply secretive. If they'd been responsible for a visitor's death, it felt entirely plausible that they would have come together to hide it. Still, my emotions wouldn't let me rest.

'Are you sure? Did your father never say anything about someone else being with them at the arches that night?'

'I'm sorry,' Jasper said. 'He's never mentioned anything like that. Why is it so important to you?'

'It's not,' I said, realizing I'd pressed too far, was at risk of revealing too much about myself. If I wanted to uncover more, I was going to have to speak to Gabriel himself . . . And that prospect was daunting. 'I just . . . I thought I'd read something about a watchmaker who died here.'

Jasper scoffed. 'Did you now? I've heard the mainland is full of ghoulish stories about this family,' he said.

I gave a wan smile. 'You have no idea.'

'It didn't stop you coming, though.' He nudged me with his elbow playfully.

'No. But it's not like I had much choice. I really need the money,' I admitted, and Jasper gave me a sympathetic smile. 'Let's not worry about the watchmaker. What happened when Edwin got back?'

'He found out that Wilbur had been working on the archway without him. Never mind that it was all Edwin's hard work and theories, Wilbur had laid claim to it. The pair of them got into a blazing row and went up to the arches, still arguing, and of course their quarrel involved something about inheritance, because that's all Wilbur has ever cared about: his role and status in the family. My pa heard the argument and then saw both of them go up – but only Wilbur came back down. Wilbur said Edwin had performed an experiment, entered a strange trance and flung himself off the edge of the tower.'

A sick feeling swirled in the pit of my stomach. 'Two brothers had a raging disagreement about something terribly important to both of them, and then one of them was never seen again. Did nobody consider that Wilbur might have killed Edwin and hidden the body?'

'If they did, they've never said so. That's not the kind of thing you say out loud in Archfall Manor,' Jasper said, pursing his lips.

'And what about you? Do you think Wilbur could be capable of murder?' I didn't mention that I'd been weighing him up as a suspect in the killing of Mr Cauldwell – I didn't need to.

Jasper shrugged, but the gesture wasn't as casual as he wanted it to be. 'How can you ever know what people are capable of? It's not as if he's the only Cauldwell to ever be suspected of murder.'

I presumed he was thinking of Mrs Temple and the recent investigation into the death of her latest husband.

'Anyway,' he went on, 'whatever happened, it was never

investigated. You remember that Edwin had been away for two years beforehand. Nobody really knew his state of mind or his real reason for coming home. They were never able to retrieve his body. There was a storm like this one, and Wilbur said it was sucked into the mire. And by the time it was safe to go out, the body had disappeared.'

Now it was my turn to scoff. 'How convenient.'

'You're missing the connection here,' Jasper said, sounding a little exasperated with me. 'Wilbur always insisted that Edwin went into a strange trance . . . And isn't that what happened to you up there?'

'No,' I said, but I wasn't sure.

When I was at the arch, I did feel . . . compelled. To pass through the window, to go into the vision. I didn't want to admit it out loud, but there had been something supernatural about the whole experience . . . especially when combined with the awful whispering that had been keeping me up at night, trying to press through with messages for me, and the way the house had at times seemed alive. I had been convinced the house was leading me somewhere. Perhaps it had been trying to lure me off the roof this whole time.

'Fantastical things have always happened here,' Jasper said. 'Look, I'm not arrogant enough to think it was my tinkering during the storm that led to this unbelievable discovery. I'm not a brilliant inventor or a theoretical thinker like Edwin. Something else happened up there. Something new.'

He was right. In fact, it was easier to believe that there was something utterly other-worldly about the whole thing than to believe I had witnessed the successful implementation of a theory using wires and the spire and the energy of the lightning. Since my first night here, my experience was too indefinable to be the result of any invention. It was something unearthly. It could not be explained, could not be mapped on paper or energized just with wires. I tried to say this to Jasper, and found the words stuck in my mouth like toffee. I couldn't bring myself to tell him about the whispers, about the door. And so I stumbled as I spoke, trying to express something that there seemed to be no explanation for.

'I think ... I think it was supernatural, what happened to me up there ... That's what we're talking about here, isn't it?' Hearing it aloud, it all sounded so clumsy, so inelegant ... and more than a little unhinged.

'I think,' said Jasper, 'if I were looking for the logic in this situation, and trying to turn it into an equation I could understand, that there were two moments in time where this phenomenon occurred. So either Edwin made his invention work all those years ago, and it's been lying dormant up there all this time. In which case, why wouldn't it work for me? Or ... there's some other force at work here. So yes, I think we're talking about the supernatural. I think it's been here the whole time, seeping into all the inventions in this place.'

We might have continued discussing it, but a resounding crack startled us. We looked at each other, both wide-eyed with trepidation. It was the sort of sound that feels cataclysmic, the sort of sound that fills your body with a cold dread, the sort of sound that informs you that something terrible has happened, something's irrevocably broken, somebody is hurt. Usually, when you hear that sort of sound, you must get away from it with haste. And so we ran towards it.

19

We set off at a sprint out of the servants' quarters, Jasper racing ahead to check the corridor of the west wing. Panic swelled inside me, and that was when I heard it – the unnerving whispering that troubled me in the middle of the night. It was faint at first, and I noticed, when I turned towards the whisper, that it grew a little louder into a disconcerting murmur. It was directing me through the house.

'Jasper!' I called as I climbed the spectacular staircase, not waiting for him to reappear.

I still couldn't make out a word the muffled murmur was saying – once again, I thought, it was as though the owner of the voice lived inside the walls – but I could follow where it led me. As I turned on to the main family wing on the first floor, the murmuring reached a crescendo, so that it felt as if there were a hundred people lining the walls, urging me onwards.

Then there was a horrible sound, a pained groaning, and the whispering receded.

On the ground was a suited body, face down, a desperate hand dripping with blood struggling to reach the door.

My heart was pounding, my throat tight with panic. The hand was grasping, straining as though the injured person were trying to pull themselves up, and there was so much more blood than I had first realized, spurting from their neck in a great spray to match a heartbeat. When the body lifted his head, I saw it was Wilbur – and a clenching horror overwhelmed me. The hole in his throat was impossibly round where a bullet had entered. His expression was a grimace of terror, a twist of pain. All the anger in him was gone, ebbing away as the fear of dying took over.

He squirmed on the floor, slippery with blood. His hand stretched up towards me. I ran, ran towards him and bent down, desperate to help, to prevent this man from dying on the floor, and yet I knew there was nothing I could do to prevent it. His death was an inevitability, closer every second.

'It's all right,' I said uselessly. 'You're going to be just fine, Mr Cauldwell.'

But he knew that wasn't true, just as much as I did. I held his hand. His blood was hot and sticky, and I fought back the bile rising in my throat. Jasper had now arrived in the corridor, and a moment later Mrs Temple too. She took in the sight of me covered in her brother's blood.

'No!' she cried as she came forward. 'It cannot be! How? What happened?'

I just shook my head, words failing me. Wilbur's hand had gone slack in mine. His head slumped, and when I lifted it, his eyes were glassy. There was not one bit of life left inside him. I let go of his hand and it fell with a thud.

Mrs Temple shrieked again. 'What happened?' She broke into a run, dropped down to the floor and attempted to lift him close to her, cradling his head in her arms. I tried to breathe. It was so hard to breathe. I somehow got myself to stand, stumbling against the door Wilbur had been grasping at in front of me, which swung open just a crack. And I screamed when I realized what I was looking at.

It was the muzzle of a gun. Somebody had shot Wilbur in the throat, and their gun was aimed at me – no, just above my head. Any bullet discharged now would go right over me into the wall behind. That was when I realized that the gun in front of me was not wielded by a person. I looked a little closer and saw that it had been fixed into a metal bracket lined with small mechanical cogs, connected so that, when the door was pushed open, a chain reaction was sparked resulting in the pulling back of a hook fastened round the trigger. The gun had been set at the perfect height to be lethal for Wilbur – or indeed any adult who trespassed.

I carefully loosened the hook and lifted the gun off the bracket, placing it down so that I could safely open the door wider. Inside was a private study, Mr Cauldwell's study. The walls were lined with books, there was a walnut-coloured bureau in pride of place, and on the floor next to it was an ornately decorated wooden chest that I already knew was impossible to break into and had only one key-hole. Thomas Cauldwell's chest.

It had seemed at one point that Wilbur was the most likely suspect to have killed his father. And it crossed my mind that somebody else might have made that deduction, might *also* have considered Wilbur responsible for his father's death, and this trap was set up as revenge. But that would have meant this person knew that Thomas had been murdered – and had discovered the little device that caused Mr Cauldwell to trip and fall down the stairs. That seemed unlikely, unless they'd seen it being placed or removed – and then why wouldn't they have told the rest of us, instead of exacting this strange method of retribution? I was certain that I was the only person who had been drawn into the supernatural vision at the arch – which was hardly likely to be taken as concrete evidence.

And so it seemed fair to assume that Wilbur's death was the murderous handiwork of the same person who had killed Mr Cauldwell – though I was disturbed to be confronted with a more confident method of dispatch this time. Gone now was the pretence of an accident. Whoever had killed them was skilled in invention, and they had turned that skill to murder.

But to what end? Who would seek to gain something from the death of both Mr Cauldwell and Wilbur? The number of us in the house was dwindling, already down by two. Was the murderer finished with their work? Or would they not rest until not a single one of us were left standing by the end of the storm? That seemed frighteningly likely given their latest kill. It was almost as if they didn't care about getting caught, or at the very least didn't fear the consequences – and that could not be good news for those of us remaining.

I backed out of the room slowly. Wilbur was still in Mrs Temple's arms. My chest tightened with a swell of emotion at her grief. The sadness that hit me was an echo. Again I was confronted by a body that moments ago was living and breathing – with all his own light and darkness – and now it was empty of everything that had made him who he was.

I had always imagined being confronted with a dead body would be the most frightening thing imaginable. I'd thought it would be an unparalleled horror. But both times, with Mr Cauldwell and with Wilbur, it had just been desperately sad. The horror was in the death itself, the awful method behind it, all that blood – and worst of all the fact that somebody in the house had knowingly taken a life, decided upon it and taken it as if they had the right to determine when it should end. The body itself was peaceful now, not a horror at all.

'Mrs Temple,' I said, making my voice as soft as I could so as not to startle her. 'Mrs Temple, we need to talk about what to do. This was a murder. Somebody set this up to kill him.'

Her head snapped up. She pointed at the device at the door, her hand smeared with blood. 'What do you mean? Was it . . . *that*?' She was utterly aghast.

'Yes. Is there anybody else who would use this room?' I asked, trying to ascertain whether the trap could have been laid for someone else.

'That room is my father's study,' she said, and then her eyes welled up with tears. '*Was* my father's study. Wilbur was in here just yesterday morning, so this, this contraption ... is new. And it was meant for Wilbur. Nobody else would come in here.'

Her throat was layered thick with grief, her voice changed from its usual crisp briskness. 'He was looking for paperwork. The will.'

Except that last part wasn't entirely true. I knew what Wilbur was really searching for – the key to Mr Cauldwell's chest. Trying to find a way to break into his secrets.

I knelt down beside her and placed a hand on her arm. She looked so confused, so lost and so distant. It was as though she were travelling somewhere else in her thoughts, and I wondered whether she'd gone to another time, another place. I wondered if her mind were transporting her to the past, the moments where she lost her husbands.

'Mrs Temple . . .' I said, and she twitched her head, as if arriving back in the room, and looked down at Wilbur with renewed shock.

She might be a liar, but I couldn't believe she was also his murderer. She wasn't that good an actress – nobody could be. I hesitated over whether to tell her that I believed her father had been murdered too, but, without evidence, what could I truly say? That there had been a murder was undisputable this time ... but with Mr Cauldwell all I had was a small hole in a staircase and a strange and fantastical tale about portals and visions of the past.

'Go, go and fetch Gabriel. He'll know what to do,' Mrs Temple said in a momentary return to her usual composure, before her bottom lip began to shake and fresh tears streamed down her face.

Gabriel. A trusted advisor to the family. Almost *like* family, but not quite. Set to inherit at least part of the family's great fortune on Mr Cauldwell's death, if a promise could be believed. In a confrontation with Wilbur before he died.

'I'll get him,' Jasper reassured Mrs Temple.

My mind was fizzing with fear. I didn't want it to be true, but out of everybody left on Sighfeyre Isle Gabriel had the greatest reason for wanting Mr Cauldwell and Wilbur dead. As I backed away from Mrs Temple, I saw Birdie peeping out round the entrance to the corridor, eyes as wide as the muzzle of the gun. My dress was sticky with blood, and I wanted to rip it off, to run shrieking from Archfall Manor and never return, but instead I kept a level head, took Birdie's hand and led her upstairs to Nora's room. Nora opened the door, her mouth twisting in horror at the sight of me covered in blood, as Birdie launched into a feverish description of what she'd seen, of what had happened to their uncle.

'I . . . I have to change,' I said, interrupting Birdie, my words brittle.

'Yes, I think you'd better.' Nora placed a steadying hand on Birdie's shoulder.

When I returned to the servants' quarters, Jasper had roused his parents. Teresa gasped when she saw me covered in blood, my dress stiff with it. I was watchful for any sign on Gabriel's face that might tell me, definitively, whether he was guilty. But his expression was inscrutable.

'You must have had an awful shock,' he said. 'Teresa – fetch the girl some tea.'

Teresa leaped up from her chair and settled me into it, before pressing a mug into my hands. The warmth of it centred me, almost touched the chill that had settled deep in my core.

'Murdered? You're sure?' she asked, turning to Jasper with bewilderment etched across her features. Was she doing what I was doing, counting the people in the house, weighing up the likelihood of their being the murderer, their possible gain? What conclusion would she come to, when she placed her husband upon the scales?

Gabriel snapped immediately into a brisk and functional manner. 'I'll deal with the body,' he said. 'You had all better stay here.'

I couldn't read him. He was practical, matter-of-fact, all useful qualities in a situation like this one. And yet I couldn't help but think that he seemed oddly detached. Almost unsurprised. I tried to push these thoughts away, and they resisted me, shouting louder in my head to listen. It would crush Jasper to know I suspected his father so. And yet who else could it be?

I finished my tea, my thoughts still confused, and Teresa took the cup from my hands.

'It's time for bed. It's so very late,' she said. 'You've had an awful shock – you must rest.' And then she guided me to my room, a hand at the small of my back.

When I was alone, I removed my dress the same way I always would, except it took some peeling away from my skin, and then I washed, the blood swirling into the basin and turning the water pink. I slipped into my nightdress, just as if it were an ordinary night, while inside I was screaming at the sheer horror of it all.

And all the time the walls whispered to me, incomprehensible but relentless, trying to push into my mind and tell me something, something I couldn't quite hear.

20

I had arrived at Archfall Manor hoping for answers, but everything about the house, the family and the entwined history of the two seemed to grow murkier with every passing day. The tangled knots were so tightly wound that it was impossible to even select which string to pick at first.

This odd and unsettling place had a secret life of its own, with whispering walls and a beating heart at the centre. Inventions could do incredible things here that didn't seem to work on the mainland. The arch at the top of the manor offered a window through time, the opportunity to see things that had been missed before, to fill in clues and reveal history and truth.

And yet Archfall Manor was also housing a murderer, while we were all cut off from the mainland and any kind of help.

I needed to puzzle it all out – everything depended upon that. I had come to Archfall Manor to change my fortune. Well, now it felt as though the flip of the coin were in mid-air, and I might decide which way it would land.

This job had been about making money to save Mam, to

rescue her from the debtors' prison and give us both a chance, and I hoped that I might get some answers about what had happened to my father, to understand what truth our circumstances had grown out of, to fill the aching void in my life.

But now . . . now there were two dead, and a seething supernatural force was nudging me and pressing at me. It had pulled me towards the archway; it had compelled me to enter the window in time; and it had washed over me as I took the key from Mr Cauldwell's neck. *Now* I felt as if the house itself wanted to pull me deeper and deeper into the mystery at every turn.

The murderer on Sighfeyre Isle was obsessed with invention and legacy, that much was clear from their methods and the path they'd carved through the Cauldwell family. Surely in time, if they got away with it, their mind would turn to the archway at the top of the house. I needed to uncover their identity so that I could protect myself from them . . . And when the storm passed, if I had solved the murders, I could turn them in. What debt of gratitude would the remaining members of the family owe me then? What rewards might there be? Fortune-changing ones, I imagined.

But I had to be careful in sifting through the evidence. The murders had cut the traditional line of inheritance of the Cauldwell family short. Could it be Mrs Temple? Her disquieting reputation as the Widow of Despair seemed to cast a shadow over everything. This was her ancestral home. Even if she, as a woman, would not inherit it herself then at the very least, with the birth of her son, she had guaranteed security for her future that she'd never had before. If she were not permitted to own Archfall Manor herself, would she now be allowed to hold the house in trust for tiny Edmund? It was entirely possible that this was something she had wanted, hoped for, *needed*.

The timing was striking – a new son, a return to the ancestral home, the swift dispatching of the line of inheritance. Was this all part of a calculated plan to force a specific outcome for herself and her children, a return to Archfall Manor as an heiress? There was benefit to be had, for not only her, but her children too, especially if she had not trusted that she would be provided for otherwise.

Mrs Temple remained a mystery. Even if she were innocent of any involvement in the deaths of her three husbands – the authorities had no evidence, even if they harboured their suspicions about her – perhaps the exposure to death and the precariousness of her situation had driven her to secure her future by any means necessary, especially with Wilbur having been so irascible, petulant and bitter. I wouldn't have wanted my future, or that of my children's, in the hands of a brother like that.

And yet the siblings had seemed to be colluding at the table the night before. Co-conspirators in the search for the key that would unlock their father's secrets. What were they hoping to find? A copy of his last will and testament? Plans for inventions they could turn to profit? And Mrs Temple had wept over her brother's body. She appeared truly broken upon losing him.

To my mind, that left Gabriel as the only other person who would benefit significantly from the deaths of both men. He'd believed in his own entitlement to the inventing work on the island, had hidden the journals of Mr Cauldwell he'd had access to in order to prevent Wilbur from getting his hands on them, had argued with Wilbur before he died. He had a temper that I'd seen first-hand. Was this his moment – destroying the Cauldwell family so he could fully step into the vision he had of himself as an inventor who should be recognized in his own right? In which case, did I need to warn Mrs Temple that she and her children were in great danger?

But this was Jasper's father, and Jasper was the only person here I could rely on. When we were together, I felt safer, felt capable of solving this. How could I tell him of my misgivings about his own father? He idolized the man – it would crush him . . . That, or he would be unable to accept it.

There was something more too. Whoever the murderer was, their methods were very strange. Brutal and dis-passionate, with a weird detachment from the act itself. Even if he had become unhinged, would Gabriel really be so reckless?

And there was a bigger puzzle as well. The events that took place eighteen years ago in Archfall Manor were still reverberating through the actions of others in this house. Edwin Cauldwell had been undertaking revolutionary work that sought to meddle with the fabric of time, and had died under suspicious circumstances. My father had come to contribute to that work, and never returned to us. People had been changed irrevocably, and yet nobody seemed to understand exactly what had taken place.

But part of it was happening again. Because the more I thought about it, the more convinced I was that Edwin Cauldwell's invention had worked all those years ago, the way it was working now.

I had two routes of enquiry to explore – the arch and the key. The arch, unpredictable and dangerous. The key, revealing Mr Cauldwell's closest secrets. Either way, I was going to need Jasper's help to move around the house and get to where I needed to be. The key, I decided, was the place to start. It came with none of the risks of the arch, none of the danger. All I had to do was figure out the mechanism to unlock Mr Cauldwell's chest, and I might find myself with more concrete pieces of the puzzle.

These fitful circles of thoughts kept me occupied through the night, so that the following morning my eyes were gritty and sore. What I desperately needed was real sleep, the kind of sleep I had always taken for granted before Archfall Manor. Deep, restorative sleep that washed over me like healing magic. Would I ever sleep like that again? Perhaps, if I left Archfall Manor and could silence the whispers that picked and scratched at the inside of my head like the sharpest of fingernails. I struggled to suppress a yawn as I entered the kitchen, ready to offer my help with the breakfast.

But instead of the usual warmth among the staff and a willingness to collaborate, what I found was a distrustful nest of swarming anxieties.

Teresa was at the sink, lathering up soap in a great tin bucket. Gabriel brooded by the hearth, the breadth of his body blocking the rest of us from feeling the benefit of it.

Molly stood with Jasper, and I could see she was clutching at his sleeve. 'I can't stay here any longer. You have to help me get away from this place. Isn't there a boat?'

Gabriel snapped his head up. 'There is no boat, but if there were, could you imagine setting out in it right now?'

Outside, we could hear the storm raging. It battered the house with all the viciousness of a personal grudge.

'Pa's right. It wouldn't be safe,' Jasper said, his voice strangled.

'It isn't safe *here*!' Molly cried. 'Mr Wilbur has been murdered! There's a murderer here on this island – why are you all so calm about that fact?'

I watched Gabriel to see his reaction, but he just shook his head in irritation at Molly. I clamped my mouth shut. It would do no good to start asking people to draw together the threads, to ask them whether they'd considered any foul play in what happened to Mr Cauldwell too.

Jasper hung his head sadly. It seemed to be causing him pain to see Molly in such distress, and yet I knew there was nothing he could do to fix this for her. 'We don't know that for sure. And we just need to get through the storm,' he said. He talked to her like he was soothing a skittish horse. 'A handful of days at most. There's more harm would come to us trying to make a crossing.'

'But couldn't we get a message out to the mainland? Can't they send a rescue party for us?'

Gabriel released a sigh as hard and crashing as the wave that had swept away the solicitor and the doctor. I was struck by his impatience and the anger that quivered in his voice as he addressed her. 'Pull yourself together, Molly. We'll cope. Sighfeyre Isle has always been this way, and it's how it always will be. It's a self-sufficient kind of place.'

For the first time, I wondered at the life he'd had before he was head of maintenance here, what kind of man it had made him to not only accept such conditions of solitude, but to accept this life for his family too. It was no wonder that the work of invention, his contribution to it, what he felt he was owed, was of such importance to him.

'"Self-sufficient"?' Molly spluttered. 'Try "desolate"! Try "forsaken"! This place is sinister and wrong, and I want to leave! When I agreed to come from London, I didn't believe Mrs Temple was guilty of what happened to Mr Temple. I know she was being investigated, but they didn't find anything. I thought she was just . . . unlucky. But now –'

'That's enough,' Teresa interrupted. She put the bucket on the ground with a great clatter and took Molly by the shoulders roughly, staring right into her eyes. 'Remember who we are, what our place is in this house. You must not start speaking ill of your employer. There will be plenty of time for all this to be unravelled when the storm is over. It would do none of us any good to start making unfounded accusations while we all must stay warm and dry under this roof, do you hear me?' Teresa shook her then, as if she could shake out Molly's rising hysteria.

'Yes,' Molly whispered, and Teresa dropped her hands.

Outside, the sound of slate crashing from the roof reminded us all of the assault on the house. Any one of us could be sliced through the head by a tile, crushed by a ripped-up tree, or consumed by the sucking mud, drowning slowly, if we ventured out. We were not safer if we tried to leave.

'We have work to do,' I said. Molly looked at me fearfully as though I might start shaking her the way Teresa had. 'Remember: as long as you're here, you're working and you're earning money for your family.' Molly's head bobbed up and down so quickly it looked as though it might come loose and roll away.

'Yes, yes, you're right. The baby will need changing soon,' she said.

'Well then. You get yourself to his room, and you take care of that sweet boy, who doesn't know anything about any of this. I'll prepare some porridge, and Teresa can get to work with that.' I pointed at her bucket. I didn't have to state what it was for. We all knew she was going to spend the morning on her hands and knees scrubbing Wilbur's blood from the floor outside the study.

'Everyone has something they need to do. These troubles, they're troubles in the family, and we must keep to our routine. It's why we're here. None of us are in any danger. We're just workers – and we must just work.'

Gabriel made an approving noise in the back of his throat. I felt the scrutiny of his gaze. I didn't dare to direct him the way I had the others, couldn't even meet his eyes. Did he know that I suspected him, that it was not out of respect that I avoided instructing him, but through fear? The longer he believed that all of us in the staff quarters were completely aligned and a closely knit company, the better it would be. The troubles were within the family, I'd said. I wanted him to think I believed it was 'us' and 'them', not revealing that he remained my greatest suspect.

I served the porridge to Mrs Temple, Nora and Birdie, the three of them draped in black. It was simple fare compared to the extravagance of earlier days on the island, before the fresh ingredients began to run out, but I'd sweetened it with sugar from the pantry and a sprinkling of cinnamon. Nora and Birdie set about devouring it eagerly, but Mrs Temple did not touch hers. Her eyes were raw with grief, her hair unkempt as though she had gone to sleep with the same style the night before. A dark exhaustion lined her face.

'What will I do? What will I do?' she kept muttering under her breath, agitated.

Nora sighed as though her mother's distress were an irritating inconvenience. I understood she had never been close to her uncle or her grandfather, and so wasn't as struck by the loss of them, but there was a remarkable lack of empathy in her demeanour.

When the meal was finished and I had cleared the plates, I asked Birdie to meet me in the schoolroom shortly, and I remained behind, waiting until Mrs Temple withdrew. I followed her to the reading room and knocked on the door.

'Come in.' She sat in a grey velvet upholstered chair, closing her book over her middle finger so that it marked her page in the slim tome. 'Miss Martin. I wasn't really reading this. I can't concentrate, it seems. My brother ... he ... he was not a kind man, but ...' Her hand was shaking.

I had wondered at her lack of visible grief on our first encounter, given that she was still in mourning for her husband, but that coiffed and polished version of Mrs Temple had been scraped away by the horrific events of the last few days, so all that remained was a wan, haggard replacement. She'd stopped troubling to apply powder to her cheeks or colour to her lips, and tears had given her face a patchy, soggy appearance. She looked haunted. I wondered how Molly could look at her, diminished like this, and imagine her responsible for the murder of her brother. Perhaps because the alternative – that it was one of *us*, one of the staff – was altogether more terrifying.

'I wanted to offer my condolences for your loss,' I said.

Mrs Temple let out a choked cry. 'Which one? My whole life is loss. I can't take any more of this. My nerves are in tatters.'

I didn't know how to comfort her. There was nothing I could offer. She had lost so much before even coming to this island, and now she was trapped in the horror that had unfolded. Her past. Her present. Filled with death and loss. But what about her future?

Surely she must also have come to the realization that Gabriel was responsible for the death of her father and brother? If so, she must have been frightened for her own life, must have been seeking a way to appease him.

Every day she was trapped here on the island was another day to merely survive, alongside the man who had murdered her family and might, on a whim, take her life as well. No wonder the panic seemed to seep out of her, bleeding into the room: *What will I do? What will I do?*

She must know that the only thing she could do right now was to wait out the storm, to make sure she was never unaccompanied, placate Gabriel where possible if he came to her with questions about his entitlement to her father's work . . . I couldn't speak a word of this to her, but I willed it to travel from my mind to hers, if she weren't thinking about all of this already.

Instead, I posed the question I had come to ask, ready to continue playing the dutiful servant.

'I was wondering what you would like me to do with Miss Birdie,' I said. 'I understand it's my responsibility to educate her, but in the light of recent events, I thought . . .'

Mrs Temple shook her head. 'To tell you the truth, Miss Martin, the most useful thing you can do is simply keep my daughter occupied as well as you can, however you can. She requires firm handling and someone who is an expert in distraction.'

I swallowed. 'You just want me to keep her distracted,' I said, feeling flat and hopeless, thinking of the way Birdie had tricked me so cruelly, outsmarted me so easily.

'Both my daughters have quick minds and are even quicker to channel their boredom or dissatisfaction into destructive actions. I fear . . . I fear . . .' She trailed off. 'Your letter was the only one that gave me any confidence, you know. You seemed the only person who might be able to help me . . . handle my daughter.'

I remembered what I'd written, how I'd so passionately entreated Mrs Temple to consider me. I thought of how strongly I had felt that all a precocious child needed was something to spark their interest sufficiently to keep them engaged. Then I'd arrived, and I'd assimilated my role as governess, trying to be something I wasn't, setting tasks on reading, writing and arithmetic, as though we were operating in a traditional school, as though Mrs Temple hadn't personally selected me for my radical ideas. I'd been trying so hard to be a person I wasn't that I'd forgotten what I could be. When the idea took hold, it did so all at once.

'Don't you worry about Miss Birdie today. I'll take good care of her,' I said as comfortingly as I could manage. Mrs Temple raised a hand to her brow as though she were trying to hold her own head together, as if it might split apart like a cracked teacup. 'Would you . . . would you want to stay with us? For safety in numbers? I am aware we don't know anything yet exactly, but . . .'

'Oh no, my dear,' Mrs Temple said. 'Thank you, but I'm not frightened of this murderer.'

A weary smile spread across her lips, so slowly that it unnerved me. I had never seen a smile so joyless, so haunted. She was still smiling as I closed the door behind me with a soft click.

21

Birdie was waiting for me in the schoolroom as I'd requested, which in itself was a pleasant surprise. 'We're going to do something dangerous and magical today,' I told her, and she raised an eyebrow at me. 'Did you know that when you boil sugar it can tear the skin from your flesh? And yet the very same ingredient, if you know what to do, can make the sweetest treat imaginable.' I knew I had her then, bright little eyes shining.

So Birdie and I made all sorts of confectionery, raiding the pantry for all its dry goods. Hard-boiled sweeties flavoured with lemon, with lavender, with peppermint. She was focused and attentive, and I was certain that using her hands and immersing herself in a practical activity was proving enough of a distraction to keep her mind occupied and away from the terrors that had been unfolding. The fact that it was a dangerous pursuit seemed to enthral her just as much as the promise of eating the sweets once they had cooled.

And all day long, in the back of my mind, was the key. It was what Wilbur and Mrs Temple had been searching for, and I'd been led to it, prompted to steal it, by the power that moved within this house. Whatever was within Mr Cauldwell's chest might well contain the answers I'd been searching for all this time. Inside, there might be something I could use as leverage to keep myself safe on this island until the storm cleared. Inside ... there could be *anything*.

That evening, after all the chores had been completed and everyone had taken themselves to bed, I presented myself outside Jasper's room, knocking quietly. He appeared in the doorway, shirt untucked, hair dishevelled in a way that made him even more handsome. I couldn't look at him a moment longer without my cheeks turning hot, and diverted my eyes to the room over his shoulder. It was simple and rustic like mine, but his bedside table was strewn with the evidence of his interests – a pile of metallic stones that clung to each other, a coil of copper wire, a small set of sharp shears.

'I have to show you something,' I said in a whisper.

He blinked, waited for me to do so, but the key in my pocket felt weighted with guilt. Not just because I felt guilty for having it at all, although I did greatly, but that the key itself indicated that I *was* guilty, of being both a thief and a liar, and neither of those were the sort of accusations I needed to face in the aftermath of two murders.

'Come back to the kitchen.'

A little fire had been left in the grate. It crackled away quietly, burning itself out. I reached into my pocket and showed Jasper the key. He visibly flinched at the sight of it.

'Where did you get that?'

I hesitated and took a deep breath. 'I . . . I found Mr Cauldwell first. At the bottom of the stairs. I was just . . . too frightened to tell anyone.'

'You took that from his body?' Jasper asked with a grimace.

I dipped my head, shame flooding through me. 'I . . . I took it because . . .'

I breathed in deeply to steady myself. I knew what I needed to tell him, but there was a part of me that felt a physical resistance to revealing my real name, my real objective.

'The whole time I've been here, I've been trying to uncover some truths.'

'What do you mean?' Jasper stared at me, hard. His eyes flicked across my face as though he were trying to read me. 'Josephine, what's going on?'

The silence between us was filled with doubt. I couldn't meet his eye any more . . . And then the truth drained out of me. All of it.

'My real name is Helena Timber, and I have never been a governess before. I stole my reference from my own tutor and borrowed her name. I took this post here because . . . eighteen years ago my father came to Archfall Manor. He was a watchmaker. I believe he was maybe involved in Edwin's work somehow. But the fact is he never came home to us. Mam always told me he must be dead because he wouldn't abandon us otherwise . . . But we never knew for certain.'

Jasper raised a hand to his forehead, rubbed his frown as though he could erase it.

'So you've been lying ever since the day you arrived,' he said brusquely.

'It was my only chance to come here,' I said, desperate to explain. 'My only chance to find the truth. And the other part – about my mother being in prison – that's all true, every word.'

A moment of realization dawned upon him. 'That's why you were asking about a watchmaker.'

I nodded. 'I . . . I'm sorry that I had to lie to you. The name and the reference are false. I work in a sweetshop. Well, I did. And everything else, everything between us . . . that has been real.'

My throat felt thick, and the awful prick of tears arrived involuntarily. I told him all of it then. About the debt collector and the bailiffs and the bone-aching fear that my mam and I would never be together again, that I would never have answers or feel whole. All the while, my heart ached inside my chest as if it didn't fit in there any more. 'I'd hate for you to think that I wanted to lie to you.'

He closed his hand round mine, and in that gesture was so much understanding that I could hardly stand it.

'I believe you,' he said. 'But why did you take the key?' The shadows and the dim firelight danced over his face, resting in the creases of his bewilderment.

'At first I thought it might open the door to the arches. I thought I'd find some sort of clue up there about how my father was involved in Edwin's work . . . But now I know that it's really for Mr Cauldwell's treasure chest. Wilbur and Mrs Temple were looking for it.' I wiped the tears from my eyes.

'He never let that key out of his sight. The secrecy of the contents of those chests has been a family tradition for generations.'

'Birdie told me about them,' I said, thinking of her serious little face. 'Why do the women in the family have them if they aren't allowed to be involved with any of the inventing work?'

'That I can't say. Mr Cauldwell was incredibly superstitious about a lot of things. He followed all sorts of odd rituals and routines that he thought would help his work,' Jasper said. 'Perhaps he thought it would be bad luck not to give the women boxes too? I know he didn't set much store on them inventing, though. When they moved back here from London, Nora asked if she could use the inventing room for her own projects, and he said no.'

'That's so unjust.'

Rage rose in my chest, and it was the rage of so many inequalities – that even at Archfall Manor, where clever, interesting Nora, who benefitted from unimaginable wealth, was barred from the work of her family when she'd expressed an interest in it. Mr Cauldwell's plans for her were an arranged marriage she had no interest in, and yet who knew what she might have been able to contribute to his work?

'We have to go and look inside the chest.'

'You don't think we should hand over the key?' Jasper sounded uncertain.

'To whom? We still have no idea who's behind these murders. We might just be giving them exactly what they want.'

'Perhaps. But I'm not sure I want to know Mr Cauldwell's secrets.' He ran a hand through his hair, leaving it sticking up. 'Don't you think a person's secrets should stay buried with them? Maybe we should just throw that key into the sea. That's more in the spirit of the chests themselves.'

'It wouldn't have stopped his children if they'd found the key first. What if there's something important inside? Something to do with the arches . . .'

I didn't voice my other hope, that there might be information about my father. People didn't just disappear. He'd been here, so there had to be something of his left behind. Maybe Mr Cauldwell had hidden it away so he could conceal the truth about what happened to Father . . . Particularly if somebody in the house were to blame for his death.

'You might have set your hopes a little too high,' Jasper said. 'The most likely outcome is that it's just a stack of rough notes and ideas. Mistakes. Failures.'

'Well, there's only one way to know for certain.' I tried to smile, but found I couldn't.

I wondered how I'd appear to an outsider, to the authorities, if they uncovered my lies. Would they consider me a suspect? I was here under a false name, searching for information on my father. If everything I'd done was viewed through the wrong lens, one of bitterness and revenge, I'd look like the perfect murderess. The thought made me feel queasy.

Jasper was hesitant too; I could see it written all over his face, but he knew I was right. 'Who do you think is behind everything that's been going on?'

'I'm hoping that if we head up to the arch again we might be able to see something else. Right now, all I have are theories.'

'Theories are good.' Jasper's eyes brightened. 'Theories are how understanding anything begins.'

'I wish I shared your enthusiasm.' Instead, all I felt was an intense dread, sending a chill through my body. Now was hardly the time to tell him that my prime suspect was his father.

'It's not enthusiasm,' he said with a flush of embarrassment in his cheeks. 'No, because it's too awful. Mr Cauldwell and Mr Wilbur are dead. But ... the arch *worked*. It actually worked. It's the most incredible event I've ever experienced in my whole lifetime. It's hard not to feel ...' He started to flounder, his hands gesticulating as though there were a market stall right in front of him where he could simply select the perfect word.

'Alive?' I offered tentatively.

Jasper's nod was effusive. 'Alive. Exactly. It doesn't feel good, but it doesn't feel wholly bad either. It's frightening and strangely energizing ...'

'The worst part is I can't stop myself feeling a bit hopeful too,' I confessed.

Did he understand that hope, so natural to him, was so frightening to me? That a lifetime of disappointments had done that to me?

'I might be able to find out what happened to my father. I feel so ... I have so many questions about him. And I think an answer would bring my mam a lot of peace.'

Saying it out loud tipped me over the edge, broke me into pieces again.

'We need to start by opening that chest then,' said Jasper. 'I'm here. I'm here with you.'

He'd said 'we'. We were embroiled in the mystery together. I didn't have to do this by myself, much as I might have assumed that was necessary when I started out. The relief of it surprised me. I didn't realize how heavy it had felt, the weight of feeling alone with this unsolved ache in my identity.

I shook my head to dispel the overwhelming emotions and tutted at myself. 'I find this really difficult, you know.'

'Anyone would.'

'No, I mean crying in front of someone.'

'Oh,' Jasper said, as though it were a strange thing to feel.

'I usually just . . . get angry instead.'

'You can be angry if you need to. Or sad.'

'I'll wager you cry all the time,' I said. 'In front of anyone. And tell them all about your feelings.'

He laughed, with a note of surprise at my friendly mocking of him, and it was a warm sound, one that I wished I could keep for later, to hear it again to cheer me when I was on my own. When I made him laugh, I did not feel like the cheerless version of myself that forgot how to hope. 'Your assessment of me isn't inaccurate,' he said. 'I suppose when I feel something it just cascades out of me, without much effort.'

'I realized that when we first met,' I replied.

He went suddenly red. 'Did you?'

'You were so excited to talk about inventions, your research,' I said, but I had a feeling there was more to his obvious embarrassment. I thought back to that first proper conversation, the way he hovered in the doorway, the thoughts that were running through my mind about the vague impropriety of being alone together . . . And here we were again, more comfortable now, closer.

Jasper cleared his throat. 'Was there anything else you . . . realized?'

His breathing was uneven, and his gaze drifted across my face – meeting my eyes, looking at my lips – as if he were admiring a painting, not me, not the sweetshop girl. Nobody had looked at me like that before. It was full of wordless longing, identical to what I felt looking at him.

'I did wonder . . .'

I struggled to push the words out of my mouth although I was almost certain now that his thoughts mirrored mine. It was just a matter of expressing them. What would I tell him – that I had felt drawn to him since that moment, that I'd imagined being closer to him than this, the feel of his hair between my fingers, the shape of his mouth on mine? How could I tell him that in all this horror and confusion he glowed like candlelight in the darkness?

'I wondered too,' he said, his voice low and rough.

The things we'd said already were sufficient. The words had gone far enough, and the way we looked at each other had bridged the chasm between what we could say and the thoughts that ran through us. We both knew.

But what I did not know was what I was supposed to do next.

I moved closer and tilted my face towards his. He moved his hands to my waist, and I melted beneath the clasp of his fingertips, firm and warm. It felt as if his hands belonged there.

And then there was the sound of a door opening upstairs, the thudding of purposeful steps. We both flinched away from each other, the way you flinch away from a hot stove. I shook my head to clear it. That had been foolish. If we had been found like this, alone, it would be the ruin of my reputation – and then I'd never work again. I needed to be more guarded.

But still. It seemed neither of us could shake the thoughts from our head completely. Sharing a glance – and a small smile – we left the kitchen as quietly as we could.

As we wove through the manor, I ruminated on what we would find inside the chest once we had it opened. 'There's got to be more than just the will,' I said, thinking out loud. I had the sense that we were on the brink of discovery.

'The only things Mr Cauldwell would keep locked up is plans or prototypes,' Jasper said. 'I cannot emphasize enough how secretive he always was about his ideas and his work, only sharing them with Pa when he was absolutely sure he was on to something. That's why Pa was so up a height when he saw us in the inventing room. I'm usually only allowed in there under supervision.'

'That sounds impossibly frustrating,' I said. 'He was so controlling over the thing that everyone in this house felt so passionate about.'

Jasper winced. 'You really have no idea of the scale of his ambition. This place looks like a manor house on the surface, but it's a workshop for invention and innovation first and foremost. There's fortune after fortune to be made here from the ideas living between the pages of notebooks.'

'But why did Mr Cauldwell keep such a tight grip on it all? So that he could feel powerful? He already had more money than anyone could spend in a lifetime . . .'

Jasper grimaced. 'I don't think it's about money. I think it was an obsession. It's an incredible feeling to be able to create something that didn't exist before, to fulfil a purpose or solve a problem. I was excited when I learned how to repair a broken cuckoo clock, but imagine being the person who invented the clock in the first place! Humans are inherently creative. We want to make things. I think it probably has more to do with that. I think Mr Cauldwell did it because . . . he couldn't stop himself.'

The nearest I'd come to that was making sweets, inventing recipes and tools to help me. Mam had always said I could engineer anything if it would achieve my aims, and it was true. If I had a problem to solve, I'd always take a look round the kitchen at the equipment we had, and I'd concoct a way to do things differently. But it had always been within the context of work or necessity – never purely for the sake of being creative.

'Maybe it can all coexist,' I said. 'Mr Cauldwell wanted to feel powerful, and he had too much money. He had a creative vision and wanted to innovate, and he was incredibly privileged to have been afforded that opportunity.

He also wanted to marry off Nora. He was broken after he lost his son and should have treated his other son better. It can all be true.'

'Who knows? He's dead. He might have been flawed, but I still believed in his vision, that we can make the impossible possible. Especially here, in this place.'

We are all made up of light and dark. That thought had become a comforting echo until a more distressing one appeared alongside it. *But sometimes people act upon the very worst of the darkness.*

22

The corridor was empty, but Wilbur's blood remained. Where Teresa had scrubbed the carpet it was stiff with soap, but no less stained. It would never be clean, would need to be ripped up from the floor, where the floorboards were no doubt soaked through too. Wilbur's blood had left an imprint of his awful last moments. From the rusty brown mark outside the study door there was a path smeared down the length of the corridor, which brought to mind the image of Gabriel dragging Wilbur's body to his room, where now it rested as though sleeping. An iron scent filled the air, reminding me of the butcher's shop in Durham.

Beside me, Jasper quietly retched. I stepped carefully to leave the mess undisturbed, not wanting to leave any evidence of our return to the scene, and pushed open the door to the study.

'There's so much blood,' Jasper said, aghast. He had gone quite grey in the face.

I wanted to tell him this was nothing; what was worse was feeling the blood pumping out of Wilbur's neck in a hot gush, wanting to help him and being unable to do anything but hold his hand. But Jasper needed me to be gentle and kind, and that took a whole new type of bravery for me.

'It's horrible,' I said, 'but the worst has already happened. This is just the echo of it.'

'You're right,' Jasper said, and a new resolve solidified behind his eyes. He copied my deliberately placed steps as though he were putting his feet on stones in a river, not avoiding leaving incriminating evidence in a trail of blood.

A whisper nagged at my ear, inviting me inside the study; a tug in my gut, as though a string had been tied round my organs, pulling me forward, dragging me deeper once again into the mystery of this family, of this house. Mr Cauldwell's chest was waiting for me, loaded with secrets, with possibility. I bent down beside it and took out the key, vaguely aware of Jasper hovering by my elbow. I arranged the bow so the twisted iron made a perfect letter T for Thomas and duly thrust it into the lock. It wouldn't move at first, not until I turned the key the other way. Finally, there was a heavy *thunk*, but the lock still wouldn't open. I leaned in closer, my gaze narrowing to the single iron fastening. A new hole had appeared on the side. I put the key in again, but it didn't fit.

'This is exactly the sort of thing I would have expected from him,' Jasper said, a fond admiration leaking out of his words. 'I wonder if they all open this way.'

I inspected the key again, and pressed in the top line of the T. Out clunked an additional prong. Placing the key inside the second lock worked this time, and there was another satisfying *clunk* as it turned.

I looked up at Jasper. 'If you didn't know that you had exactly the right key and exactly the right chest, you would have just given up, wouldn't you?' It was about as secure as I imagined anything could be.

'Probably, but people in this family tend to be pretty determined about things.'

The latch slipped off the chest, and although the lid was heavy and unyielding at first I managed to heave it up. Inside, there was a folded envelope, sealed with wax. I turned it over, not hugely surprised by what I read: *Last Will and Testament*. There was no way of knowing whether it was a recent document, reflecting Mr Cauldwell's final wishes before his death, or an older version. Not without tearing open the seal, which wasn't what we were here to do.

I put the envelope down again because Nora was right: the will was the least interesting item inside the chest. Fixed into its back wall was a row of five hooks, and each one of them held a key, just like the one I'd used. On each key, the bow formed a different letter – E, W, C, N, B. I don't know what I'd expected, but it wasn't this. A key for Edwin, Wilbur, Caroline, Nora, Birdie. Nothing for the baby, I noted – who would make one for him now?

Mr Cauldwell believed that everybody should be able to keep their own secrets, except, it appeared, from him.

'There's a key for each one of them,' I said, my words coming out breathy and strange. It was an intense betrayal on Mr Cauldwell's part, and now I was involved. 'I have no doubt that Mrs Temple and Wilbur would have been shocked to discover this. I think they knew the will would be in here, but hoped they were also going to find some valuable patents, or a prototype they could cash in on. But this . . .'

'There was only meant to be one key for each box,' Jasper said, disbelieving. He crouched down next to me.

'Do you think he used them?' I asked. 'Or was this a form of insurance?'

Jasper winced. 'I would have liked to say he never used them, but I would also have bet against the existence of these duplicate keys with everything I have and considered it a certainty. What should we do with them?'

'I think . . . that we take the key for Edwin's chest, and we lock the rest of them away again for now. And maybe when this is over we can make sure they don't exist. Maybe the best thing to do will be to throw them into the sea. But we can't know that yet.' I was impassioned, my voice had got too loud. I reined myself back in and brought my voice to a gentler hush. 'We are dealing with a murderer. A murderer who could be one of a number of people on this island, who we are trapped with while the storm cuts us off from the mainland, and who may or may not be finished with whatever it is they're trying to achieve. Are these keys part of the puzzle? We just do not know yet.'

'Right,' Jasper said, pinching the bridge of his nose as if steeling himself for the task ahead.

'But we need to take the key for Edwin's chest. If the arch truly did work the last time he was here, then he might have left some information as to how. Don't you think that would be valuable information to have before trying again? Especially if it's as dangerous as you believe it to be.'

What I didn't say was that I was thrumming with a particular excitement. Surely I was closer than ever to discovering what happened to my father? Edwin *must* have documented his involvement and presence somehow. I pinned all my hopes on there being answers in that chest.

'I know where it is,' Jasper said. 'Edwin's room has been left entirely undisturbed for eighteen years, same as his mother's. Like I said – Mr Cauldwell could be oddly superstitious about certain things.'

'Take me there,' I said, snatching up the key whose bow made the letter E.

The door to Edwin's bedroom had a heartbeat. I felt it the second I touched the doorknob and its unsettling warmth. A faint pulsing, the sense of something living, moving, shifting beneath the surface.

When we entered, we saw that the room had indeed been left unaltered in his absence, but there were very few signs of the sort of person he might have been – no trinkets, or mementos, or the sort of contraptions that adorned the rest of the house. Given his reputation, I had imagined Edwin's room to be full of cogs and springs and prototypes. A jacket had been neatly folded on top of the bureau, so many years ago, but that was the only evidence of somebody having lived in this room, breathed in it. There was no question that Mr Cauldwell had been changed irrevocably by the death of his elder son, but whereas the room his wife had left behind felt like a shrine, with its creepy memento mori, this one lacked any personal touches.

But then Edwin had left the island, left his home, had been gone, researching, for nearly two years. Was it really for research purposes, looking for a watchmaker, finding my father? Or was it more sinister than that? Had he been estranged from his family? In the end, he had returned for his invention, only to die. It didn't seem as though he'd come back here with the intention of staying for any length of time. It seemed like he had just been passing through.

But even if the human residents were indifferent to this room, the house was not. I felt the press of it the moment I entered, a weight on my shoulders.

It didn't take us long to find the chest resting at the foot of the bed, his name carved upon it. Jasper and I crouched beside it, looking at another complex locking system. It took us some time to manipulate the key in the correct manner – much longer than it had with Mr Cauldwell's. But eventually our patience was rewarded with the crunch of the spring-loaded pins in the cylinder. I lifted the lid, my heart rising with anticipation, my hands fast and clumsy in their eagerness.

Inside, there was yet another box. I turned to Jasper, disbelieving, making a hollow approximation of a laugh. It felt like some kind of joke at our expense. I lifted it out, grunting a little at the weight, and placed the box in front of Jasper. His face twisted in confusion. 'Helena,' he said.

The sound of my real name in his mouth made me fizz and crackle and bubble inside. It was a teaspoon of bicarbonate of soda, transforming me into something new. I felt like I'd waited so long to hear him say it.

'Yes?'

Jasper shook his head. 'Helena.'

And the whole room whispered *Helena* back to me.

Jasper turned the box round. There, etched into the wood, was my name. The shock of it struck me through. I began trembling involuntarily.

'What's a box with your name on it doing in Edwin Cauldwell's chest?'

My mouth moved wordlessly. A box with my name on it. The whisper grew. *Helena, Helena, Helena.*

I shook my head as if I could shake the sound from my ears. I reached out for the box, and Jasper placed it in my hands. My name was indeed carved into the wood, and beneath that, fastened where a lock should be, was a small watch face and a dial to enter a date, month, year. This box did not require a key. Running my hands over the polished wooden lid, my fingers fell into more etched grooves along the edge.

For you, and you alone, the moment you changed my world, I read.

The box was made for me. It had remained here for eighteen years, and not one of the people who lived here would have been able to open it . . . But I knew what I had to do. A great shiver of anticipation surged through me. It was strangely energizing, as though I could do *anything* – climb the outside of the building right up to those arches, or run right across the submerged causeway, my feet skipping over the water.

'It can't be,' I said.

My mind was whirring faster, faster, faster. My father had made this box, of that I was certain. But to find it here ... and why had Edwin hidden it for him? I could scarcely find my breath, but the warmth of Jasper's hand against my back steadied me. I twisted the dial so that it would show my date of birth, pulled out the crown of the watch face, and turned it until the hands were pointing to the hour and the minute I was born, and then pushed the crown back into place.

I met Jasper's eye before I opened the lid, and could tell that we both had a sense that this box contained something monumental. I lifted the lid, my heart stuttering and missing a beat, an odd sensation that felt a little like being struck internally.

Inside was a thin, slight, silver key and a folded piece of paper resting on top of a stack of leather journals. The key was simple and traditional – no obvious tricks about it – and tied to it with string was what looked like a sort of receipt with a long number upon it, and the address of a bank in London. I hesitated before unfolding the piece of paper, as if I knew that it would change everything.

It was a marriage licence, dated five months before I was born, between Edwin Cauldwell and my mother, Nancy Timber. Jasper was reading over my shoulder, and his breath was warm against my ear, sweet and honeyed.

'She always called him Ned,' I said, my voice quavering.

23

I thought that answers would bring me peace, but this was cataclysmic. Everything I had ever thought I knew about myself shifted irrevocably. I was a legitimate daughter of the Cauldwell family, the daughter of Edwin Cauldwell.

I sifted through the journals. Page upon page upon page of ideas, of designs, of potential. Inventions my father never had the chance to complete. The watchmaker and the inventor – they were the same person. My father was Edwin Cauldwell. He'd left the island and fallen in love with my mother, magicked me into existence. The heir and the sweet-maker. I could imagine how his family might have reacted, and yet it seemed they didn't know.

But then he'd come back here . . . to tell them? Tell them that he'd married Mam, wanted to elevate her to a respected status that his family would understand and acknowledge, and brought his wedding certificate as proof? Or did he come back for one last piece of unfinished business, before turning his back on them forever? He'd made a box for me, no doubt using the inventing room and resources here, was preparing to gift me his life's work. In the meantime, he'd argued with his brother and returned to his greatest invention, the theory he felt strongest about pursuing.

And he'd died before he'd had the chance to resolve any of it.

Mam had kept this from me all my life, and I couldn't help the seething resentment that lined my veins like thick, sludgy oil. How could she have kept me in the dark about who I really was, even when faced with the debtors' prison? I'd always felt incomplete somehow, as though all the questions I longed to ask had eroded an abyss inside me, a dark and empty cave that I'd never had the courage to venture into.

Now I felt a purpose in the pull I'd felt to Sighfeyre Isle, despite Mam's warnings. This *was* where I was meant to be. The house knew I belonged here. It had been reaching for me all this time, calling me in.

I wanted to talk to Mam so desperately in that moment. Why hadn't she wanted me to know the truth? I knew she blamed the Cauldwell family for my father's death, and I could understand why that might be. Her new husband had left her with their tiny baby to go and break the news to his family, and he never returned. It was clear from her warnings before I came here that she suspected foul play. Was that why she kept the truth about my identity a secret, made us both go by her maiden name? Did she believe I was in danger from the Cauldwells too, if they were to discover who I was?

And I couldn't help but ache at the thought of how different our lives might have been if my father hadn't died.

Would we have lived here, in comfort and ease? Even if we hadn't, even if he'd chosen a life back with us in Durham, at least we'd have been sustained by his love, and his apparent genius for invention.

'Did you know?' Jasper asked. 'Or suspect at least?'

'Not at all,' I said, my face crawling with embarrassment. Should I have? I looked down at my hands, tired hands that looked older than they were. 'What do I do now?'

'I have no idea,' Jasper said. 'What do you want to do? You've got evidence that you're a legitimate heir to Edwin Cauldwell right here. He was married to your mother. You need to find out if he made provision for you both.'

'Provision?'

Jasper pointed at the box. 'This was a gift to you,' he said. 'I can't believe he wouldn't have made plans to provide for you.'

What would that mean? That we had access to wealth, to security? My head was reeling. I thought of the key, attached to the receipt with the long number and the bank address. Would it lead me to a deposit I could claim?

'Even if he did,' I said, 'what would I do then? I just . . . I can't believe that this is true. That I'm a Cauldwell . . . Do you know what it means to be one of them? How am I supposed to prove myself? I'm just . . . just the girl from the sweetshop.'

'You're not "just" anything,' Jasper growled. 'They're not better than you because they had money when you didn't. Look, I know I'm just as creative, just as innovative and more practical even than most of the inventors that used to visit Mr Cauldwell here. I just toil away in secret around the edges, hoping one day I'll do something worthwhile enough to earn some respect.'

'It's different for you,' I argued. 'I've never even had the opportunity to figure out what I might like to do, what I might be good at. I warrant your father gave you a wrench instead of a rattle.'

That made him smile a little, his joyful glow returning. 'But maybe there's no acknowledgement that would make either of us feel worthy. Maybe we don't have to strive to create it. Maybe we're already enough.' I raised an eyebrow at him, and he lifted his hands in surrender. 'I didn't say I live by my own wisdom.'

'Maybe you're right. But it sounds like the sort of thing Mam would say to talk me out of doing something dangerous ... like presenting myself to a supernatural arch, with potentially fatal consequences.'

'Or the sort of thing somebody would say if they could see your determination and bravery, and they felt you mattered, just as you are, without you *proving* anything.'

His gaze was so earnest that I could not meet the warmth of his amber eyes any more. A wave of guilt for having deceived him, even temporarily, washed over me again.

'Stop it,' I muttered, although what I really wanted to say was, *I feel the same way about you. Don't you think we were supposed to meet each other, right now, as all these events collide? That together we could unravel this mystery and achieve everything we've hoped for?*

'I mean it,' he said.

'I know you mean it. That's why it's hard to respond,' I said. 'You're just so ... good ... and optimistic ... and, and ... sincere. And that's why it's so improbable that you would even want to be around me, because I'm cheerless, and distrustful, and not hesitant to be deceitful when I need to be, as you've already discovered.'

He looked crestfallen. 'All right,' he said, his hands raised in surrender. 'You can't see what I see right now. But I *do* want to be around you. And remember that I did before I knew who you really were. Both as Helena Timber ... and Helena Cauldwell.'

I smiled – I couldn't help it. 'So will you help me go back to the arch?'

He flinched at the suggestion. 'The arch? But why? You've found your answers. And now we know why it worked for you. It's because you're Edwin's daughter. There must be something about the arch that means it won't work for anyone else.'

I realized he was probably right. The house had spoken to me and led me to the truth about him. It had worked because the force in this place had *wanted* it to work. My instinct had been right – it had all been connected, all along.

'But you don't have control over yourself when you're up there,' continued Jasper. 'It's dangerous. I can't believe you're even thinking about it.' He was so distressed at the idea that his voice was shaking.

'I need to go back,' I said, but it felt impossible to find a way to articulate why it was so desperately important.

The house was humming in the back of my head, the noise of it throbbing like a headache.

'It's late, and we're both too tired – and too stunned, I'd warrant – to talk about this sensibly now,' Jasper said. 'Will you just . . . sleep on it at least?'

I acquiesced, knowing that not only would I not sleep that night, my mind would not be changed. I had to find a way to convince Jasper to change his, though, to help me go back into the window through time, to uncover who killed Wilbur.

We walked swiftly to our rooms, and I crawled into bed, utterly exhausted. It would have been a relief to succumb to the sleep that Jasper thought would soothe me, and yet my mind refused to stop chasing itself round and round. Like it or not, the knowledge of my true identity filled in a piece that had been missing all my life, answered questions I had desperately needed answering. I couldn't stay angry at Mam for keeping it a secret – she must have been so frightened when my father disappeared and fearful of what it meant for me. She had been trying to keep me safe all this time.

And yet I was always going to arrive at Archfall Manor. It was inevitable.

Uncovering the truth about my life felt like reading by candlelight – the words slightly blurred, partially illuminated, with shadows threatening to obscure them. I'd found out the truth too late to speak to Mr Cauldwell or Wilbur about exactly what happened on my father's last visit to Sighfeyre Isle.

But I did have the arch and the supernatural thread tying me to my father.

If I had known who I was all along, if provision for my future had already been made, if there had been no pull for answers deep within me, then I might never have come to this place. The arch had worked for me after all this time, which surely meant I was destined to go back up there and use that remarkable phenomenon to uncover the murderer on Sighfeyre Isle.

I also knew my work wasn't finished because the whisper kept trying to speak to me all night long. I tossed and I turned in the bed, the sight of Wilbur dying resurfacing over and over again. His hand, grasping so desperately as if trying to cling on to this life, the blood draining out of him, each burst of his heart stealing him closer to death. I was beginning to think that, new-found family member or not, there was no way I would ever leave Archfall Manor with my sanity intact.

It seemed there was something else the house still wanted me to know, still wanted me to do.

24

The following morning, the house was quiet, a tense spiderweb of dread hovering over everything, but while the insides of the house were hushed, the elements outside continued to roar, and the rage of the storm somehow brought even more of its wrath down upon Archfall Manor.

There was nothing to do but keep up the semblance of normality, so I decided to stick to my usual routine, no matter how much my thoughts were in turmoil. I was making my way to Birdie's room when I heard a dreadful crash from the top-floor landing behind me. It was thunderous. My whole body tensed, flinching, bracing, preparing for the worst, as the resounding clatter shook the very walls of the manor. I swung round, and immediately saw the terrible damage.

The landing was covered in debris: parts of the ceiling, large stone blocks. Weak from inattention over the years, the roof had been struggling for days, and we'd grown used to the clattering of slates shooting down, but this . . . This was a fearful catastrophe. The forceful arm of the wind had dislodged bricks from one of the ancient stone arches, it seemed, and under their weight the roof had caved in, yielding to its exhaustion. Like intruders, the cold and the wet burst in through the gaping wound in the ceiling, circling round the chaos, giving me a chill.

Birdie and Nora appeared from their respective rooms to investigate, and I gestured for them to stand back out of the way.

I rushed down the servants' staircase. Despite my apprehensions about being around him, there was only one person who would be able to handle this.

'Where's Gabriel?' I asked Teresa, who was busy polishing silver in the kitchen. The incongruence of the scene disturbed me – what use was it, making every knife and fork sparkle and shine while the manor fell victim to the aggressions of the weather, when its inhabitants died at the hands of a murderer?

'Why?' Her head snapped up quickly. There was a tremor in her voice. 'What's wrong? What's happened now?'

'One of the arches has come down. It's crashed through the ceiling on the top-floor landing. Nobody's hurt but . . . it's all open to the elements, and there's stone and debris everywhere.'

Teresa let out the breath she was holding. 'I thought . . . I thought it was going to be . . .' She'd reacted so intensely because she thought I had been about to tell her of another death.

'I'm sorry. I didn't mean to frighten you,' I said with a note of apology.

'No, no, it's fine. I'm just rather tightly wound. Gabriel and Jasper are both in the drawing room, trying to clear up another great mess. A tree came down, smashed through the window.'

Despite the warning, the sight of the tree still shocked me. It sprawled through the centre of the drawing room like a dead body, surrounded by shards of glass. The wounded window gaped and the freezing outside air rushed in.

When I told them about the state of the landing, the pair of them followed me back upstairs. Gabriel insisted on heading up to the tower immediately to see what he could do to stop the damage from increasing, despite Jasper's protestations to wait for the calm we knew was coming, would be with us shortly. As the pair of them argued on the top-floor landing, Birdie peered down the corridor, her darting eyes surveying the damage of the caved-in roof.

'Go round,' I told her. 'Take the staff staircase, and I'll meet you in the kitchen.' It seemed the best place to keep her out of harm's way, and, as Mrs Temple had requested, to keep her distracted.

When we reunited, taking our separate pathways round the house, Birdie had a nervousness about her, the worries bubbling up beneath her skin causing her legs to twitch and tremble when she sat down.

'What's happening to the house? Will we have to go back to London?' she asked.

I didn't know how to answer her. The future was uncertain for us all. Each one of us would be thrown on to a route far different to what we'd ever anticipated. Would that involve Mrs Temple taking her children back to

London? Would she find her ancestral home too haunting from now on? Or would the financial freedom and independence she would no doubt be granted be everything she'd hoped for? It all depended on how the authorities interpreted the situation – I didn't think she was guilty of murdering Mr Cauldwell and Wilbur, but perhaps the police would find it a convenient way to neatly tie up their investigations into the deaths of her husbands too.

And what would happen when I revealed to them my true identity?

'Your mother will decide on the best way forward for your family when this is all over,' I told Birdie.

'And you . . . will you leave us?'

She was welling up with tears, angrily blinking as if she were furious at herself for showing me she cared. The roundness of her face, the way her feet didn't touch the floor from the stool, these little details reminded me of how young she still was, desperate for reassurance.

I'd been working hard to build the foundations we needed for her tutoring, against her rebellion and determination to unsettle and wrong-foot me. My persistence was finally paying off. And yet I couldn't make the promises she wanted to hear. I would not be her governess forever. I was something else to her instead – we were cousins; we were family. That counted for something, and however the debris settled I wouldn't let her fall.

'Birdie, you don't need to be worried about what happens next.'

'But what if the house falls down? It makes such awful noises in the night, and sometimes I feel as if . . .' She brought her hand to her head as though it were aching. I watched her carefully as she folded the rest of her sentence back into her mouth.

'You feel as if . . . ?' I willed her to continue, but Birdie refused to elaborate, picking at the edges of her fingernails instead.

'Never mind. I just have nightmares. I don't want to talk about it.'

The house – did it press and push at her, the way it did at me? Did she worry that she was losing her mind, the way I had? Had anyone warned her before she came, told her that this place affected its inhabitants, leaned on them and imbued their creations with its power? When she'd seen the impossible magic entwined in the inventions within its walls, she'd accepted them willingly with a childish naïvety.

'This house . . . has anyone ever talked to you about it? About the way it's different?'

She wrinkled her nose. 'I don't know what you mean. And I don't believe in servants' superstition.'

I couldn't resist a small smile. Here was the supercilious Birdie I knew. In any case, it wasn't my place to tell her the truth – or at least the truth as I understood it – about her family and Archfall Manor. Not here and not now.

'It's not going to collapse about our ears. With an old house like this, there are always bound to be weaknesses, places where the structure is vulnerable, that's all. And the storm raging round us is fierce.'

Birdie listened and looked at me with trusting eyes, momentarily soothed. 'The house is just like those of us inside it then.'

I managed to catch Jasper alone for a moment in the drawing room as he was gathering up pieces of glass, collecting them in a large towel.

'I have to go back into the arch,' I said, closing the door behind me. He turned and let out a weary sigh. He looked depleted, his shoulders heavy.

'I was hoping you wouldn't say that. Please, Helena. It's utter chaos up there. There's a huge structural weakness on the side where that arch came down this morning.'

'Not the arch we need.'

'No, but . . .'

I needed to make him understand. 'I know you believe in the supernatural energy that moves through this place. Well, I feel as though I hear it. It's been reaching for me, nudging me forward, all this time. The house . . . it's not finished with me yet.'

My chest began to loosen a little, confessing this truth. I knew I could speak freely with Jasper.

'I'm a Cauldwell, and if I'm going to try to claim anything my father might have wanted for me, then I'll have to reveal who I am. But somebody has been murdering the heirs to this family's legacy. I'm not safe.'

'You're not safe,' Jasper echoed. He pressed his lips together.

'And I won't be until we know who the murderer is.

The last time I was at the arch, I saw what happened to Mr Cauldwell. What if there's more it can show me?'

'But it's dangerous, and it's the reason your father died. You didn't have control of yourself last time. You looked possessed moving towards it. *That's* what's not safe.' His voice was low and urgent.

'It would be worse if you didn't help me,' I said.

He looked wounded. 'Of course I'll help you.' He brushed a wayward curl of hair behind my ear, and I grabbed hold of his hand and pressed it to my cheek.

'You've utterly upended everything since you got here,' he said, his voice rumbling like the storm outside.

'I have to do this,' I said. 'I have a feeling I was always meant to.'

He stroked my cheek with his thumb.

'I'll do whatever I can,' he said. When he smiled, it didn't quite reach his eyes, even as his dimples creased. 'We'll tie a rope round your waist. I'll hold on.'

I trusted him. And more powerfully than that I *wanted* him. The immediate attraction I'd felt when I first saw him had been building, like a wave reaching its crescendo, inevitable, and sweeping me away. If heading up to the arches was so dangerous, then what was the use of being coy when just being near Jasper made it feel as though my insides were effervescent?

'Before . . . before we go . . . will you kiss me?'

There was a swoop of anticipation sliding through me as I said it. Before I went up to the arch again, before I took the risk, I wanted to know the feeling of his lips on mine.

His eyes brightened, and the dimples deepened as he smiled. He blew out a stream of air, looked up at the ceiling and then met my gaze. 'You want me to be completely broken if it goes dreadfully wrong up there? Because that's already on the cards, I can assure you.'

Every part of me felt alive, the nerves mingling with the anticipation. My hands were on his arms, firm and strong beneath my fingers, and he stepped closer, one hand still on my face and the other on my waist, and my eyes closed instinctively as he dipped down and his lips met mine.

Even as the freezing cold blew round us from the open window, a current of warmth flowed through me. I sank into him, and I don't know what I thought it would be like, but it was so natural, so easy to follow the movements of his mouth, my head spinning. All I could think about was the way it felt like I was melting, that I was made of fizzes and crackles, whisked up and transformed, as though sugar crystals were sparkling beneath my skin.

25

This time, we were prepared, gathering resources from the workshop first. Jasper took a gas lamp and a heavy coil of rope that wrapped round his arm like a python. After everyone was in bed, we ascended to the arch, up those twisting, uneven stone steps, and the feel of the pull began, weak at first and then stronger. It was as though a fish hook had speared me, and I was being reeled in.

At the very top, Jasper forced the door open against the blustering wind that seemed to want to keep it closed. I tried not to take this as an omen, a warning to stay away from the weather itself. The sky was filled with pinprick stars watching us, peering round the voluminous clouds.

'Here we go,' I said, bracing myself against the spattering rain that was almost falling sideways with the power of the wind. Jasper got straight to business unravelling the rope.

'Are you sure you want to do this?' he asked again, and, when I firmly nodded, he fastened the rope into a loop. 'Arms up,' he said, and I lifted them for him to guide the loop of rope over my head, and it was too much like the way I would stand if he were slipping off my dress. Then his hands were on my waist, tightening the rope, and I almost couldn't bear the way I felt drawn to him.

He looked in my eyes, and I was struck by this feeling, as though he'd reached into the centre of me and sparked an unsatisfied longing. The rain poured around us, but I could barely feel the way it drenched me because he was close, and he smelled like he'd taken another toffee from the tin, and I wanted to be closer.

'I won't let go,' Jasper said, backing away with the end of the rope in his hands. I tried to breathe more slowly and compose myself. He looped the rope round his wrist to tighten his grip.

'What if nothing happens?' I said, suddenly feeling self-conscious. I looked up at the dark and rumbling sky. 'What if the lightning doesn't strike again?'

'It didn't work because of the lightning,' Jasper said gently. 'It worked because of you.'

I took a deep breath. I'd always wanted to feel as though there were something more to my destiny, and now it seemed I hadn't been wrong. I looked at Jasper, so tall and strong and devastatingly captivating to me, and I trusted him. He wouldn't let me fall. He met my eyes, and my insides twisted with yearning.

'I understand you feel you have to do this, but it frightens me.'

'It frightens me too,' I admitted. When we kissed again, it was full of the desperation of a goodbye, of something unfinished.

But as much as I felt a pull towards Jasper, from the moment I stepped on to the tower roof, the tugging sensation back to the arches was stronger. I separated from him before I would have wanted to otherwise, and moving towards the arch all I could think about was Wilbur and the way he died in my arms. He had been my uncle, and neither of us had known it. I felt certain that it was Gabriel who had killed him. It was the only thing that made sense to me – the struggle for power between the pair of them, the angry words they had exchanged before Wilbur died.

'Show me,' I whispered to the house.

It did not feel voluntary, the wrenching sensation dragging me forward. A strange humming filled my ears. Walking towards the arch, I was doubtful it would work again, but incredibly, astoundingly, impossibly, it did.

The arch was no longer an arch, but a portal, with the same ethereal surface as before, shadows shifting beneath the intangible layer. The surface quivered as though it were trembling with a blend of anticipation and terror, just like me. The sky was strange, and I had a sense that it might fall down on top of me, that there was no way the multitudinous stars above us should be able to remain suspended where they were when everything else was turned upside down.

I touched the rope around my waist, the anchor that kept me in this moment and not the one that waited ahead for me, although I felt its pull. I was desperate to hold on to myself, to choose, consciously, every single movement I made, but my steps became dreamlike and I began to lose any sense of the tower, of Jasper, of the wind and the rain.

I peered deep into the scene unfolding beneath the incorporeal window into another time.

The argument between Wilbur and Gabriel. Those clenched fists, clenched jaws. But the moment was frozen, a still image.

I was close to the surface. It took a staggering effort to plant my feet on the ground and stop myself being swept into the scene ahead of me like a piece of flotsam or jetsam caught on the tide. I would not move. I was not driftwood. I gritted my teeth, my feet aching with the urge to press onwards.

Reaching forward, I let my fingers skim the surface that had formed over the arch instead. It was an odd viscous texture, an awful sludge tough to move through when I pressed it. But then, most startlingly, my hand passed through. Cool air hit it on the other side. I looked down at my feet – would they pass through too? Would I land in the scene ahead of me, in this other moment in Archfall Manor? Or was it all just a figment of my imagination, a vision and nothing more tangible, that – given the opportunity – would send me plunging to my death over the side of the tower? It was as if I were a ship that had been seized by mutineers, an insurgent force taking control of my body.

Instinctively, I took a deep breath and screwed my eyes tightly shut, as though immersing myself underwater. I pushed my face into the surface, felt it ripple and undulate against my nose, my cheeks, my lips, an unbearable ooze. Through sheer effort of will, my lungs beginning to scream out from the lack of fresh air, I continued to press. It was like passing through a deep, gelatinous syrup, so much like plunging head first into the contents of my pan in the sweetshop kitchen that it felt as though my skin should be burning.

Something broke across my face. Now the still image was alive, and I could hear the detail of their argument.

'With all due respect,' Gabriel was saying in a tone that communicated he believed none was due to Wilbur at all, 'I remain the head of maintenance in this house beyond the passing of Mr Cauldwell, and it is my responsibility to take care of his workshops, his inventions and his materials, Mr Wilbur. I –'

Wilbur interrupted, sharply reprimanding Gabriel. 'Do not call me that.'

'Very well, Mr Cauldwell,' Gabriel said evenly. 'But my opposition remains and so does my guardianship over the late Mr Cauldwell's work until I have been informed of his express instructions.'

Wilbur sneered. 'No. No, you will not be. Because there is no last will and testament. The only existing copy was swallowed up by that wave you so narrowly avoided. The copy held by Mr Harris the solicitor is submerged at the bottom of the sea with the solicitor himself.'

He was lying, bluffing, relying on the impenetrability of Mr Cauldwell's chest, the lost key. Whatever the will actually stated was irrelevant if no one could get to it. Nobody would dare dispute Wilbur's claim to his own father's wealth and property; nobody would uphold Gabriel's aspirations.

'Whatever you thought my father was going to gift you

is gone, long gone, so you can forget about it. Everything in this household is mine by rights and you ... you are dismissed with immediate effect. You and your family will leave this place the next time the causeway is viable.'

He might as well have stuck a knife into Gabriel and twisted it round.

'I'll make sure you get what's due to you,' Gabriel said in a threatening growl.

I was pulled back with all the force of genuine terror, yanked out of the moment by the rope round my waist and the panicked strength that only arises in an emergency. The sudden tug snatched all the air out of me as I returned to the present, gasping for breath like a fish hooked out of the river. A glance at the arch showed me the surface had dissipated. The disruption, like last time, had stolen the vision away. The tower around me came into focus, Jasper at my side, his expression horrified. It frightened me.

'Helena! Are you – are you all right? The parts of you that went inside ... they disappeared,' Jasper croaked. 'And now ... now ...'

I looked down at my hand, and it was the shape of a hand still, but all made of stardust, twinkling, vaporous and no longer mine. My hands, my chest, my neck and head – they had all been submerged.

My scream was internal. The sound wouldn't come out of my mouth; it was stuck somewhere inside me, reverberating around without escape. The skin and muscle and sinew of my hand had been replaced with shifting smoke, ghostly and inhuman. My face ... I couldn't bear the thought of looking in a mirror or even touching my cheek in case it was the same. The arch had transformed me.

'H-h-help . . .' I faltered when I tried to speak. I fell to my knees, feeling like a crumpled-up piece of paper.

'What can I do?' cried Jasper.

'Help . . . me . . . down,' I said, every word an effort.

I needed him to get me away from the arch. The physical proximity seemed to make it worse, the time I spent in the arch increasing how compelling it felt to return. And this time the surface had not vanished. It flickered in the corner of my eye, as if to tempt me back inside.

Jasper wrapped my arm round his neck, and I gripped on, as if my life depended upon it, as if I were drowning out at sea and he'd swum to my rescue. He scooped up the rest of me, and as he held me the shifting vapours solidified. My skin trembled as it re-formed, knitting back together and wrapping me back inside the safety of my body, connected to the physical world once more. I thought I might be sick as I became encased within myself again.

'I've got you,' he said, and I could feel the rumble of his voice where my head rested against his chest.

My vision went black around the edges, and I felt as if I were walking into a dark tunnel. Although I wanted to hold on, I knew that I was going, and as the beat of my heart roared in my ears I grabbed hold of Jasper, gripped his shirt tight in my fist as my mind whirled, spinning circles and seeing stars.

26

Jasper carried me back to my room and laid me on the bed. I could not stop shivering, the cold so deep in the marrow of my bones that it felt like it would never shift, that I would never warm through again. Jasper's eyes were full of a tenderness that made it hard to look at him. I was broken somewhere inside me, as if I had been cracked open and made weak. How could I ever be whole again when there remained an insidious call to head back up the stairs, to become lost through the arch?

'Stay with me,' I said. 'Please.'

Jasper didn't hesitate. He lay down next to me, folded his body round mine, his legs tucked up underneath mine, one arm beneath my head and the other across me, our fingers intertwined. His breath was hot against the back of my neck, and I willed that heat to spread throughout the rest of me. I don't know how long we stayed there, but the longer we did, the more human I felt.

When I looked at myself, and the flesh of my skin appeared fully returned, I started to cry, great heaving sobs. It was terror and relief mingling together.

'I feel empty,' I said. Not physically. In a more complicated way than that, as though something were missing, as though I were forgetting something, as though I left something behind when I was pulled back out of the arch.

'You looked like you were made of magic,' he said. He stared at me, his face filled with awe. I couldn't stand the heat of his gaze.

'Magic,' I repeated, feeling numb to it all.

It had been horrifying, looking down and seeing myself transformed. It didn't feel like magic, or at least not the magic of fairy godmothers bestowing wishes upon princesses. No, it felt more like being cursed, like discovering there was something awful and wrong crawling just under the surface. Was this the truth of my father's legacy rippling unseen beneath my skin? The arch had only ever worked for him, and worked for me, and was that a gift or a curse?

'You reached your hand out and it vanished,' Jasper said. 'It was gone – your arm just started at the wrist . . . And then, when you leaned forward, your face disappeared too, and you were this headless spectre standing there. And when you went to walk inside fully, I just . . .'

'I went to walk inside?'

I hadn't been aware of that. It must have been utterly involuntary. What would have happened to me if I had? Would Jasper still have been able to pull me back?

'I thought . . . I pulled you back because I thought you'd disappear entirely if you went right in, but I was so frightened. I didn't know if the bits of you that were gone would come back.'

'I did go inside a bit, I think.' I tried to explain to him what the arch looked like when it transformed, and it sounded like a fairy tale told to children, like a portal to another land created by a supernatural being. 'From the outside, the scene is suspended in time, still. It is just a moment. When I immersed myself, though, time began to move in there. I could *hear*. I think . . . I think that's what happened to my father. I think he went inside a moment.'

'A moment?'

'That's how I think of them, the visions in the archway. They're moments in time. They're not just still images, they unfold as though time were as easy to stop and start as a pocket watch . . . And I just wonder if the reason they never found a body to bury was because my father didn't plunge over the edge. He went inside a moment, like I did.'

'What . . . what would that do to him?'

'I really can't be sure. I think it could go one of three ways. He might have joined the moment in time he saw and been able to continue living inside it . . . like starting off another set of events in another timeline, so here he was just . . . missing. Or maybe he simply disintegrated. Turned into stardust and smoke. Or – and this is what I think I believe – maybe it's like being a ghost, and he got trapped inside and couldn't cross back.'

I didn't tell Jasper about the whispering murmur that

had guided me since I first arrived at Archfall Manor, and I didn't tell him how it felt as though a force of life were pulsing through the walls, like a soul lost or trapped within the boundaries of the house itself.

'I think . . . I think my father might still be inside there. I think it's all connected. There's a reason this is happening now.'

'Did you see him?' Jasper asked, and I shook my head.

'No, no, this is just a theory. You like theories, remember?'

I tried to whisk up some of the lightness between us again. All of the ease we'd sunk into had evaporated. Was it the kiss? Or the horror of what he'd seen rippling beneath my skin? Both had shifted the equilibrium between us, sent us off balance as though we were training to walk on tightropes in a circus and had attempted our first performance off the ground.

'Where did you go? *When* did you go?'

I scrunched my eyes closed because I didn't want to remember, didn't want to tell him. And yet I had to. I was certain that it was Gabriel who was responsible for the horrors that had unfolded at Archfall Manor. A grasping greed had overtaken him, turned him into a monster willing to kill to take what he believed he was owed.

'The argument between your father and Wilbur,' I said, relieved to be facing away from Jasper because his gentle eyes would have made it impossible to utter.

I felt him freeze, holding his breath for what I was about to say next, and a prickling sensation crawled all across my arms and chest as if my very skin were distressed.

'Wilbur dismissed your father. He was going to send your family away from the island when the storm lifted.'

'What?' Jasper sat up, pulled away from me to sit on the edge of the bed.

'Your father was threatening to hold on to the work he had done with Mr Cauldwell. But Wilbur was adamant that he wouldn't get to keep any of it, that whatever your father thought he was entitled to was lost when the lawyer, and the will, was swallowed by the sea. I think that *is* what Wilbur and Caroline were looking for in Mr Cauldwell's study after all – a copy of his will.'

Jasper went very quiet, his lips pressed together as he thought.

I continued carefully, sitting up to join him on the edge of the bed. 'Your father . . . he said he'd make sure Wilbur got what he was due. I think . . . I think he's behind the murders, Jasper. I'm sorry.'

'You think?' he asked, his eyes narrowing. 'Or you *know*? You deduced this from an overheard conversation, or you saw incontrovertible evidence?'

'He was threatening him.'

It was Gabriel. I was sure of it. He believed he was due to inherit from Mr Cauldwell, and he couldn't wait any longer to take ownership of their work together. But after he'd killed Mr Cauldwell, the solicitor had drowned and the will had been lost. Wilbur had been willing to exploit that, had been about to destroy everything Gabriel had worked for. He'd lost his life as a result of that display of dominance.

'I'm telling you,' Jasper said, beginning to sound exasperated and desperate, 'my pa isn't capable of it. He might be hot-tempered, but he's not a murderer. And certainly not the sort of person who would plan the calculated murder of one of his oldest friends.'

'But he and Mr Cauldwell weren't friends, were they? Mr Cauldwell was his boss.'

'Don't say it,' Jasper said, his voice turning icy. 'Don't tell me my pa is "just staff", because you're wrong. You haven't been here all this time. You think you know, but you don't.' He clung to the vision of his pa.

'Jasper, I know this is hard – but who else had both the skills and the opportunity to create those contraptions, and a motive to be rid of Mr Cauldwell and Wilbur?' I asked, but my words fell into the uncomfortable silence between us. A case could be made to have both murders blamed on Mrs Temple, because she was seeking security for her family, but there was no possibility she could have come up with those inventions.

Jasper stood up and walked away from me, breathing heavily. His back was half lit by the lamp, the other half in shadow. 'I can't convince you,' he said, 'but I refuse to listen to this any more.' He left the room with purposeful strides, but still closed the door gently.

A well of sorrow opened up within me. My stomach churned. There was a part of me that wanted to be wrong, for Jasper's sake. But there was a much larger part that knew I was right, that erupted with pride at having unravelled the mysteries of Sighfeyre Isle – the questions about my father, the identity of the murderer of the Cauldwell line. I had pieced it all together. My experience through the arch was an other-worldly encounter, but the murders were a very human crime.

Now all I had to do was stay alive.

27

I was beginning to turn my mind towards sleep – the hour was so late. My thoughts were preoccupied, not really in the room at all, when a brisk knock at my door startled me. My heart panicked and sought an escape route out of my mouth, or so it felt, and any calm thoughts seemed foolish now because one of the people under the roof of Archfall Manor was very dangerous indeed, and I had no idea who waited outside my room.

I could not steel myself to open the door so I stood behind it, breathing heavily and listening. A silly thing to do; this would not tell me who the person outside was or what business they had with me at such a frightful hour.

'I know you're in there,' said a female voice. With that sharp, demanding tone, I matched the voice immediately to its owner – Nora. I opened the door with relief.

'Come in,' I said, glancing round the corridor and ushering her in.

'You're rather skittish,' she said, folding her arms across her chest. 'Anyone would think you felt you had something to be frightened of. But really – what would the murderer want with a governess like you?'

She said it all with a smile, as though she were teasing me, as though we were friends. Clearly, Nora's brand of friendship came with a dash of cruelty. I flushed. Of course she didn't understand why I was so petrified. Why would I be of interest to anyone in this house, where a legacy was being wrestled over? She sat on the edge of my bed, kicked her shoes off.

'Why are you here so late?' I asked.

'Who do you think is responsible?' Nora asked, ignoring my question with a ghoulish expression that reminded me of her little sister poring over the anatomy guide. 'When you think of everyone in this house, who could be capable of murder?'

I gave a weary sigh. 'I truly couldn't say. I'm tired. It's all been so hideous.'

'I know you have a theory,' she said. 'I've been listening this evening.' She reached into her pocket and casually pulled out a tiny tube.

My mouth went dry, and my skin chilled with fear. 'You . . . you've been listening?' I started to rake through my memory for everything that had passed between Jasper and me since we'd returned to my room. What exactly had we said? 'That's not fair. You can't just go eavesdropping at people's doors.'

'Can't I?' Nora pulled her legs up beneath her. 'Isn't that exactly what you've been doing these last few days?'

I blushed – I could hardly deny it.

Nora gave a satisfied smile and carried on. 'So . . . as I understand it, Gabriel Wright believes he was willed something by my grandfather. And he didn't want to wait for it any longer.'

I hadn't wanted anyone else to know my suspicions – not least because, if Gabriel thought I suspected him, it might draw his attention to me in a terrible way.

'But my uncle intended to obfuscate my grandfather's wishes so he could keep everything for himself. He threatened Gabriel, dismissed him and his family from their employment here. So Gabriel murdered him too . . .'

Wearily, sorrowfully, I nodded. 'Did you hear everything I said to Jasper tonight?' I asked.

The thought of her listening to the private confession of our feelings about one another made me feel vaguely nauseous. But more than that I needed to ascertain if she'd heard me talk about the arch, if she was now aware that I'd seen glimpses through time, knew things I should never have known.

She folded her arms, an inscrutable expression sliding across her features. 'Oh yes. Everything. Including about the arch, if that's what you're wondering.'

My mouth went dry as I spoke, and there was a quiver in my voice. 'That's what I feared.'

Nora smiled, her incisors flashing. 'Why would it be fear? All I've ever tried to do is welcome you here. Haven't you felt welcomed by me?'

'I have,' I said. 'But . . . it sounds so impossible, and I can't prove it. You believe me? You don't think me mad?'

'This is not a house where we are frightened by impossible things,' she said, breathless and excitable. 'And somehow you've managed to unlock something incredible.'

'Incredible and dangerous. It did something strange to me ... I think it did something strange to Edwin too. I think he's trapped inside there. Broken apart somehow.'

'Possibly. But that's not all you think about Edwin, is it ... Helena?' Nora said.

She pressed her lips together. Her eyes challenged me, and that was when I realized she'd used my *real* name. A cool horror swept through my body, but there was no opportunity to compose myself. I recalled what I'd said ... She'd heard my theory about Edwin entering a moment in time, she'd heard me say that there was no body to find, and she'd worked out who I meant.

Nora went on, not waiting for my reply. 'Clearly, you came here under false pretences, pretending to be a governess. So who are you really?' She fixed me with a stare. My cheeks went hot at the accusation. Regardless of who I knew myself to be now, I had been lying from the moment I came to Archfall Manor, and she knew it.

'My name is Helena Timber,' I said. 'And I did use a false reference to come here, but I didn't know then that Edwin was my father. I'd always been told that my father died when I was a baby, travelling to this island. My mother said he was a watchmaker, and I thought he had been brought by Edwin to work on his invention and his theory of time. I never imagined they were ... that he was ...' My breath was getting hard to catch, and I stumbled over my words. She watched me, with the appearance of a surgeon eager to begin a dissection.

'Helena *Timber*.' Nora sounded out the syllables of my name. 'Not Cauldwell. So even if Edwin was your father, and I'm not entirely convinced of that, you're not an heir of the family. You're not legitimate,' she scoffed.

I bristled at the judgement laced through her words, at the implication that I was worth less somehow. And I clutched tight to my chest the knowledge that she was wrong, that she didn't know my parents were married. That Mam had chosen to call me Timber as I grew meant nothing – she was frightened of the Cauldwells, had wanted to hide the truth of my identity. One day I hoped to have the chance to talk to her about it all, but in the meantime it was a good thing that Nora didn't have the full facts. The fewer people who knew the truth about my identity, the safer I was. My identity was an added complication in a series of murders motivated by legacy and inheritance.

'I must admit that is a relief,' I said. Nora looked at me coolly.

'You mean you wouldn't want to be a part of this family?'

'I should not feel safe if I were a potential heir to any Cauldwell legacy right now.'

'You're right,' Nora said with a sharp nod. 'But this news, Helena, it still makes you family. It makes you our blood.'

The image of Wilbur's blood pooling on the floor rushed back. How much of me was Cauldwell inside? What sort of life might I have been destined for if my father had not disappeared? The questions were almost painful. Life in Archfall Manor might have been bestowed with the kind of luxury I could have only dreamed of when I sank exhausted into sleep at the end of a long day working in the shop, but it didn't make any of them happy. Every member of the Cauldwell family was miserable and tormented in their own way. By comparison, I often found an easy joy in the simplest moments making sweets side by side with Mam, despite the hard work – tasting from her spoon, finding satisfaction in creating a new tool, a good day of sales meaning a chunk of meat braised over the fire.

What did it truly mean for me to be a legitimate heir to the Cauldwell name? In the light of the murders and the turmoil of the line of inheritance, it was fear that accumulated, resting on me like falling snow. My potential claim to my father's portion of the estate would be the last thing anyone would want to hear about, and would even put my life in danger. Easier to remove me completely than to deal with me. A shudder went down my spine, each bone struck through with reverberations of dread.

Mrs Temple had said she was not afraid of the murderer, but was that because she was not afraid to die, or because she believed that Gabriel Wright was no threat to her? Perhaps they already had an agreement, a deal, that he would receive the things he believed he was owed, and her family would take the rest ... What would it mean to place me in the middle of their plans for the division of the inheritance?

Jasper thought my father would have made provision for me – it could be completely life-changing, depending on what had been recorded before his death . . . I had arrived at Archfall Manor desperate to change my fortune, and a new life might be within my grasp so long as I managed to keep my secret and stay alive.

Nora broke my thoughts with a cheerful conjecture. 'Do you know, I rather think my grandfather would have been delighted to know about you. Especially given your affinity with the power of this island. The way it blends with innovation, creating such remarkable things – that was what set him alight. He was a remarkable man.'

'And yet he never let you fulfil your interest in his work. I think you're being a bit optimistic about how he would have reacted to his son having a hidden child.'

It was my turn to be scathing, and I could see what pleasure Nora found in being cruel. When her face dropped, I felt powerful.

'Perhaps you're right,' she said. She mulled it over a little. 'At the very least I know Wilbur would not have welcomed you. The rivalry between the brothers ran deep. And we both know of another person who wouldn't appreciate the added complication right now.' Nora looked thoughtful, fixing me with an intense focus. 'I think it best if we keep your secret between us until Gabriel Wright is safely dealt with, don't you?'

She said his name like it was a curse.

'Please, Nora,' I said, 'you mustn't tell anyone until the island is reconnected to the mainland, until we're all safe from him.'

We agreed not to confront him, to lie low until the

storm subsided, at which time a full police investigation could begin and we could present Gabriel as a suspect, confirm his motives, his capacity for invention, and sow suspicion so the police could unravel a physical trail of evidence. In the meantime, he needed to believe that none of us posed a threat to the things he wished to lay claim to.

Then, it seemed, Nora couldn't resist one final act of teasing cruelty. 'When this is all over, maybe you'll be able to mend things with Jasper,' she said. 'The pair of you are very sweet. Although I'm sure Molly will be very disappointed when it comes to light.'

I flushed at the thought of Nora eavesdropping on the moments we thought were private. If Nora wanted me to press her on this, wanted me to ask more, I ensured she was left wanting, although it did make me bristle just a little.

'I really must get some sleep.' Even saying it, a yawn crept out of my mouth.

'You must.' Nora placed both of her hands on my shoulders, surprising me with the firmness of her grip. 'Just remember: even if you're not an heir, we are family. I'll keep your secret for now, but we are irrevocably bound. We won't be like Edwin and Wilbur. We'll be something new. Together.' She was almost patronizing in her reassurance. She pressed her cheek against mine with a final whispered goodnight and then left.

Family. We were family. It was an incredible thing . . . So why did it feel so hollow?

28

The following day, Nora wanted to join in with Birdie's lessons after breakfast. I sensed that she felt we were safer together, that to move through the house in each other's company made us less vulnerable should Gabriel decide his murderous inclinations were not complete.

Birdie had requested we spend the morning in the library, and we'd not long been settled when we saw Gabriel march past the open door, striding down the corridor towards the reading room, where Mrs Temple had been headed after breakfast.

Nora and I exchanged a glance. It was unusual for him to be in this part of the house at the best of times, let alone when he had been tasked with clearing the wreckage and rubble of the collapsed roof. Nora slipped her hand inside the pocket of her dress and pulled out the small listening device. I nodded swiftly.

'Birdie, I want you to read the rest of this chapter independently,' I said. 'Your sister and I . . . we'll be right back.'

She seemed to pick up on the tone of my instruction and

did not argue. We shut the door behind us. If I needed to, I'd make a barricade with my own body before I let Gabriel get to Birdie, though I doubted he would dare to try and hurt any one of us with his own hands. His methods so far had been clever, but also cowardly.

Gabriel had closed the door to the reading room. Under any other circumstances, it would not have been proper for him to be behind a closed door with the lady of the house, but in that moment my fear was for Caroline's life far more than her reputation, a great swelling fear.

Gabriel's voice reverberated out through the door. 'Where does it end?' he roared. 'You know and I know what's been done here. Do you truly believe it's over?'

There was a mumbling in response. Nora took out her listening device and pressed it against the door, leaning in so that she could hear her mother's reply. She frowned in concentration.

When Gabriel spoke again, the parts that reached me were just a rumbling through the door. Whatever he said, however, it was something that made Nora freeze, as if she'd had ice-cold water poured over the top of her head. It was a look I'd seen come over her before – a hardening of her insides, a detachment.

Nora listened. Then she quickly gestured for me to move, move away, move quickly.

I scrambled back as Gabriel bitterly exclaimed, 'Well then, you are more of a fool than I took you for. I urge you to reconsider.'

Nora and I slipped into the room next door, pressing

ourselves up against the wall just in time to see through the crack in the door that Gabriel Wright was stalking away down the corridor, pausing only to slam an angry hand against the wall, his aggression spilling over.

'What were they saying?' I asked Nora, desperate to understand the missing pieces of the exchange.

'He's blackmailing her,' Nora said. 'If she doesn't give him everything he's asking for from the estate, he's going to frame her for the murders.'

'Frame her?'

'He's got all the evidence hidden away. He said that given what happened to my stepfathers it'll be easy. He said she's got a day to make her decision . . . or . . .' She bit her lip.

'I dread to think,' I said, and I did.

But I still had no idea how terrible things were about to become.

At lunchtime, Mrs Temple had come to visit Birdie and me in the schoolroom, and the three of us were sitting around the table when Nora burst in, breathing heavily. Her clothes were wet with splatters of rain, her hair tousled and her eyes wild.

'Nora!' cried Mrs Temple. 'Good gracious! What have you been doing? Where have you been?'

But Nora seemed almost frenzied. 'He's dead,' she said, gasping for breath, her eyes filled with tears.

My heartbeat thundered away in my chest. 'He' could only mean one of two people now – and every part of me weakened. *Please, not Jasper.*

Birdie gasped, and Mrs Temple stood so quickly that her chair fell back with a great clatter. She was at Nora's side in seconds, guiding her to a chair. 'Who is dead? What do you mean?'

'Gabriel! He was ransacking the inventing room, searching for something, and then he marched up to the tower to interfere with that contraption built into the arches up there. I know I shouldn't have followed him, but I did. I told him to stop, that none of it belonged to him. And then he grabbed me, and he dragged me to the edge. He . . . he confessed to everything. He sounded mad!' She dissolved into sobs.

Mrs Temple brushed the hair out of her daughter's face and wiped her tears. 'Oh, Nora.'

'But listen, Mother – it's all right. He can't hurt us now,' Nora said, and the words sounded as if she had to force them out. 'I . . . I pushed him. He lost his grip on me right as we got to the edge of the house, and I didn't think. I just reached out, and . . .'

'Pushed him? From the tower?' Mrs Temple flinched back from her daughter. 'So . . . he's really dead?'

'Yes! I saw him die. It's over. It's over now,' Nora said. She reached out for her mother, and Mrs Temple gathered her to her chest, before reaching for Birdie too, who ran tearfully to join the embrace.

So it was finished. Gabriel Wright was dead. He had done terrible things, and he had met a terrible end. I didn't need to be frightened any more. The shadow he cast over the island and our entrapment had been lifted, and hopefully the storm would soon lift too. I was desperately sorry for what this would mean for Jasper. But I couldn't stop the relieved smile from creeping on to my face. We were safe – it was over.

'It's done then? Does that mean we'll stay here forever?' Birdie asked.

Mrs Temple shushed Birdie, pushed her face deeper into her shoulder to make her stop talking, and a tiny suspicion raised itself inside me like a baby bird peeking its beak out of the nest.

Birdie was precocious – I'd known that since I'd met her – but there was something in the way she'd spoken just then that sounded odd. It made it seem as though all of this were something she'd been hoping for. The day before, she'd seemed so concerned that she'd have to return to London.

Mrs Temple looked me straight in the eye. 'Remember what you heard here,' she said. 'I would imagine the authorities will want to talk to you when they come to the island. My daughter acted in self-defence to save her life from that awful man who betrayed our trust and murdered members of our family.'

'Yes,' I said, and I felt a warning in her words. 'Of course.'

Mrs Temple pulled back from her girls and began smoothing Nora's hair again. 'Oh, Nora,' she repeated, and this time there was something else in her voice. It sounded almost like resignation. Then she looked at me once more and said, 'Will you send Mrs Wright to me in the library?'

I nodded silently and left the room, thoughts throbbing. I had been flooded with relief knowing that we were all safe, that Gabriel Wright was dead and there would be no more murder … But now I was filled with a nagging sensation that I had missed some vital piece of the puzzle. I'd been so certain that Gabriel was the only person capable of the murders. But as I tore through the corridors of Archfall Manor to find Jasper and his mother, I lost all my certainty that I'd done the right thing in planting the seed of his culpability in Nora's mind.

Jasper was stoking the fire, keeping it alive, while his mother pulled ingredients out of her pantry, lamenting how little remained from the last delivery, before we were cut off.

'When does your father's contraption say all this will end?' Teresa was asking.

'I thought you said you didn't have any use for it,' Jasper replied over his shoulder with a grin. 'I thought you said –'

Teresa harrumphed. 'I know very well what I said, but these are desperate times.'

'Tomorrow,' Jasper said. He lifted his gaze and met my eye, losing his smile.

'Mrs Wright … Jasper … I'm sorry,' I said. I was about to shatter their worlds, and I knew it, wished it weren't true. Even if there were a way of proving that Gabriel was guilty without a shred of doubt, this would have been awful. 'Mrs Wright, Mrs Temple would like to speak to you in the library.'

Teresa frowned, and put back the sprouting potatoes she'd been inspecting. She slipped off her apron. 'Did she say what it was about?'

My mouth gaped, and I found I couldn't form the words. 'She . . . she didn't, no.' It was a lie, but I couldn't face being the one to tell her that her husband was dead.

Teresa's frown deepened, and she headed out of the kitchen at the pace of someone under summons.

'What is it?' Jasper said, his voice a pale version of what I was used to. He put the poker down by the grate.

I couldn't bear it. After this, his life would be split into the moment where his father was alive . . . and after. He would be changed, a piece of him gouged away. I hated to be the person to tell him, to forever be the one who told him the worst news of his life.

'Come on, Helena, it's all across your face. What's happened?'

'Jasper . . . I'm so sorry. But . . . your father is dead.'

He blinked at me, his mouth dropping open as slowly as the first tender flakes of snow falling from the sky, before a true flurry begins.

'He . . .' Jasper's eyes were a question.

'He fell from the tower.' It was a horrible echo. My mind conjured up images of Gabriel falling.

'No,' Jasper muttered. 'No!' He spun away from me, brought his hands to his head. My heart simply ached. Jasper had believed the best in his father the whole time. When he looked at me again, I could see the pain swelling up inside him, choking him, crushing his heart.

'It was Nora,' I said in a quiet murmur. 'Nora went up to the tower to confront him about stealing from the inventing room. She said that he attacked her, that he confessed to the murders and tried to throw her from the roof, so she . . . she pushed him.'

Jasper's eyes turned fierce. 'Last night you were the one who branded him a murderer. You thought he was a threat to you. Well, you must be feeling a lot better now.'

I hated seeing this wounded, suffering version of him. I hated my part in it.

'Jasper, it's not like that. I think –'

He lifted a hand to silence me. 'I don't want to hear one more word about what you think. I've heard far too much already.' Shaking his head, he left the kitchen and, when he was out in the corridor, I heard his sob break loose as he ran to his mother.

29

The agony of Teresa's wails reverberated down the corridor as I took myself to the inventing room at the top of the house. Gabriel had left it unlocked – he'd never returned to close it up. In the doorway to the room, I closed my eyes and breathed deeply, reaching out in my mind to that other-worldly presence I'd felt ever since I arrived at Archfall Manor. I knew that I had an idea of something that would work, but I was going to be more than a little reliant on the impossible energies of the house.

'Please,' I whispered. 'Help me. I've done everything you asked me to.' I pressed my hands against the door frame, listening in the silence.

When the whisper began, indistinct and faint, I could have cried with relief. All this time, I'd been dreading it reaching out to me in quiet moments, felt sick with the way it intruded on my mind. But now I needed it. I had the idea, but I couldn't do it all by myself.

The whisper let me know I wasn't alone.

I thought I might know what I was looking for when I saw it, and tore through drawers, searching for the pieces

I needed. I knew exactly what I wanted to make, and I'd spent enough time listening to Jasper talk about the principles of his work to know how I could turn my idea into reality. It just required a certain logic.

The little mechanical timer had been shoved into a drawer, forgotten again. Jasper had never worked out what he wanted to attach it to, so it had never completed its purpose. But I knew that if I could assemble a weighted pulley with enough of the loose bricks at the top of the tower, and fasten it to trigger at the end of the timer, I could set it up to yank me back out of the arch without needing somebody to hold the end of the rope.

I sketched it out quickly on a piece of paper. The rope round my waist would pass through a pulley looped over the top of the arch on the opposite side. This would be held down with enough bricks to exceed my weight, precariously balanced on the very edge of the tower. The wire pressed against the bottom layer of bricks, connected to Jasper's mechanical timer, so when it flicked to trigger the bell it would tip the counterweight over the edge – and pull me back out. I'd have to make sure I kept my wits about me enough to grab hold of the arch to stop myself from rebounding off the opposite edge.

I removed the back from the timer, knowing that the more I prepared before I got to the top of the tower the better, as I knew the arch would try to draw me in. I gathered the rest of the tools I would need – wire, rope and circular metal loops like curtain rings – and then I was ready.

The landing with the great circular window had been left in a state of terrible disrepair, plaster and roof slate still littering the floor. It reminded me of the chaos when the bailiffs ransacked the shop. A whistling chill boxed me round the ears as I took careful steps towards the bottom of the winding stone staircase. Each pace I took felt fated, as if once again everything had been leading up to this moment. The door had been kept open with a stone brick from the debris – Nora was planning on returning. If I'd found it locked, I'd have needed to beg Jasper for the duplicate key, or steal it from him, and it was a relief to not have to resort to either. Instead, I could continue with my plan with all haste. What was I hoping to find in the arch? I had started to think that maybe it was connected, that whatever dominated my thoughts as I plunged through the portal directed where – *when* – I would end up. I'd thought about Mr Cauldwell, and I'd seen his fall. I'd thought about Wilbur and Gabriel's argument, and I'd watched it unfold.

And now there was something else I needed to see.

Nora's unsettling tale felt wrong . . . She knew I suspected Gabriel. She knew that with my unfounded conviction in my theory, bolstered by my experience through the arch, she could count on me to back up her story during the inevitable investigation when we reconnected to the mainland. Except I had a way to dig into the past and see for myself what really happened. I would press my way through the window of time into the events of this morning, and find out what really had transpired between Nora and Gabriel.

Because I couldn't shake the feeling that something had passed between Mrs Temple and Nora earlier. Mrs Temple had looked at her daughter with such devotion, but her voice had also been filled with that exhausted resignation. Mrs Temple, Nora and Birdie had returned to their ancestral home with the new baby, and now they were set to take everything in trust for baby Edmund – the house; the Cauldwell family fortune; every patent and prototype and plan; and a freedom that most women could only dream of.

I still believed that Mrs Temple's grief was genuine. But there was another possibility I'd not previously considered, one that was beginning to make sense the more I examined it.

Nora.

Her stepfathers had both died under mysterious circumstances, with no satisfactory resolution. Her mother had been subjected to the suspicious gaze of the authorities, but of course one of the first things I'd learned about Mrs Temple was that her children meant more to her than anything. Returning to the island, Nora's wishes for her future had been trampled on by her grandfather and uncle. She'd harboured a desire to engage with their work, to learn from them and walk in their footsteps, a request that had been brutally denied and rewarded only with the prospect of a marriage to one of Mr Cauldwell's inventing hopefuls.

I'd never considered that Nora could have been responsible for the terrible events at Archfall. And yet, once the thought had occurred to me, I couldn't shake it. My mouth dried up.

I needed to know, once and for all – had I been right, and were we now safe from Gabriel Wright? Or had I made a terrible mistake? Had an innocent man lost his life thanks to my attempts at puzzling everything out?

I had to get to the bottom of it, not least because, if it had been Nora all this time, I couldn't guarantee my own safety if she decided I was a threat to everything she'd created – especially if she discovered I was indeed a legitimate heir, and my father had made provision for me that might disadvantage her tight family unit.

The door at the top of the staircase had been left wide open, and it smashed against the wall aggressively. When I stepped out on to the top of the tower, the glimmer in the arch was already there as if it were waiting for me.

I had to move quickly to set up my new device, looping the pulley and lugging the bricks, balancing them so that they teetered at the edge, ready to be whipped by the wire. I figured that if they fell too soon that was no terrible thing. Better too soon than not at all. I looped the rope round my waist and set the timer for five minutes. That ought to be plenty of time. My last experience through the archway had been enough to stab me with an icy shard of fear about what would happen if I stayed in too long.

I couldn't allow myself to contemplate not going through with this. I knew what it was like to live with unanswered questions, unresolved stories. I'd arrived at Archfall Manor seeking a resolution to the questions that kept me awake at night. I'd uncovered the truth about my father, and I wasn't about to let another unsolved mystery haunt me for the rest of my days.

I drew closer to the arch, and the image reflected back at me was of Gabriel Wright, his face contorted in shock, and of Nora, her arms outstretched, and I knew the arch had responded to my intentions. I pushed through all at once this time, every part of me immersed in the world through the portal.

Nora and Gabriel were standing by the arch, but there was no violent tussle, as she'd described in the schoolroom. Instead, they were simply talking, the dark sky thundering above them. Gabriel was standing by the broken stack of bricks, his hand outstretched in warning. He wasn't trying to steal anything. He was saying: 'You had better head back down those stairs, Miss Nora. It's no place for you to be up here.'

'I could say the same about you,' she retorted. Everything about her demeanour was ominous. She was perfectly in control, a stream of menace trickling through every word. 'You think there are things in this house that belong to you, that are due to you?'

'I know you killed them,' Gabriel said. His voice was steady, but his eyes were flashing fury. I'd seen that look in Jasper's face when I accused his father of being the murderer. 'I never should have given you access to the workshops. I believed you when you said you just wanted to learn. I felt sorry for you. I should never have taught you a thing. You've destroyed this family. You're a murderess.'

'You don't have any way to prove it,' Nora said. 'You tried to get my own mother to turn me in, and you failed.'

'I'll find a way,' he growled. 'You will face the consequences of your actions. I'll see to it.'

'No, you won't,' Nora cried. She ran at Gabriel with all her strength, arms outstretched, and gave him an almighty shove. For one second, his face was full of fear, a shocked mouth, two disbelieving eyes, and then he was gone, over the edge. Compared to Nora's other kills, it was simple – but just as effective.

I had been wrong, so terribly wrong. When Jasper trusted his father, I thought he was so naïve, but it was I who had made the most terrible mistake. And I knew my misplaced suspicions had emboldened Nora to commit this final murder. Might it have been avoided if I hadn't meddled?

The truth chilled me to the bone.

Unaffected by what she'd just done, Nora marched over to my father's arch and began to feel round the edges of it, probing, testing. She wanted to know if she could make it work too, but I knew that it would not. I thought with intense pride that the arch was a connection between me and my father – Nora could not get her hands on its power.

Then, at the thought of him, everything changed. My whole world seemed to shudder, the illusion in front of me rippling as if it were a reflection in a pond, the surface disturbed by a splash.

The murmuring voice that had haunted my nights broke through the howl of the wind, became clearer, calling my name. *Helena.* Just beyond Nora, I saw a figure far out in the distant grey of the storm, a ghostly apparition hovering over the sea. It was a dark shadow of a thing, vaguely human and yet incorporeal. It felt familiar somehow, reached into a subconscious part of me that recognized it. Recognized him.

Father?

Was it him? Had it always been him? The essence in front of me didn't seem human any more, more like parts ripped from a person. Broken. Torn. Incomplete. He was sustained by the force of the house, by the supernatural power that was woven into the lives of everyone in Archfall Manor.

Where did he end and the house begin?

I reached out, felt a pull as though I might step outside my own body, be freed of the constraints of my arms and legs, everything that made me human, slip out of my skin and go to him . . . And I wanted to, so very badly.

But just as I felt myself reaching, reaching . . . an almighty heave at my waist yanked me off centre, and I crashed forward on to my outstretched hands, my face smashing into the ground as I was dragged back, back into reality. I opened my eyes, back in the present, and saw that every part of me was vaporous and lost, watched as my whole body shivered with the effort of forming back into itself.

Nora stood over me. A shudder of revulsion chased down my spine, and she saw it.

'So now, Helena, what did you see?' she asked, her eyes narrowing.

30

'Gabriel was right,' I said, the bitterness of acid on my tongue as I writhed in discomfort, feeling my body sewing itself back into the fabric of the present. The truth tasted horrid. My anger spewed out of me before I could consider the wisdom of revealing what I knew. But now that her scapegoat was dead, I hoped she felt she was limited in what she could do to me without provoking suspicion. 'You killed them. You killed him.'

'I did what I had to do,' Nora said. 'You, of all people, must understand how painful it is to be unacknowledged.'

The inside of my mouth felt like sandpaper, my throat so dry. I couldn't stop shivering, the cold seizing me. I shot a glance at the arch over her shoulder. It glimmered temptingly. It wanted me to cross back over. It wanted to absorb me, to steal my soul. And my father, he was trapped in there. Or at least whatever was left of him.

'Please,' I said. 'Take me inside. We can talk about this. I'm so cold.' I didn't want her to know that the arch was already pulling me back, that if I just had the strength I would fling myself through the portal unwillingly. If Nora knew, she would surely try to manipulate me.

'We can talk,' Nora said. She loosened the rope around my waist, hoisted me to standing. The further she helped me get from the arch the easier I could breathe, as it lost its proximal power over me, released its tight grip. She slipped off her cloak and wrapped it round me, hiding the unsettling effect of seeing my skin rematerialize over the swirling darkness that being in the arch revealed.

Nora helped me down to my room and closed the door behind us. A trapped, panicky sensation surfaced in me. She was truly a creature to be feared now, rounding on me like a predator staring down its prey.

'We're family,' she said. 'We're in this together. We can do this together.'

'Do what together?' I wrapped my arms tight round myself. My bones felt brittle, my stomach clenched, and all the tiny hairs along the back of my neck were raised. 'What are you suggesting?'

'I've been thinking. We can tell my mother who you really are. Our grandfather and uncle are gone; the will is gone. Everything they left is ours. Nobody has to know what it took to get us here. We tell them it happened just as you thought. We realized that Gabriel killed my grandfather and Uncle Wilbur. You were right – nobody could deny he had a motive, not even his family.'

I had given her this theory, this scapegoat. I'd had the best of intentions, and I had been wrong.

'We blame Gabriel,' I said. My voice felt pathetic, weak against her.

'We say exactly what I said earlier: he tried to kill me, tried to push me over the edge, and it was a tussle, it was self-defence. Believe me, I've had hours of interviews with detectives. They'll just be happy to tie it all up with a neat bow. It will make a brilliant tale for them to share with the newspapers. Imagine the eager public getting hold of this one.'

'Gabriel didn't have to die,' I said.

'But he did.' Nora nodded eagerly. 'Don't you see? He's the perfect cover for us.'

I flinched at the word 'us', tried to hide it. 'You want me to lie.'

'We could even say you saw it.' Nora was warming to her theme. 'You saw him threaten me. You heard him confess to the murders. You saw him try to push me. I know you were with Mother, but she would back it all up. She always does. She always will.'

Mrs Temple, whose name had become the subject of horror stories and penny bloods, who had lost three husbands, her father and both of her brothers, had steadfastly protected her children. Mrs Temple smoothing Nora's hair.

'Nora, I . . .' I didn't know what to say and my breath was ragged. I was backed against the wall.

'In return, I'll protect you. I'll make sure you have everything you've ever dreamed of. Money? You'll never have to worry about it again. Renown? We could become the first female leaders of the Institute. But I like to think this is more than just a business transaction, because, you and I, we're the same, aren't we? Ambitious. Creative. Unafraid of deception when it's necessary. We're family. You'll be part of our family.'

My mind swirled with a chaotic concoction of thoughts. Wasn't this everything I'd come to Archfall Manor for? I knew who my father was, I knew who I was, and with the money I could save Mam from the debtors' prison and give her the freedom to live however she chose. It should have been a simple choice, but it was not.

Writhing inside me, like a ghoulish serpent, was a terrible guilt and a sense of responsibility. Did this all happen because it was always going to happen? My father's theory of time suggested so, if the future was also layered on top of us like the past was, and the arch a window to peer through. But that absolved me of responsibility, and I felt responsible for what had happened to Gabriel. Perhaps he and Nora had always been going to end up at the top of the tower together – Nora might have come to the same conclusion about him herself. But my theories had given her time to think, to plot, to steel herself to do it.

'Why?' I asked. 'If family is everything to you, then why did you do this?'

Her answer came easily. I didn't doubt she had justified this to herself over and over again.

'We lost my father to tuberculosis when I was young and I often wonder how things would be different if he had survived. Birdie's father was very cruel. I was protecting

Mother. Edmund's father was very stupid. He'd squandered away all his money – we were about to lose everything.' She was so angry, but her voice remained even. It all seethed beneath the surface of her skin. 'And then we came back here, and my grandfather and my uncle were ready to crush my chances of ever fulfilling my potential. I have a brain for inventing. I didn't want to use it for murder, but they left me no choice. They didn't see me, didn't see what I could do, given half the chance. I had to clear the slate.'

I stared at her, trying to understand how she could still appear so human when she had done such awful things. She believed wholly in what she had done. There didn't appear to be an ounce of regret. And Gabriel had paid the ultimate price to cover up her crimes. The hurts she described made me angry on her behalf, but murder? I couldn't believe there had been no other way.

'You wanted them to acknowledge you,' I said. 'Did you know you were going to do this all along?'

'No,' Nora said simply. 'I gave them both a chance to see me. I've been planning it for weeks, though, and this storm seemed the perfect opportunity. I couldn't have imagined you, though. You've opened my mind to so many new possibilities. Do you know I tried to use the arch up at the top of the tower? I wanted to see if it would work for me, if it was something in our blood. But no. It's all just about you.'

A judder of fear brought my whole body to full alert – did that make me more important to her? Or was it a reason for her to feel bitterness towards me?

'I think my father – whatever's left of him – is still in

there. That's why. It's not about me at all . . . It's about him. He haunts this place.'

'Fascinating! We could investigate together,' she said, her eyes shining. 'There are so many things about this house and this island and its power that we don't understand. There's so much we don't have the answer to, but we could uncover it all together. Perhaps there's even a way to free your father?'

Hearing her talk like that was like looking into a broken mirror, the pieces shattered and distorting my image. She reminded me . . . of me. And yet she was a person who had gone to the darkest extremes, and she terrified me.

Could I . . . could I go along with the lie? Could I live with myself, painting Gabriel Wright as a murderer when I knew who was truly responsible?

I couldn't stop picturing Gabriel's shocked expression the moment before he fell. I was wrong. I was wrong. I was wrong!

'What about Jasper?' I asked.

She looked at me with a pitying expression. 'I think you know whatever there was between you is already over. When you're ready to claim your Cauldwell name, I can assure you that you won't be interested in dalliances with staff. If it's romance you're looking for, we can find you a much better match.'

More to the point, I doubted Jasper would be able to look at me the same ever again.

'Perhaps. But, Nora, I don't know if I can do this,' I said, my voice wavering.

'Helena.' Nora took my hand. 'What other choice do

you have? Keep this all close to your chest for now, and, when the storm lifts, everything will be ours.' Her lips pulled back from her teeth in a smile that could just as easily have been a snarl.

She was right. What choice did I have? I'd found the truth – but at a terrible cost. The answers I'd gained chilled me to the bone, and I was no closer to being free of this nightmare. Nora had twinned us together now, bound us to each other inexorably. To think I had once pitied her loneliness. She had woven the threads of our lives together, and I was about to be trapped, forced to hide her awful secrets forever . . . There was no way I could return to my old life, and she was capable of such detached horrors I would spend the rest of my life waiting for her punishment.

Either I must fully commit to Nora's lies, or I had to find a way to prove her guilt. Her words – *close to your chest* – lodged in my mind.

It was then that I knew exactly where Nora would keep the evidence of her crimes.

31

The storm was beginning to lift, but in the staff quarters the mood was as melancholy as the darkest depths of the tempest we'd lived through. Teresa had taken to her bed after Mrs Temple had dosed her with a sleeping tincture, and so it was Molly who stood in front of the hearth, preparing a very simple stew. For one more night, at least, I was to perform the role of governess, of staff, with Nora determined that we would only reveal my identity after the inevitable investigation had been resolved.

I went to Jasper's room and gave a soft knock on the door. I half expected him to ignore me, but he opened the door, his eyes bloodshot and his shoulders slumped with the weight of his devastation. 'What do you want?' He sounded so dull and flat, the light inside him extinguished.

'I just wanted to say that I was wrong, and I'm sorry. I'm so sorry.' The words were not enough.

Jasper wept openly then. 'I don't want it to be real,' he said. He wiped his eyes with the back of his hand. 'And I can't believe it was him.'

'I don't either,' I said, lowering my voice to a whisper, remembering all too well Nora and her listening device. 'This is what I wanted to come and tell you. It was Nora all along.'

'Nora?'

He turned back into his room, went and sat on the window ledge, staring out of the window. I followed him in and sat next to him, telling him about returning to the arch, setting up the pulley system so that I could go through the portal by myself. As I spoke, he melted into me, his head resting on my shoulder, tears sinking into my dress.

'You went up there alone? Didn't you think how dangerous it could be?'

'I just knew I needed to see what really happened.'

'And . . . what did you see?'

I explained what his father had said to Nora, that he'd been teaching her all this time. Without dwelling on the upsetting details, the look on Gabriel's face that kept repeating in my mind over and over, I told him that Nora confessed to the murders before she pushed him.

'I was wrong.'

'It's not your fault. It's hers,' he growled. 'What she's done is despicable.'

'But I was wrong about him, and I feel like this is all my fault. I was so determined to be right, to get the answers, to solve the mystery of what was unfolding here . . . I gave her the opportunity to kill him.'

'I don't blame you,' he said, resigned. Even his breathing seemed a heavy chore. 'I just wish it were different. I wish I could bring him back.'

'I'm so sorry.'

'She needs to pay for what she's done. Where do we go from here?'

'Nora wants me to lie for her,' I said. 'She was the one who killed her stepfathers, and Mrs Temple has been covering for her all this time. Nora wants me to be part of the family.'

'And everything that entails,' Jasper said, raising his eyes to the ceiling and letting out an exhausted sigh. 'Ma and I will be dismissed. You'll be trapped.'

'Nora will want to keep me close forever, and maybe I deserve that. But to know she would just be living her life, with no consequences at all? It's not right. I know I can't bring your pa back, but I'll do whatever I can to make sure she doesn't get away with it.'

Jasper gazed over my shoulder out of the window again. 'I think I could make it across the causeway this evening. If I go now, if I take one of the horses without a carriage and don't take any luggage, I could probably make it.'

'Probably?' I swallowed hard. The storm was beginning to recede, but I couldn't forget the sight of the sea swallowing the doctor's and solicitor's carriages.

Jasper sounded convinced of his ability now, a new conviction settling into his voice. 'If I was fast enough, I could make it back with reinforcements while the tide is still out, or tomorrow morning at the latest.' I realized he needed this, needed to feel there was something he could do. Even if that meant risking his life, he was willing to do it, for the sake of justice.

The way I'd been prepared to plunge myself into the danger of the arch, for the sake of answers, only to find that the answers by themselves weren't enough, brought us no peace. We both wanted Nora to be held accountable for what she'd done.

But even so – did we have enough evidence to bring the authorities to Sighfeyre Isle and accuse Nora? There would be an investigation, and I was sure that Mrs Temple and Nora would tighten their stories, close ranks and find a way to make me pay if I didn't comply.

'It's a risk,' I said. 'Even if you managed to get across the causeway, and return with the authorities, there's no guaranteeing that they would believe us. The family are powerful. They questioned Mrs Temple when her last two husbands died, but they never took her before the magistrate.'

Jasper looked pensive. 'You're right. Nora's part of an important family. We're just staff. They're going to want to believe her.'

'Exactly. And if I produce the marriage certificate to elevate my status, I just complicate things, make myself seem more suspicious. Nora might twist it all on me, make me look guilty. After all, I came here under a false name, with a stolen letter of reference. I'm already guilty of that.'

'So we need proof,' Jasper said. 'Incontrovertible evidence that she did it. Enough to get her locked away, otherwise . . .' He trailed off. In the pause, I began to imagine the worst that Nora could do. Ruin me. Destroy me. Kill me?

'Anything incriminating, she'd keep inside her chest,' I

said. 'And I'm the only person besides her who can get inside it.'

'If I'm going to do this, I need to go now,' Jasper said, standing quickly. His body seemed full of a purposeful energy that propelled him across the room to grab his thick coat and put it on. He dashed to pull on a weighty pair of boots, and I was struck by the urge to stop him, to beg him to stay safe.

'When they're all seated for dinner, I'll go to the chest,' I said.

Between us, I thought perhaps we could manage it. If only he could just make it across unharmed by the vicious whipping of the waves and the crumbling fragility of the causeway path.

'I need to go,' he said, and tears sprang to my eyes, all the regret and desperation and fear leaking out of me.

'Jasper.' The shape of his name in my mouth was all I could form. We had navigated such a dark, twisting forest together, with tearing thorns and gnarled roots that made us stumble and fall. He kissed the top of my head, the firm press of his lips like a permanent branding.

'I need to go,' he said again. Neither of us could bear to say farewell.

When the family were seated for dinner, with Molly's limp attempt at a stew dished out in front of them, I dashed to Mr Cauldwell's study, determination and resolve springing up where there had been an utter loss of hope. The chest was just as Jasper and I had left it, and I performed the trick with the key once more, again marvelling at the cleverness of it. The keys were all there resting in a row. Before, I had been aghast at the invasion of privacy, but now all I felt was relief that there was a way for me to get to Nora's most secret possessions.

I took the key with a metal N fashioned inside its bow. Then I closed the chest and slid it back into place, locked it and slipped both keys into my pocket, where they jangled next to each other.

I headed to Nora's room and opened the door, taking a quick glance along the corridor first. Empty. The room was opulent, beautiful, a room I could only have dreamed of when I was lying on the sagging, miserable mattress above the sweetshop. Gathered velvet was draped in curtains round the four-poster bed, promising a thick warmth, despite the cold of the rest of the house, and on every surface were expensive trinkets – necklaces in silver and gold, a mother-of-pearl hairbrush, an emerald brooch – but her passion for invention was hidden away, along with her true nature.

Nora's chest rested at the foot of her bed. I knelt down beside it and followed a chain of unlockings, turning the key this way in a lock on the left, that way in a lock on the right, and fiddling with the N in the bow to release it to unlock the centre. Each of these took precious time and concentration, and my palms were sweating, making the key slippery and difficult to manoeuvre.

When I finally got the chest unlocked, I listened gratefully to the heavy clunk of iron pins releasing their catch, and I breathed a sigh of relief. Swiftly, I flung the lid open and inside . . .

Nothing.

I gasped aloud in shock, and a terrible dread pooled in my stomach. I'd been hoping for all the evidence we'd need to prove her guilt – plans in her handwriting, murderous designs, perhaps even the tools themselves that she'd used. If they weren't here, where else could she possibly keep them?

I realized then that she was ahead of me somehow. She knew. She knew that I had Mr Cauldwell's key, that inside his chest were the keys to each of their secret chests, that I would come here. The listening device, the skulls in the walls that meant she could watch me unseen. She knew. She'd already moved the evidence.

I needed to get out, leave everything exactly the way I'd found it, and wait, bide my time until Jasper returned with help.

But just as I was closing the final lock on the chest, I heard the intentional clearing of a throat in the doorway.

I looked up, and there, of course, was Nora.

She shook her head, disappointed. 'Now I know you can't be looking in that chest by accident.'

'I . . . Nora . . .' I scrambled for the right thing to say, for a way to placate her. She was so very dangerous, and from the way her eyes flashed I could tell she was so very angry with me too. She almost seemed hurt, hurt that I would betray her.

'You really thought I'd just leave the evidence here for

you to find? You little idiot. But then again this is exactly the sort of simple thinking I'd expect from you.'

My face grew hot. I'd thought I was ahead of her, but she'd always been smarter, faster, and she would always be more cruel.

'It's such a shame. You had so much potential. With my guidance, you might have made something of yourself. But now . . . Well, it's very clear that I can't trust you.'

She rushed at me, sank her fingers into my hair and tightened her grip. She yanked my head back, and I yelped with pain. I tried to fight, but I was on my back like a beetle, and she avoided my flailing hands, pulling me back and out of the room, dragging me towards the little alcove in the corridor.

'Nora, stop, please!' I screamed.

'Shut up,' she hissed in reply.

At the bottom of the stairs, she gave a kick to my ribs, winding me. The pain was like a hot, blinding light. I was so desperate. We were close now, and I could feel the urge to walk of my own volition up the stairs and fling myself through the arch once more. I called for help. 'Help! Please! Somebody!'

It was useless. The mansion was so sprawling nobody would hear us unless they were already nearby. I let out great gasping sobs, and screamed anyway, screamed as loud as I could, begging for help . . .

And then I had a moment of hope. As Nora stepped over me at the bottom of the stone staircase, I glimpsed the outline of a small figure that had appeared on the landing, hovering behind the bannister. It was Birdie, her mouth wide with horror as she witnessed the viciousness of her older sister. Nora hadn't seen her, was roughly grabbing at my wrists, and I didn't want to draw her attention to her little sister, who might be my only chance. Instead, I tried to speak with my eyes, to plead, to beg with Birdie to fetch help . . . She backed away down the marble stairs, taking my last hope with her.

Nora kicked me again, and while I was winded, gasping, she grabbed my wrists, lifting them above my head and pulling me. The stairs scraped my back, and I struggled and wrestled until I . . . didn't. A calm draped over my entire body, and I had no fight in me, no desire to resist.

At the top of the stairs, Nora was exhausted from the effort. She caught her breath and looked at me – surprised by the way all the resistance had seeped out of my body. I followed her lead willingly, but inside I was screaming. My body wouldn't do what I wanted it to do. I could picture the way I wanted to resist and flee . . . but I was a marionette, my limbs controlled by the supernatural pull of the archway.

'What's wrong with you?' Nora spat. 'Why aren't you fighting?'

I let out a cold laugh. 'I see you don't know everything. It's the arch,' I said. 'This is what it does to me. It calls me in: it wants to devour me.'

'Like your father.'

'I saw him in there,' I said, the surface of the arch glowering at me from across the tower, and I stood up and walked towards it, powerless to resist its pull, caught in the surging, invisible tide. 'I saw my father.'

I moved towards the arch, untethered, drawn in, and the surface was frozen with an image of a young man staring at the arches, creating an odd sensation like a mirror reflecting a mirror. I took one last look at Nora, but she was just watching me, fascinated, her grin a spiteful tear across her face. When I reached the archway, it took no effort for me to plunge through the surface – and, inevitably, to my own demise.

32

My father was standing at the base of the arch, running his hands over the stone, fastening a complex clockwork device to the surface. I would have placed him in his late twenties. He had an eager face, full of wonder and curiosity. His hair was thick and unruly, his eyes a deep brown.

'You were gone for nearly two years with no word!' A shout came from behind him. It was Wilbur, a younger Wilbur, with a face with fewer lines, but just as much bitterness and rage. 'And now you've been back a week, tinkering around in the inventing room, gathering things and stealing them away to your room, squirrelling yourself away in the study with Father and that lawyer of his ... You think you can just come back here and lay claim to everything? I'm the one who has been here.'

'Wilbur, do you know why I started looking into theories of time?' my father asked.

'Why should I know why you do anything, Edwin?' Wilbur scoffed. 'You baffle me with your entitlement and your arrogance.'

'For her,' my father said quietly. 'I wanted to see our

mother again. I thought . . . When I landed on the idea, I thought that if I could find a way into the past, I'd find a way to see her again.'

Wilbur did not reply. He looked as though he were fighting to suppress the strong tide of grief. He wordlessly shook his head.

'I left because I *had* to leave here to be able to step out of Father's shadow. But what he didn't tell me – what he hasn't told *you* – is that our magic doesn't work off the island. It's tied into this place. This thing that we can do, with cogs and springs, when we make the impossible happen, it isn't because of us. It's because of Sighfeyre Isle. We whisk it into being with our intentions and our creations, but it isn't real the moment we step off this island.'

'It . . . it doesn't work on the mainland?' Hurt and confusion crossed over Wilbur's face.

'That's why I've come back. Because I'm certain of my theory, and I'm certain it will only work here. Our family has a special connection to this place. We always have. We can do things here that are unimaginable for the rest of the world. Us. We've been given an incredible gift. There are such wonderful things we could do if we could just . . . listen to what's already here.'

He spoke with such passion, it was impossible not to get carried away with him. *Listen to what's already here.* He expressed it so eloquently. That's what I'd been doing ever since the night I decided to stop resisting the whispers, began following the nudges of the house. The arch didn't work for anyone else because they weren't *listening*.

'I never managed to make it work before. I have a theory on that. I wanted to try it before I leave. I think . . . I think if there's a powerful emotional hook, an intention . . . the house will respond to it.'

'An "emotional hook"? What are you talking about?' Wilbur blustered.

'Tell me you don't still grieve for her every day. Tell me you don't hate the way Father keeps her room like a shrine, but won't let us in, won't let us even talk about her, remember her the way she should be remembered. Tell me you wouldn't give anything to see Mother once more.'

He turned towards the arch, and then it was clear he was seeing something that Wilbur and I could not. The strength of his intention and his grief had brought the magic to life. It was the same magic that had responded to my desperate desire for answers, that lived because of him and echoed down through the years to me. He'd left many things for me, financial provision, a legacy of ideas and invention . . . and this, this force of magic he'd conjured one night eighteen years ago.

Edwin took a step forward, and then another, a strange serenity across his expression as though he were hypnotized.

'What are you doing?' Wilbur asked. 'Do you . . . Do you see something?'

Edwin did not reply, just continued his march towards the edge of the tower.

It was striking to behold what I had experienced happening to somebody else – the way it seemed as though he were being pulled into an undertow, the invisible ebb drawing him in. Even though I knew he was going to slip through the arch into another moment, my heart was in my throat seeing him like that, as though he were possessed of the notion to fling himself off the roof.

Wilbur cried out to him. 'Edwin! Stop!'

But Edwin went through the arch and was gone.

Wilbur wore a horrified expression and he let out a yelp. He rushed to the edge of the tower, peering over the side and shaking his head in disbelief when there was no body on the ground below. 'I don't understand,' he murmured, touching the stone arch Edwin had passed through.

I drew closer to it myself. This arch was the same one that had unfolded my own fate, but here it was eighteen years earlier . . . It was dizzying to think that, in another moment in time, I had passed through it, and it existed here too. As I got closer, it began to shimmer and ripple, and it made me think of holding a mirror up to a mirror. A figure appeared in the centre of it, the shadowy husk I'd seen before, the remnants of consciousness that used to be my father.

The husk shifted and reached out. There was a deep sadness and longing in that gesture, and I felt profound grief at his being so lost for so long. I too reached out my hand, the edges wispy and insubstantial like smoke.

'I wish I had known you,' I said simply. It was the heart of the matter after all – the heart of it all.

And as I took hold of the place where his wrist should have been, as I found him, the scene around me began to shift and shake, and there was the sensation of being ejected, like being flung from a horse, and everything went black.

I collapsed on the ground and lay on the hard stone, staring up at the moon, high and bright, no longer obscured by thunderous clouds or blinding rain. The wind that stirred around me was no longer a vicious lashing. The darkest part of the tempest had passed over us at last. The wind had receded, and in the ensuing silence I realized I could hear the sounds of a struggle. I turned my head, and saw that Teresa was restraining Nora, fastening her hands behind her back with rope. Birdie had gone to fetch help after all.

Birdie hovered in the doorway, biting her fingers nervously, and she screamed when she saw me, a ghostly being that had emerged from the arch. Jasper had told me I looked like magic, but to Birdie I must have appeared as a spectral horror. She turned and ran away, and that was the last time I saw her.

I had not come through the archway alone. The haunting shadow of my lost father was beside me. As my body went through the shivers and rigours of re-forming, I waited for his to do the same. But it seemed that he was incapable of it. He'd been in the arch too long. Even though he was no longer lost, his body had forgotten the shape it was meant to be in. Instead, it was like he was drifting away on the wind, becoming more shapeless with every second that tethered me to our world once more. Before my eyes, he turned into nothing, and I remembered my mam saying, *Surely you can't miss what you've never had?*

But the echo in me that I knew to be true said otherwise. *You can, you can, you can.* I'd found him, I'd brought him back, and it still wasn't enough. He was already gone.

'No!' I cried out. My throat clogged with grief, my vision swimming as tears filled my eyes. It felt so cruel, that everything had brought me to this moment, and I couldn't bring him back.

Nora was screaming, and flailing from side to side, but Teresa had her firmly pinned, with a knee pressed into her back, her hands tied.

'You'll hang for this,' Teresa hissed in Nora's ear, and for the first time I saw what Nora looked like when she was frightened.

I turned back to the arch. Nothing shimmered or flickered. It was just two stone pillars meeting at the top, decorated with the debris of invention. But it had never been about the invention, it had always been about the *intention*. The house was finished with that piece of magic conjured up by my father. I was not afraid. But I was filled with a deep sorrow at everything that had transpired.

And now it was over. It was finally over, but I would never step back into my old life again.

33

Even on the mainland, there is no such thing as feeling safe any more. I wake in the soft bed that Harry's mam made up for me, wake from dreams where Nora's hands are round my throat.

She's not here. And yet it feels like she'll never leave me.

Archfall Manor is many miles away, but I still have a crawling sensation that runs all over my arms and legs, a restless tugging at my limbs that feels like it belongs to the house, calling me, calling me back. I thought, when I recovered my father's soul, or what was left of it, from the place where it was trapped inside the window of time, that I'd done everything the house wanted me to do . . . And yet it still wants me back. Archfall Manor has planted tiny barbs beneath my skin, and I have no way to rip them out. I am like a dog trying to pull burrs from its fur with its teeth, gnawing away at itself.

When the police arrived on Sighfeyre Isle with Jasper and saw the bodies – Wilbur's soaked in blood, Mr Cauldwell's broken and twisted, and Gabriel splayed out in the mire – the inspector had ruled that the case needed to be heard.

That we already had Nora locked away in a room, that we'd taken the precaution of restraining her, that every member of staff closed rank and pointed an accusatory finger, was enough for them to arrest her.

Nora gave a hideous scream as they wrestled her away, and the way she looked at me gave me chills.

'Not to worry, miss.' The weathered bobby took hold of the rope that tied Nora's wrists together. 'With her being as distressed as this, they'll get her sedated sharpish.'

He took her off in a carriage before the sea covered the causeway again, and Molly, Teresa, Jasper and I set about gathering our belongings. Jasper helped me haul down the chest with my name on. I gripped his hand tightly as I turned my back on the manor, and I could not bring myself to look over my shoulder as we crossed back to the mainland, away from the fevered dream we'd been living.

We left Mrs Temple and Birdie, and I couldn't bear to see if their faces watched us from the window. But I longed to let Birdie know my gratitude for what she'd done, for the way she'd fetched help for me, even realizing what it might cost. A deep sorrow took root in my chest and has not stopped growing there since.

I've been rehearsing. Whether or not there is a conviction remains to be seen. There is no tangible evidence of Nora's crimes. We never did find the tripwire device, or any prototypes to link her with the murders. It is my word against hers.

She made an attempt on my life. She tried to push me from the roof. I believe she did the same to Gabriel Wright. I believe she made the contraption that killed Wilbur Cauldwell. I believe she was responsible for the death of Thomas Cauldwell . . .

I dress myself all in black, fastening the buttons up to my chin, tame my hair into a twist at the nape of my neck. It is important that I appear respectable, that I look like somebody who can be trusted. I must be prepared to be questioned on every aspect of my standing, must prepare to stand in front of a jury and be interrogated. Under oath, I will tell them every truth I'm able to.

And when all of this is finished I'll be able to start a new life. The things that my father had placed in the chest for me are going to turn my fortunes around. When the trial is over, I'll go to the bank in London with the the key and the receipt. Father could never have imagined that he wouldn't be able to make it home again to ensure Mam and I had access to the money held in his name there. I'm hoping there will be enough to buy Mam's freedom from the prison, to settle her debts . . . I haven't dared travel to London yet in case I miss Nora's trial; the bobby had made it clear that with a high-profile case such as this the magistrate would want to have it handled quickly.

Beyond whatever money there might be, the chest had been filled with jewels of another kind – Father's ideas and prototypes and inventions, each with a value of its own.

The marriage certificate still troubles me, why Father took it with him in the first place. In the conversation I saw in the window through time, it was clear he had always intended to return to Archfall Manor as its heir, and questions have swirled in my mind – had the plan been to have my legitimacy documented, to ensure that one day I could be considered an heiress? Wilbur had mentioned meetings with a lawyer. Had my father had a chance to tell Mr Cauldwell about me? Had he ever tried to find me after my father disappeared?

Mr Cauldwell's last will and testament still rests in his chest, and as the person holding the key I'm the only one who can lay hands on it. Whatever it states, I have an eerie sense that Archfall Manor isn't finished with me yet.

Downstairs, Jasper and Teresa are waiting for me. They've been staying at a local inn where they managed to secure rooms. They're arranged in the comfortable armchairs by the fire, Jasper's long legs stretched out. Harry sits on the window ledge while his mam pours tea for everyone. Sally Mirren is all soft edges and round plumpness, the sort of mother who looks like home should. There is a tense feeling in the air – we all know how important today is. Today Nora will be hauled in front of the magistrate.

Jasper gets to his feet and offers me his chair, while Sally presses an earthenware mug into my hands. The tea is steaming and a rich ochre shade, not too much milk. I bring the mug to my lips and allow the liquid to warm me.

'Are you ready?' Harry asks, patting me on the shoulder.

'As ready as I can be,' I say.

'I should tell the magistrate I saw it all,' Teresa says. Whenever she speaks, her words tremble now. 'I should say

I saw her try to push you. If that's what will bring her to justice, then –'

But Jasper interrupts her. 'Lying wouldn't help. Pa was an honest man, and he wouldn't have wanted you to make false oaths in his name. You're more likely to create inaccuracies they can pick holes in, and they'll be wondering why you didn't say it when they first questioned you on Sighfeyre Isle.'

Whenever the Wrights talk about their loss, an echo of regret crashes through me. I did not kill Gabriel, but he is dead because I blamed him. I believed him responsible for the murders on the island, and Nora fed on my theories. What happened to Gabriel might never have come about if it weren't for me. I was altogether too trusting of the power within the window through time – I thought there was a plan, that I was a crucial piece of the puzzle and I just needed to unravel the mystery. But what was shown to me through the arch was altered by my own preoccupations and presumptions.

I know Jasper doesn't blame me, but my heart aches whenever I hear Gabriel's name. All I can do is try to bring Nora to justice.

'We have to hope the jury can see the truth,' Jasper says earnestly. His eyes are red, but there's still enough of him that glows with trust, that believes the best.

The jurors' ability to see the truth is not the only thing I have to hope for. I sent a letter to Mrs Temple across the causeway with their delayed delivery from the local grocer. I begged her to come to the trial, to tell the truth about her daughter. *You might not be able to save Nora from who she's become*, I wrote, *but things could be different for Birdie and Edmund*. So much depends upon Mrs Temple, whether she comes, what she will say.

Harry begins to prepare Treasure, and when the carriage is ready for us Jasper and I sit next to each other with Teresa opposite. Jasper taps his foot, the juddering of his leg moving the whole seat. His nerves are contagious, so I rest my hand on his knee to steady him.

When we arrive, the first thing I notice is the sheer number of people gathered outside the towering building, intimidating with its polished stone and fluted pillars. Their faces are unkind, ravenous for stories of the worst kind, eager to collect the gory and gruesome details. I want to grab them by the shoulders, tell them it's worse in real life, worse than they could ever imagine. I want to tell them that their nasty little pamphlets could never capture the horror of a man's blood pouring out over you, or the terrible angle of the twist of a neck, or how, in the moments before a person falls to their death, they realize it is going to happen.

But I say nothing. I save my words because it is only inside that building that they will truly matter.

I resolutely grit my teeth as Jasper offers me his arm. I take it and let him guide me past the crowd. When I don't answer their questions – *Are you here to speak of the murdering heiress? Do you think she did it?* – they quickly lose interest in me. Another carriage is arriving. I peer over the bustling bodies to see who it is that steps out.

Mrs Temple.

She is smoothed over once more, her make-up neatly applied, her clothing elegant, a black veil covering her hair. When she catches sight of us, I cannot tell what feelings are stirring inside her. She has come after all, but why is she here? What will she say? Will she stand and condemn her own daughter? Or will she rip our accusations to shreds, use her status to push us down? Her word in this court will make the difference to all of us, which way our paths lead next. I went to Archfall Manor so that I might change my fortune, but it was all of us who were changed during my time there. Lives were altered, lives were lost, and in front of the magistrate the lies will be unpicked, the truth uncovered, and the direction all our lives will go in next determined.

I step forward, step into my fate.

And still, still the house pulls at me, waiting for me to return.

Acknowledgements

Thank you to my agent, James Wills, for always championing my creativity and for helping my writing dreams to become a reality.

Thank you to my editor, Naomi Colthurst, for developing and crafting this story with me and for the way our ideas sessions always leave my mind fizzing with inspiration. It is always a delight to work with you on these dark and twisty mysteries.

Thank you to Shreeta Shah for guiding me through the copy-editing process with patience and encouragement, and to everyone whose careful reading made this a better book – Jane Tait, Debbie Hatfield, Sarah Hall, Petra Bryce. Thank you also to Jenny Glencross for your guidance over the final stages of this book.

Thank you to all the team at Penguin working to get this book into the hands of readers – with special thanks to Chloe Parkinson and Michael Bedo for creating such exciting opportunities to share my stories.

Thank you to Andrea Kearney for another beautiful cover, Saskia Nichols for the interior design work and to

Emily Faccini for illustrating the map of Archfall Manor and bringing it to life from my scrawled floor plans.

Thank you to my friends for all the ways in which you support me and my writing. A special thank you to Laura, for our conversations about craft that challenge me to keep growing as a writer, to Danny, who never fails to help me problem- (and puzzle-) solve, and to Prayer Quad for sharing these seasons of life with me with so much encouragement.

I am so blessed to be part of a large and wonderful family – thank you for all the ways you've supported me, practically and emotionally. Thank you to my parents, my granny and my sisters for always believing I could do this. Sharing a love of books with you is one of the great joys of my life. A special thanks to Mum for going through this manuscript with her teacher pen.

Thank you to my husband, Jake – this one is for you. The things you do for our family make this whole writing journey possible, and I'm eternally grateful that we get to go through life together. We really are the best team. In the time this book was in progress, we also brought a whole new human into the world. I delivered a draft the day I found out I was pregnant, completed a round of copy-edits the day before going into labour, and I'm writing these acknowledgements with our newest family member sleeping on me – welcome to the world, Barnaby, and thank you for all the joy you've brought with you. Thank you to Imogen, for inspiring me daily with your creativity, your imagination and your love of stories – the ones you tell are my favourite.

Thank you to God, who has a plan, with hope and a future.